My Casino Lover

Julia Burgman

Dedications

I would like to dedicate this book to my Husband, Owen, as well as my Children Gregory Sr., Jackie, and Tyrone LIGE. Also, to all of my grandchildren and my daughter in law, Rita.

My greatest dedication goes to My Mother, whom I know if she were still living, would be very proud of me. I also dedicate this to all of my siblings, the ones that are still living, and the ones that have passed away.

This also goes out to all women and men, to keep an eye on their relationship with the opposite sex when there is a little too much closeness going on. Keeping it real.

Acknowledgments

First and foremost, I give honor to GOD because without him, this would not be possible.

Again, I acknowledge my Husband, because he encouraged me to keep on going, along with my children. I would like to thank my best friends, Wanda Martin, Beverly Benson, and Melinda Dixon. Also, Larry Pado. All of your encouraging words stayed with me.

MAY THE LOVE OF GOD KEEP US ALL.
JULIA LIGE BURGMAN

I've always jumped in the tub and soaked when things weren't going the way that I thought they should. I thought that I could soak away my problems or troubles whatever it was that was troubling me. But this time, I don't think that soaking is going to be enough—no, not this time; only God and time will heal my heart and the pain that the children and I are going through even though it's been seven years since my Shawn was murdered, though at times it still feels like yesterday. When the police came to the house, I wasn't there, but my daughter Shawnda was.

Shawnda called me on my cell phone, which was strange in itself because I was at work, and she would always just call the office when it was an emergency. I answered the phone.

"Hello, Ma," Shawnda said.

"Yes, what is it, baby?"

"Ma," Shawnda said.

"Yes," I said again, this time with a little attitude.

"Ma." Shawnda just kept on saying Ma and hollering, so I said, "Little girl, if you don't stop all that hollering—"

Shawnda said through her tears, "Ma, you need to come home now."

I said, "Stop hollering, Shawnda."

Right away she said, "Ma, we have an emergency here, so please come home right away."

"Well, all right but calm down, and I'll be there in about a half hour."

"No, Ma, now."

"Shawnda, if you holler again like that—" Then another voice came on the phone.

It was a male voice, and he said, "Is this Mrs. Brunson?"

"Yes, it is."

"Mrs. Brunson, this is Officer Peters. Can you return home right away?"

"What's going on?"

"Mrs. Brunson—"

"Look, Mr. Peters, you're upsetting me. Is there something wrong with one of my children? Oh my god. There's something wrong, isn't it?"

"Who is it? Shawn Junior? Jaylen? Who is it? What is happening? Is it my husband? What?"

"Mrs. Brunson, I'd rather talk to you face-to-face. It's going to be better that way."

"Okay. I'm on my way. I'll be there in ten minutes."

"Mrs. Brunson, please try to keep your mind on driving carefully."

"What?"

"Take your time driving, that's all."

"Oh, all right."

As I was driving home, I was thinking if one of those boys had done something that they should not have done; I'll wring their necks. Or could it be both of them? I remember one day I found a joint in Shawn Jr.'s pocket. So I was thinking maybe he got caught smoking a joint. He and Jaylen are getting older, and it seems like they're getting more devilish as they're getting older. Well, anyway, this time I'll let their dad handle this punishment because I've got enough on me with all my lying and cheating clients.

As I was pulling up in the driveway, I saw two police cars. Boy, I thought those two boys are really gonna get it; and if I think that their dad's letting them off too easy, then this time I'll handle it. And they'll be on a punishment for the rest of their life. Then I noticed that one of the police cars belonged to Big Shawn's friends, Kirt and Wendal. So when I got out of the car and I walked up toward the house to where they are standing, I looked at them, and it looked like they all have tears in their eyes, so I said, "What's going on?"

"Rachael," Kirk and Wendal both called my name at the same time, and then they said my name again.

I stopped walking and said, "What's going on? Will someone please tell me what the hell is going on? What is it?"

"Rachael, please go inside."

"No. No. What is it? Is there something wrong with Shawn Jr.? Jaylen?"

"Rachael, it's Big Shawn."

"What about Big Shawn?"

"Rachael, he's gone."

"Kirk, what are you talking about? Just what are you saying when you say he's gone?"

"Shawn's dead. He's dead, Ray."

"What?"

"Shawn's been shot."

"What do you mean he's been shot? Oh no. I just talked to him, and we plan to have dinner together since we missed having lunch together, so how could he be gone when I'm meeting him for dinner?" I kept saying. That was all I could say.

"It looks like there was a break-in," Ray said.

"A break-in? Where?"

"At the office," Wendal said. "Shawn was shot three times, and Sharon was shot once."

After he said that, I didn't remember much of anything. When I woke up, I was in the hospital.

"Oh my goodness, I had a terrible dream." I was thinking out loud until I really opened my eyes and saw that I was in a strange place, someplace other than my bedroom. People were all around me—my children, Kirt, Wendal, and even Officer Peters; and after looking around at everyone, I realized that it wasn't a dream, and tears started running down my face. Reality hit me. It was true. My life was no more.

"Mama, are you all right?" Shawnda said.

Tears were running down my face uncontrollably. By now, all my children hugged me and said, "Ma, everything is going to be all right."

All right, I thought. *My husband is dead.*

But I didn't say a word to them; I just looked around. And everyone in the room was crying.

So I thought, *I'm going to have to pull myself together and find out exactly what is going on. And why am I in a hospital bed?*

So I said to my babies, "I know that everything is going to be fine, but first tell me, why am I here?"

So through teary eyes and weak voices, they said, "You passed out, and we thought that we were going to lose you too because when you fainted, your breathing slowed down, and Uncle Kirk picked you up and rushed you here."

"Okay. Okay. I'm going to be fine." I laid my head back and thought someone has killed my husband, the father of my children. My partner, my lover, my friend. And just when things seem to be going good and we were at our best and I was trusting and believing in my heart again, someone has come along and changed my life completely.

Kirk, Wendal, and Officer Peters all said, "Rachael, this is not over until we find out what happened and why. We're going over as soon as we can and talk to Sharon to see if she knows who it was that did this."

Then they each hugged the children and I, then said, "Now that we know that you are going to be all right, we've got our work cut out for us, so we'll be going. But we will keep in touch. And if during the night or day you or the kids need anything, don't hesitate to call either one of us because he was our brother too."

Then Officer Peters said, "We will not stop until we have caught whoever it was that did this."

They each kissed us all and left.

A couple of hours later, after being checked out by the doctors, I was released from the hospital; so we went home and cried and cried some more until the kids fell to sleep.

The following week went by in a blur. At the funeral, I had them play "Missing You" (instrumental), which made it a little tougher on me than I knew; but we made it through. About a week after the funeral, Kirk and Wendal came to the house and said that they had made an arrest.

I said, "You're kidding. So soon?"

Kirk said, "No, we are not kidding. We had practically everybody, every officer—black and white—out asking questions in the area. Because Shawn's office was in the heart of the city, somebody had to have seen or heard something, so as we were questioning these two young men, they began to look at each other. Well, I wouldn't call them young men but young boys. They said that they were on their way down to the police station because they had heard on the news something about a murder, but wasn't sure, but the picture that they seen and the construction site or building that they were showing on the news was the same place that they had met this lady at. They said that the lady offered to pay them five thousand apiece if they would do her a little favor. She wanted them to shoot both her and her husband with a blank gun that she would supply them with."

I was beginning to look a little nervous; then Wendal said, "Are you sure that you want to hear the rest of this? Because you are not going to like it."

"Go ahead. I'll be all right."

"The boys said that this lady wanted them to meet her at four thirty back at the office right before it was time to go home. That way, when they did get back home, he would reassure her of his love. Sharon told them that you know how sometimes when you have been married for a long time. And the love seems to have disappeared, and you want to put the sparks back in the marriage, so you do things to make it happen. Sharon said, 'Now I'm not asking you to kill either one of us. That's why I'm going to supply the gun that you will be using. I only want to get him to love me even more. So after you shoot him, then I will give you the money, then you can shoot me and then make it look like there was a break-in so no one will think anything different.' The boys said it sounded a little crazy to them, but they were looking at the money, and after all, it wasn't murder."

"Okay, wait a minute here. You mean to tell me that Sharon paid to have my husband shot?"

"Yes, that's right, Ray, but it gets even better. The boys said they were going to confess because they didn't want the lady to come back and blame them for murdering her husband. So after we arrested them, we went to have a talk with Sharon who was packing up to leave town, thinking that she had made a clean getaway. Oh yeah, the boys said that they had done a lot of things in their lives, but they had never murdered anyone or done anything that serious before. But anyway, back to Sharon. When Kirk and I got to her house, we acted as though nothing was wrong so that there wouldn't be a big scene. So once we got inside, Sharon was still packing. She had the nerve to ask if we had found whoever it was that had murdered her 'bighearted' boss. We told her that we had. She stopped packing and said, 'Oh, did you really find them? I mean, did you really find whoever it was that did it?' 'Yes, Sharon, we did, and it was two of them, just like you said.

Sharon, we are here to read you your rights.' 'What are you talking about? Read me my rights?' 'Sharon, the game is over. The two young men that you hired confessed.'

"At that point, she started to run. But we grabbed her, and she just started screaming and screaming like she had lost her damn mind. But when we got her down to the station, she started pouring her heart out, saying that she was not sorry, and if she had to do it all over again, she would. Because she was tired of hearing about how much Shawn loved you. Sharon hated you for being so forgiving of him when you thought that he had fucked up. Sharon said that if she couldn't have him, you were not going to either.

"Rachael, she really hates your guts. Sharon said that she kept him out on purpose, hoping that you would get so mad at him and put him out. But after so many times of keeping him out didn't work either and you still didn't put him out, Sharon started having her friends call the house and act like they had slept with him in hopes that, once again, you would get so mad and put him out. And then he would become all hers, but that backfired. And she was just tired of watching him go home to you and make love when it should have been her that he was going home to make love to.

"The thought of him and you together only made her angry, so she decided to put a stop to it once and for all. Sharon just kept on repeating over and over, 'Shawn loved her and those damn kids. But I know that deep down inside, he really wanted my son and me. I just know it, but Rachael wouldn't take her slimy hands off him no matter what. Man, Shawn would tell me to order his wife some flowers and have them sent to her office and have the card to read, 'From the one who loves you the most.' Damn, I hate that bitch.'

"Sharon said that she wanted to have you killed, but it was hard to keep up with you on your job, and she wasn't sure of your work hours. Sharon said she would ask Shawn where you were at certain times, and he would say, 'She's at work. What do you want with her?' Then she would say, 'Oh nothing.' 'That bitch,' she kept on saying. So finally, the idea came to her to hire a hit man, but she would play it off and tell him that she would supply the gun. Sharon said that she had no intentions of putting blanks in the gun that Shawn kept. Sharon said that she just had to find the right person to do the job. Sharon said that Shawn kept blanks in the gun that he kept in the office because he didn't want to hurt anybody if they tried to rob them while they were there in the office. He said he only wanted to stop them."

I began to shake and cry and yell, "That bitch! That bitch has ruined my life, my family. Everything is ruined! That bitch! Just wait until I see her."

Then Kirk said, "Rachael, Sharon has been put into a mental hospital."

"That's good because when I get in to see Sharon and break her fucking neck, she'll already be in a hospital, and I'll just say that she was trying to attack me when all I was doing was trying to talk to her."

"Now, Ray," Kirk said, "you know that no one is going to let you near that crazy bitch."

"Oh, Sharon ain't crazy yet, but she will be as soon as I'm through with her. She's gonna wish that she never met any member of my family. There has got to be a way for me to get in to see her, and when I do, she's gonna lose a lot more than that little potato brain of hers. I know I'll just wait a few months and let her think that I have forgiven her. Better yet, I'll start to write her letters, telling her that we both lost someone that we loved. I'll make her think that he did love her as much as her little make-believe mind had her believing. Oh, that bitch has fucked with the wrong household this time."

"Rachael, do you think that Shawn would want you to do that to her?"

"Hell yeah and then some."

Then I said, "Maybe not really, but it would make me feel better, if nothing else. But I do have to do something because Sharon has taken away my life and my children's life with their father. Now what are we going to do? Because that crazy bitch couldn't find someone unattached."

"Rachael," Wendal said, "the kids have already lost one parent. Don't make them lose another." Then Wendal put his arms around me, and I cried for all of us.

Some months have passed now; and Kirk, Wendal, and Officer

Peters helped us struggle through the roughest times, but it's better now. Just a little but it's better. I've gone back to work; the kids are doing much better also. And time just keeps on moving on; although it's been seven, almost eight years, I can't let go. It always seems like yesterday, and Shawn and I are planning on doing something either with the kids or by ourselves. I'm always daydreaming about that horrible day that my daughter called my cell phone. I keep thinking what if—what if this never happened, what if I had divorced Shawn, thinking that he had cheated or was doing drugs or just smoking weed again. What if?

I know now that I should have believed him when he told me what he was really doing when he was gone. He offered to take me with him so that I could see for myself. But I thought that he was only saying that because he knew that I was not going to go. I thank God for my family and coworkers for sticking with me and the kids. I'm glad they cared enough about us to continue with us; after all I put them through, they helped me deal with Shawn's death and go on with life.

Lisa tells me daily that Shawn would never believe that I would behave like this. Lisa said, "Girl, you never sat at home long enough to watch a complete movie on TV. Now you can rewrite any movie that comes on cable. Rachael, all you do is sit around, making dates with the TV and the tub. Then off to bed. Rachael, it's been a good while since Shawn's death. One minute, you were okay. Then the next, you went back into your shell. And now it's been almost a year since you've dated anyone or been out with anyone. Come on, now let's go out to a lounge, church, bowling—something." We started laughing. "Rachael, even your sisters asked me if I could get you to go out because the kids were worried about you."

"Okay. Okay. Let's go out this weekend. How about this Friday after work?"

"Okay. Good. We'll go to Happy Hour down at the riverfront."

"But I'll need a quick bath before we go because I can't stand wearing the same thing all day and night."

So I promised Lisa that we would go out on Friday.

"That's my girl." Then Lisa turned and left my office, smiling.

And so was I.

I knew that I had to get back on track. And I had to start somewhere. Damn. The days went by so fast it was already Friday, and I know I had promised Lisa that we would go to Happy Hour. But like I said, I was gonna need to have a bath first because the case that I had today really made me sweat.

So here I am, soaking and thinking about the last week that Shawn and I spent together. It started out the usual. For some reason, I just can't seem to let go of my Shawn. But I know that it will pass. And I'll be able to live my life with him being only in my thoughts occasionally. But here I am, taking one of my long baths, when I'm supposed to be meeting Lisa in a little while to hang out; so as soon as I get comfortable in the tub, the phone rings.

"Damn, who could that be?"

I got out of the tub and answered the phone without looking at the caller ID. I said, "Hello."

"Ray, it's me, Lisa."

"Hey, girl."

"Ray, I'm sorry, but I'm going to have to pass up tonight."

"What? What do you mean you're going to have to pass up tonight?"

"Girl, because Eric and I have been on the outs. But now he wants to talk. He asked me if I could do him a favor and stay home and talk to him so we can try and work things out. So, girl, do you mind if we go out tomorrow after work? Will that be all right with you?"

"Yeah, girl, that's fine with me. You go ahead and get your thing together, and I'll see you tomorrow—I mean, on Monday."

We hung up the phone. And I said, "Damn, I was kinda looking forward to going out tonight, but that's all right. I'll just get back in the tub and soak awhile."

So here I am again, soaking, with too much time on my hands to just soak and think. So as I'm just sitting and relaxing in the tub, I started to drift off, thinking about the time that Shawn and I spent together, our ups and downs, the good times as well as the bad times. I'm just relaxing and thinking about everything because I've always been a dreamer—always believing that people, places, and things would someday be just the way that I wanted them to be.

So that's why I always jump in the tub as often as the need arises. I would burn scented candles and just relax after a long day at work. I really enjoyed my job so much that sometimes my clients' problems would become a part of my problem; it was as though I could feel their pain along with them. I was such a softie. Boy, I had to toughen up because I was bringing too much of their stuff home, and I really didn't need that because Shawn and I have our own set of problems. When I look back over the years of our lives—all the lying, cheating, drug abuse—man, I thought that after having three beautiful children for him and showing my husband just how much I loved him, he would stop all the outside activities that kept him away from us so much. But showing him all that love was just not enough.

But I thank my heavenly Father because, like it is said, He will put no more on you than you can bear. Because I didn't know just how much more of Shawn stuff I could take. There were women calling the house, telling me all the things that they were doing with him. Now I am not one to just believe anything that they were saying, but when personal things about my husband's body was being said—like where his birthmark was and his favorite foods, things that went on in a course of a day at our house—these types of things were things that I know could only come from someone living in our house. I knew that I didn't tell anyone, so it had to come from Shawn telling someone, and when I would try and talk to Shawn about it, I already knew the outcome ahead of time. I knew what he was going to say before the question was even asked. So a lot of time, I would just bite my tongue. Because I didn't want the children caught in the middle of us arguing with each other, because sometimes the children would say, "Ma, you fuss at Daddy too much."

So all I could do was try to keep the piece by keeping my mouth shut until the last straw came when my son broke his arm and fractured his ankle. When I got the call at work, I panicked. When I got down to the hospital, there was Shawn, he and his lady friend who was supposed to work for him down at the construction company. So I thought about what he told me,

"Today it's just going to be my boys and me."

I was thinking that if we were not in a public place, I would raise all kinds of hell. Because of his lies, now my baby is hurt.

Shawn saw the look on my face, which pretty much told him that all hell was going to break loose when we got home.

Shawn acted like it's not enough that they're together damn near 24-7. Shit, now the bitch had my husband during the weekend too.

Now it looks as though my weekends with my husband—the only time that we really have to spend together—is gone because my job keeps me going all the time. That's probably why. I have not had the time to sit down and really realize that my marriage is nothing more than having the convenience of lying in bed with someone next to you because sex was down to almost nothing.

I don't think that we even realized how far apart we had become; I'm going right, and he's going straight to hell whether we prayed or not.

When we were done at the hospital, Shawn said, "I'll meet you at home. I'm going to drop Sharon off at her house, and I'll meet you at the house. I'll be right home, I promise. I'll be right there."

"Whatever," I said as the attendant rolled our son out in the wheelchair. I told the attendant that I would be just a minute while I got the car.

While driving home, I asked Shawn Jr. and Jaylen what happened; they looked at each other and said, "We asked Dad if we could take our skateboard out and play on the hill with it."

"Hill? What hill?"

"There's a hill that they are working on near Aunt Sharon's house. But at first we were just running up and down the hill, then I thought that we should try it with the skateboard, but that didn't work."

"So I see that, but I still don't understand how you fell so hard."

"Well, Ma."

"What, little boy?"

Shawn Jr. said, "I'm not supposed to say anything. But Sharon's son, Derrick, ran up behind me and pushed me as hard as he could. Jaylen was trying to tell him not to get so close-up behind me while I was trying to get my skateboard to sit right on the hard dirt, but he pushed me before Jaylen could finish saying what he was saying. But, Ma, please don't say anything to Dad because I told Dad that he did it by mistake, but I know that he did it on purpose because I wouldn't let him play with my skateboard. Ma, I don't want Dad to be mad at me because of what happened."

"Junior, your father will not be mad at you."

"Ma, please don't say a word. Just let it go, okay? Please."

Now I am really boiling because I can't cuss him out like I want to, the way he deserves to be handled. *Or I'll look like the bad guy once again if I say anything*, I'm thinking to myself as we are pulling up into the driveway. As we are pulling up, here comes Big Shawn looking so stupid he was looking like he was about to get a beating. But if I could, I would rip his head off. But instead, I will make him wish it were off. Damn, I started to feel so tired I didn't know what to do, so I made sure that he knew how I felt without saying a word with my mouth. I just looked at him hard.

The kids were there, and I knew that they were looking right at me, waiting for me to go off, because I could see the tension in their faces, just waiting for me to blast off; even Big Shawn was looking scared. But I kept the peace and said, "If anyone needs me, I'll be in the bathroom, soaking in the tub."

When I walked into the bedroom and started undressing, Shawn walked in and said, "Baby, I'm so sorry."

"Sorry," I said, but I didn't look at him, and I said it again. "Sorry is not good enough. How could you let your children see you with another woman?"

"Another woman? Sharon is not another woman. She works for me, and you know that, baby."

"Baby my ass."

"Baby, please listen. The boys and I were at the park, just the three of us, when Sharon paged me. I had left my cell phone in the car, so when she kept on calling me, I decided to call her to see what it was she wanted. Sharon wanted to see if I could come by and sign some contracts that needed to be signed by Monday morning. The contracts needed to be shipped out much earlier than I usually get to the office. Sharon gets there way before I do. Baby, we were not doing anything. I promise you that we weren't, baby. I have not cheated on you since that time in high school. I swear it may look like it because I'm not home a lot. But, baby, I love you and only you. I couldn't even see myself lying down with anybody else. Baby, please believe me, I love you. And don't forget that. I have asked you to hang out with me one day so that you could see for yourself just what it is that I do all day at the job and at the counseling center."

"Shawn, you know I have really had it with you after all these years. You know, Shawn, I bring home just as much money as you do."

"Where did that come from?"

"It came right out of my mouth, and what I am seriously thinking about right now is us and our lives and what we mean to each other."

Before I could finish saying what I was saying, Shawn grabbed me and kissed me like we were teenagers.

And I just froze; he was kissing me all over my face and neck, then back to my lips until I opened my mouth to kiss him back. I was opening my mouth to tell him to stop, and when I did, he stuck his tongue down my throat. His hot tongue felt good and tasted of mint. I slowly stopped fighting and squirming, then put my arms around his neck. I started running my hands through his hair and gave in to his passionate kisses. He continued to kiss me all over with his tongue running in and out of my ear and up and down my neck. He had taken off my bra, and I didn't even realize it; he was kissing my nipples so tenderly. Damn, how I loved it when he made love to my breast. I started to moan and kiss the top of his head while letting my hands explore his body until I felt his erection; he was getting harder by the minute. He just continued to make love to my breast because he knew just how aroused I got when he did that.

"Oh, baby," he said after feeling between my legs and seeing how moist he had gotten me. I whispered, "Ooh, baby." Shawn started to move his kisses down to my stomach, placing light little kisses down the way to my navel, and continued down until he reached the top of my kitty cat. I still had my panties on, and he kissed and tongued my panties as if they were off. I loved that. Then he slowly slid my panties to the side and slowly started letting his tongue run up and down and in and out of my kitty. He slowly slid my panties off and went to town. He was so smooth I didn't realize that he had taken off his clothes and was entering me at the perfect moment. "Oooo, baby, you know just how to make me forget any and everything."

After being inside of me for a few minutes, he said, "I want to taste you again." And he did, tasting all my juices that had begun to flow. He was really enjoying himself; then he raised my left leg to his shoulder and stuck his tongue in me a little deeper.

"Ooh shit. Ooh shit, baby. You're gonna make me cum, baby."

"Hold on one second, don't cum yet." Then he stood up with his penis in his hand and slowly guided it into me, saying, "Ooh, baby, you feel so good." And with a few more strokes, I could feel Shawn getting harder and harder. Then he said, "Okay, baby, let's cum together." And we did.

Sweat was pouring off him as he lay on top of me.

"Baby, you take all my strength away every time. So how could I have anything left for someone else?"

"I just know that you better not."

He kissed me on my cheek and said, "I love you too much for something like that. I just work a lot, baby, you know that."

"I just know that I get too jealous sometimes when you spend so much time with Sharon."

"Baby, I promise that I am going to cut down on my hours at work and spend more time with you and the kids." Then he kissed me on the cheek and rolled over.

We just lay there awhile, enjoying the moment.

Until I got up and went into the bathroom to freshen up a bit.

When I came back into the bedroom, Shawn was looking at me as if he could eat me up all over again. He acted as though we had not just had a session of hot lovemaking, and damn, was it good. And at the spur of the moment.

I guess that made it better, but he was always good at any time, day or night.

Shawn kept on staring at me as I was coming out of the bathroom. I looked down at him and damn if he didn't have another erection.

"Honey, please sit on me."

"Hey, come on now. You know you just wore me out. I need a minute."

"Oh, baby, please."

"No, not now."

"Okay then, just lie next to me then, and we'll see what happens, all right?"

Damn, I began to smile because my insides had begun to warm up again at just the thought.

I headed toward the bed, but I told him that I was not going to do anything. He said okay with a smile. So I lay next to him. After a second of me lying next to him, he took my hand and laid it on his protruding big piece of beautiful meat.

"Please, baby. Can you just rub it for me please, baby?"

Damn, I was thinking every time that we did make love it was always good. I was stroking him up and down when he leaned over and started licking on my breast. Just like he was licking an ice cream cone. Then he started to run his hands along my stomach, inching his way down to my kitty cat where I had gotten wet all over again.

He just let his hand run up and down my kitty, giving it a massage. I started to moan and move my hips. I just couldn't believe what I was doing because I was already sore. But just the touch of his hand moving ever so slowly up and down my kitty cat made me forget that I was already sore.

But I didn't care how sore I was; I needed him inside of me.

I was feeling no pain when he let one of his fingers slide up inside of me. Shawn was heating me up and getting me ready for big daddy, and boy was I ready.

He continued to kiss me all over my breast.

Then he eased his way on top of me, slowly inching his way inside of me; he felt marvelous.

I thought that I had died and gone to heaven. Oh, Shawn knew just how to please me; he knew exactly what got me going after years of experience with each other. We knew exactly what turned each other on.

He was working his charm very well. There were times when I would have to push Shawn off me a little bit because he would get so excited. And because of his size, it would hurt.

But he still knew what to do, so he would move very slow until I could get with his rhythm; then we would go to town. Shawn and I worked each other so well that it seemed like the very first time.

We were sweating up a storm, and I felt him getting harder and harder; he started whispering my name and saying, "Ooh, baby. Ooh, Rachael." I knew that he was ready to break loose, so I squeezed my kitty even tighter.

As he came, he whispered, "Ooh, baby, that felt so good. But you are always so damn good." Then he kissed me lightly on the lips and said, "I love you and only you. Baby, always remember that, okay?"

Then he turned over and pretended to be going to sleep so that I wouldn't continue the conversation that we had earlier, before he made his sneak attack on me.

"Damn you, Shawn. You sleep now, but tomorrow we will talk, do you understand me?"

"Yes, baby, I understand."

The next morning, when I woke up, I was trying to beat Shawn out of bed. But he was already up before me and had been in the shower and was half dressed. He said, "Good morning." He leaned over to kiss me, but I had my hand over my mouth because I knew that my breath was reaching out. He said, "Like I haven't smelled that mouthpiece of yours a million times before."

I punched him on his arm as I grabbed my toothbrush and began to brush my teeth.

As he was walking out of the bathroom, he said, "Can we meet for lunch, or will you be in court all day?"

"I don't know. I'll have to check my calendar book. Hey, go ahead and look in it and see what I've got going on around noon."

He looked in there, then hollered, "It looks as though you have a break right at noon."

"So I'll see you at noon. Where is it that you want to meet up?"

"Hey, how about Sinbads?"

"Naw, let's go for some real home-cooked food."

"Oh, I know. We'll go to Callies's Kitchen."

"Hey, that sounds great. Okay, honey, I'm leaving." But he ran in, kissed me real quick, and grabbed my butt.

I told him, "Quit playin'. Don't start what you can't finish. Don't forget I'm the boss. Now what?"

As he was hugging me, I said, "Get out of here." He kissed my nose, then said, "I'll see you at noon. I love you." He then left. As he was closing the door to our bedroom, I tried to catch a glimpse of him. "Damn, I love that man."

But he has been acting kinda funny lately. Something going on with him, I can feel it. It's as though a light kicks on in my head, and I wonder what he's doing.

But if I didn't know better, I'd say that he was on those drugs again. But I don't even want to go there with that thought.

It's just that the sex was out of this world; it was the way it used to be when he was on drugs, the way that he keeps coming back one after another—dammn—over and over again.

And that just wasn't like him. Lately.

Then again, we have not had sex in about two weeks, so maybe that's it. But whatever it is, I'm going to be more attentive to my husband's needs.

Maybe he's been reaching out for me, and I'm not there for him.

I am going to cut down on my hours so that I can spend more time with him.

I won't mention my feelings to Shawn about thoughts of him on drugs; I'll just keep my eyes open and watch his behavior. Because he just might have forgotten that he told me how it makes him act, so I'll just be cool.

Damn, I'm getting mad at myself for even thinking about it because I know better.

When I got out of the shower, it was already seven o'clock, so I got dressed, then went to wake up the kids for school.

When we were all dressed and ready for school, we all hugged and kissed before going out the door; that was a big deal with me because my mother always made my sisters and brothers and I hug before we went out of the door even if we were mad at each other. She would say, "Get over it and kiss before you leave out this house." I just kept the tradition going, and it works.

When I got to work, I was swamped with new cases on my desk; in addition to that, I had a court appearance, and I had to visit a client in lockup.

My day was moving right along. Before I knew it, it was time to go meet Shawn for lunch.

I wasn't going to make it, so I called him and said that we were going to have to change our lunch to dinner for sure, just the two of us.

He said, "Okay, honey, I'll meet you at home. Anyway, I'm kinda busy myself. Sharon stepped out of the office for a minute, and I'm answering the phones, so I'll just see you tonight. We can still go to Callies Kitchen, and we won't have to rush."

"Sounds good to me."

"Honey," Shawn said.

"Yes, dear?"

"I love you so much."

"Well, I love you even more, but don't be tryin' to sweet-talk me because we've got to talk about our boys and you."

"Okay, love you." Then we both said, "Talk to you later," and hung up the phone.

But later never came. That's been almost seven, going on eight, years now; and I still can't shake the day that the man of my life was taken away.

I've been married again, but the feelings were not the same as they were for Shawn. Those kind of feelings can never be replaced.

And I know that. So the people that I have dated have been totally different.

Robert was the next guy that I fell for.

I met him through Lisa. She's good at trying to hook people up, and I don't know why I'm going out with her again just so she can try and hook me up with Mr. Wrong.

I can feel my bathwater getting cold. So I hurry up and get out. I think I'll just call Lisa and tell her that I can't make it, but I can just hear her mouth now.

"I'll bet you were soaking in that damn tub and started to feel sorry for yourself again, and now you want to stay home and mope."

But we are going to hang out tonight. I never let Lisa forget how my second marriage turned out even though she didn't make me marry him.

Robert was so easy to get along with; we laughed a lot, and we got along just fine. I'm thinking about Robert while I'm dialing the phone to call Lisa. She picks up the phone, sounding so dry.

I said, "Lisa?"

"Yeah, Ray?"

"Girl, what is wrong with you?"

"Rachael, I don't know. I started feeling bad after work, so I just came home to rest up before we went out. But I don't think that I'm going to make it."

"Girl, do you need me to come over and do anything for you?"

"Naw, Ray, I'm just going to rest. It's probably just gas."

"All right, if you need me, just call, but I am going to check on you later, okay?"

"Okay, Ray."

Then we hung up the phone. Dammn, I was ready to put up a fight; but now that she is not going, what am I going to do?

I want to do something outside of thinking about my past life. Even though I cared a lot about my husbands, it was time to let go. What is wrong with men and me? All the ones that I seem to run into are either on drugs, alcohol, or other women. Damn, with Robert, I knew that it was not going to work when I found out about his drug use.

I really should have known sooner, but I guess I was too busy enjoying the sex and looked past the signs that Robert had displayed.

But I guess that since Shawn had passed and time had passed on, I tried to just block out everything, even the signs that Robert had showed when he was using.

But I never thought that he would lie to me about such a serious matter, so I hung on in there for two years before I had to break myself away from him and his good loving.

It was kinda hard because on top of the good sex, he was all good to me, and I knew that he really cared about me and my children who are all grown and gone on their own now.

Shawn Jr. and Jaylen still run the construction business and have branched out into a clothing and jewelry store, with their sister handling the books for them.

So they are all doing just fine. But I am still a little overprotective of them sometimes, just as they are about me, but it's all good.

Now back to thinking about Robert. For the most part, he was a good man.

But I just couldn't sit back and watch him destroy his life slowly, then tell me that he was only hurting himself.

But anyway, Shawn and Robert are both a part of my past, and it's time that I move on.

I had just walked back into the bathroom when I heard the phone ringing.

I started smiling to myself, just thinking about the life I've had; the phone seemed to want to jump off the hook. "Hold on!" I yelled as if they could hear me; I picked up the phone without looking at the caller ID.

"Hello?"

"Hey, Ray, what's up?"

It was my sister Denise. "Oh, girl, nothing much. Lisa and I were supposed to hang out, but she isn't feeling good. Why? What's on your mind? What do you have planned?"

"I was wondering if you wanted to go across the water because I am bored as hell myself."

"Girl, you haven't said nothing but a word. All I was doing was falling asleep and having memory flashbacks."

"What?"

"Denise, I can't seem to let my past stay in the past, I just keep thinking about Shawn and Robert."

"You know what? When the right person comes along, you'll let go. It won't go away completely, but it will go away."

"I hope so and soon."

"Girl, you called at the right time. I can't wait to get out of the house."

"You know, that's another thing. I'm going to start getting out of this house. I'm going to put it up for sale."

"Like I said, Lisa and I were going to go out, but Lisa wasn't feeling well, so yeah, let's go. Are you gonna pick me up or what?"

"I know. How about I just come to your place and I ride with you?"

"That's fine."

"Oh yeah, did you ask Wanda if she wanted to go? She is already on her way over, so we'll be at your house shortly."

"Okay."

"All right."

We said our goodbyes and hung up. I walked back into the bedroom and started to get dressed.

I started thinking I've got to change my way of life because my life consists of my job, my children, and my husband coming over once in a blue moon when he thinks that I'm horny enough to sleep with him.

But that's all going to change even if I have to start hanging out by my damn self. I just keep feeling sorry for myself because of other people's fuckup.

As of this day and the rest of my life, I'm taking control.

I'm even going to stop my clients from treating me like I'm their therapist.

Because I'm a damn good lawyer who's about to get even better. Damn, I was on a roll thinking about getting my life in order when I heard someone at the door.

I go and open it without asking who it is. But it's Robert.

"Hey, Rachael, how are you? Fine, I hope."

"What are you up to?"

"Nothing much. I just thought that I would stop by and see how you were doing since I haven't seen you in a while."

"Well, I'm doing just fine, thanks for asking."

"Well, I can see that you're fine."

"Look, Robert, do not think for one minute that there is going to be any sex going on because there won't be any sex going on—not today or ever again. So you can stop all the buttering up, there will be no sex."

"Rachael, I am totally shocked at you. What are you talking about? I only stopped by to see how you were doing. Not for any sex even though that doesn't sound like a bad idea."

"Man, please. You know you want to try and get my panties off. Well, this time, it's not going to happen."

"Girl."

"Girl my ass." He started to laugh.

"Ray, I only stopped by to say hi."

"Yeah right."

"Anyway, Ray, why are you trippin'? Because every time that I do stop by, you are all over me just as hard."

"Well, that's true, but we are no longer going there."

"Why not?"

"Because."

"Because what, Rachael?"

"Look, Robert, you and I are not together anymore because I am tired of the three-hour stands with you."

"We can make it a one-night stand, but you always put me out afterward. Anyway, I'm still your husband."

"You're right, but that's in name only."

I turned to go into the kitchen to get a drink of water out of the fridge when Robert walked up behind me.

I had on all my clothes except my blouse. Robert put his arms around my waist and started touching my breast.

I said, "Stop. It's not going to work."

Robert said, "Oh, come on, Ray, just one more time?"

I could feel him starting to rise. I was just about to give in when there was a knock on the door.

"Who is that?" he said.

"It's Denise and Wanda. We were about to go out."

"Damn," he said but continued to play with my breast. He was still trying to put his hands down my pants; then he started to take them a loose.

But the knock got louder; he said, "Don't answer the door. Let them think that you are not at home." Then he took my hand and rubbed it across his erection.

"No," I said and pulled myself away from him.

"Shit, they would have to show up now," I said to myself just as I was about to give in for one last time.

But I am glad that they did show up. I opened up the door, and Wanda said, "Girl, what took you so damn long to open up the door?" She looked and saw Robert, then looked at my blouse that wasn't there.

She and Denise looked at each other and started laughing. "Sorry we got here a little too soon."

"Huh?"

"Sure did," Robert hollered from the back.

"No, you didn't. He was just about to leave."

As Robert walked past me, he touched my butt and said, "See you later."

Denise and Wanda said, "What's up, Rob?"

He said, "Nothing now."

Then we all laughed. I said, "See you later, Robert."

Then he took off.

When he was out of sight, they both asked, "What's up with you and him? Are y'all gettin' back together or what?"

"No, we are not. He just stops by every once in a while and gives me a touch-up. He was just about to when y'all stopped by, thank you."

"Well, you are very welcome." And we laughed.

I said, "I'll be ready in a minute."

"Make it two and wash your ass because I know that thang's wet."

"Shut up," I hollered back; I could hear them laughing.

Finally, we were all headed for the car. And as soon as we were all in the car, Wanda said, "I'm glad that everything is all right with you and Robert even after the breakup."

"Why wouldn't it be?"

"Well, you know, with what happened with Shawn, and he turned around and was doing the same thing."

"Well, I thank God each day for strength because now I'm in a place where I'm looking out for myself, because—as you can see—the kids are all fine and have gone on with their lives. So now it's my turn."

"Well, good for you" Denise said. "So have you found you someone else? Or are you interested in anyone of the hundreds of lawyers that you work with?"

"No, I have not found anyone. And I am not looking for anyone. Not right now. Hello, I'm still married."

"That's right," Wanda said.

We all laughed because my sister Wanda was not one to just settle for one man, whether she was married or not.

"Mama always said that she took after Daddy. She's just hot in the ass."

When we reached the casino, everyone was excited and ready for fun. When we got inside, we decided to all go our separate ways and to meet again in a couple of hours in the lobby.

Then off we went.

Before I started playing the slots, I watched the table games just to see if I would be interested in playing the tables instead of the slots; but I went ahead and played the slots, vowing to come back and play the table games.

Time was going by so fast. And I really didn't realize just how long it had been since I had enjoyed myself. I really had a good time. I had been to the casino before, but it had been a long time ago.

I thought, *So this is where I'll start hanging out all by myself. Yep, this is where I'll be. I'll be back.*

I was really enjoying myself. I was talking to all kinds of people; I would hit a little bit, then play it back.

Then before I knew it, it was time to meet up with my sisters. Two hours had passed by so fast it was almost time to go, and I knew that I would be back soon.

When we were all accounted for and back in the car, everybody was kind of quiet and laid-back, just enjoying the moment.

We started to talk about the fun we had just had.

Then Wanda said, "Hey, y'all, I met this really cute guy. Shit, if we were not in a public place, I might have let him taste a little some'in, some'in."

We all busted out laughing, and Denise said, "Bitch, you probably did."

Wanda was laughing so hard that she started coughing and said, "I just let him get a little feel and gave him my cell phone number. Maybe we'll hook up and have a one-night stand. Who knows? I mean, after all, we use it or lose it, right?" Boy, did we laugh. We laughed and talked all the way home about men and sex.

Denise and Wanda said, "Sorry, girl, for breaking up your—how can I say? Your almost touch-up job because we're headed home to pick up where you left off."

We laughed again; then I said, "Fuck both y'all, now get out of my car."

"All right, don't hate. He'll be back to give you some."

I said shut up as they were getting into Denise's car.

The next few days, time just dragged along. After leaving Wanda and Denise that night after the casino and feeling lonely, I decided to go to the casino by myself.

Starting this weekend, after work on that Friday, I decided that I was going to go out by myself. So I did just that.

I had myself a ball. One day, while I was there playing, this guy sat down next to me and asked, "Is anyone playing this machine?"

I said no and continued to play my machine. He sat quietly for a while, just sitting there.

Now, I'm thinking, *Lord, don't let this man be crazy. Just let me be cool, and in a minute or so, I'll just get up and leave without looking scared out of my mind.*

So I did; I just played it off.

I got up and attempted to walk away.

But he said, "I hope that I didn't scare you away."

"No, you didn't. It was the machine." I was lying because the machine was doing fine.

He just kept on staring; that was why I left, but for a few minutes, I did look at him in the face and up and down. He looked like everything that you would want on the outside of a man.

But looks isn't everything, and everything was in all the right places, but for some reason, he still made me nervous.

So I finally got enough nerve to leave without looking scared.

I went away for about an hour and a half then found my way back.

But I didn't see him. Damn, where was Mr. Tall, Dark, and Handsome? Was he standing somewhere looking at me? I thought, but he wasn't. I said, "Oh well," and just played my machine.

I kinda felt relieved that he wasn't around.

So I just played my machine as if nothing ever happened.

But his little smile stayed on my mind.

I threw him out of my mind and continued to play my machine. All of a sudden, it hit for six hundred tokens; and as I was thanking the machine, who walked up was Mr. Handsome himself.

"Hey, you're pretty lucky, huh."

I turned, looked him in his eyes, and said, "Hope so, but we'll see in a little while I'll play this machine a little longer. Then I'll be able to let you know just how lucky I really am. That is, if you are still around."

"Oh, I'll still be around."

"So how is your luck coming?" I asked him.

He said, "Let's see. On one hand, it's doing okay, and on the other hand, it's doing great."

I smiled and said, "I hope that I can say the same thing by the time that I leave."

"Hopefully you will."

After he said that, he paused as if to say something else, but he didn't. He just walked away.

I continued to play for a while, looking around occasionally to see if he was anywhere in sight. But he wasn't.

I didn't see my handsome stranger anymore that night. And I didn't feel scared of him anymore. But then again, I didn't see him anymore either.

So finally, I decided to leave. By the time I looked at my watch, it was already twelve thirty. And I had to be at work the next day earlier than usual. And here I was—in another city.

"Well, I won't be doing this again, not on a work night."

And then when I do get home, there's no going straight to sleep right away because I'm going to have to take a shower. Then look and see what's on the TV. Then look and see what's in the fridge even if I am not hungry.

Then I'll go back into the room and let the TV take control of me.

I'm just thinking of all the things to do while driving home, and when I got there, I did all the things that I said on the way home.

Then the thought of Mr. Handsome came to me. Why?

I don't know. It was just a passing thought. I finally went to bed, and sleep came before I knew it.

When I woke up, I felt so good that I couldn't even tell you why.

The week went by so fast. I was in and out of the courts, moving like I was gliding on ice.

It was Friday already, and I thought about going over to the casino but decided against it because I really didn't feel like driving that far.

So I went home, took a shower, got in bed, and watched TV. I was thinking about my grandbabies.

So I called my daughter and asked her if she wanted to take the children shopping tomorrow. She said that would be nice. So that's what we did.

The next day, I picked them up, and we rode out to the new mall that had recently been built out in Pontiac.

When we got there, we walked around a lot just looking. Then the children spotted a store with all kinds of games in it. There were a lot of different games and slot machines. They even had a machine that looked like one of the machines that I play at the casino.

I played that machine for a while, but it wasn't doing much for me; plus it only gave out tickets that you turn in for prizes. But I was doing pretty good; I had won a lot of tickets that I gave to the children. They were pretty excited; we had a lot of fun, and I enjoyed shopping with my daughter and her children.

My boys didn't have any kids yet, so I spent as much time with Shawnda and the kids as often as I could.

Being in a room full of slot machines only made me think about going to play the real slots since it had been a few days since I had been there.

The more I thought about the casino, the more I wanted to go.

But I didn't rush because spending time with my daughter and the kids was special to me. When we left the game room, we walked around the mall, going in to different stores, buying all kinds of outfits for the kids and ourselves.

I even picked up the boys and their girlfriends something.

I had told Shawnda that I was treating even though she could afford whatever she wanted.

Well, the time came for us to go.

By now, I was thinking about going home alone; but after being with Shawnda and the children all day, I actually loved being by myself at times. Then there were times when I wanted to be with someone even after being married two times.

Sometimes I still felt alone because Shawn was always doing things to please his customers and buy us whatever he thought we wanted.

To compensate for lost time with us, Robert, on the other hand, did a lot; but it still seemed like we were going in different directions.

One day, I thought, *I am going to sit down and figure out just what went wrong with my marriages so that when number 3 comes along, I would know what to look for and be more attentive to him and not my job.*

While driving home, I decided that I was going to drive over to the casino for a little while just to relax my mind.

So after dropping off Shawnda and the kids, I headed home. I got there, took a shower, then tried on one of my new outfits, trying not to look like I was on the prowl.

The traffic was kind of heavy; it looked like everyone had the same thing on their minds, to get away.

I call it relaxing after a long week at work. And with the long hours that I had put in day after day, it's no wonder that I was going over more than I realized. Some days I did well, and some days I didn't do so good, but it was still fun to me.

Any way you looked at it.

At last, I had made it across and was in the parking structure.

And on my way to play my favorite machine, but when I got there, someone was already playing it. So I just stood and watched for a while. Then I started looking around for one of the other machines that I like to play.

As I walked to one of the other machines that I like to play, I saw that someone had a coat on the seat but was playing the machine that he was sitting at. So I walked up and asked him if someone was playing the machine that he had his coat lying on.

"Well, kind of. I am playing both of them." He turned and looked at me, then did a double take, then said, "Oh, you can go ahead and play. I'll just move my jacket."

When I looked down at him, I saw that he was handsome. I said thank you and sat down and started to play.

I started wondering just how often he came over. Feeling relaxed, I started asking him questions about the machine, if it was hitting or just giving enough to keep you playing.

He said, "I really don't know. I really wasn't playing it. I was holding it for someone."

"Oh, you were?"

"Yeah, but you're here now."

I gave him a little glance and said thanks, wondering just what he meant by that.

But I just let it go without giving it another thought.

I was beginning to get nervous not because I was scared, but because he was so pleasant to talk to.

And I didn't want to give off the wrong impression, you know, like I was flirting with him even though deep down inside of me I was. So I began to slack off on the small talk and move someplace else.

So as I stood up to play my last few coins in the machine, he stood also. When I dropped my last coin into the machine, the spinning started. I got one gold 7, then another; I started getting excited. Then it happened. The third gold 7 fell, and the machine started singing. I was saying yes, yes and started to turn. As I was turning, Handsome was right there and gave me a hug; and in my excitement, I hugged him back. I looked up into his eyes and said, "It's about time."

He looked down at me and gave me an unexpected kiss—a little light kiss on the lips—and said, "It really is about time that you hit."

Then realizing what had just happened, he said, "I'm sorry, I was so happy for you."

"Apology accepted." We were still in each other's arms when the attendant walked up and asked, "Whose machine was this?"

Not really realizing that we were still hugging, I turned and said, "Oh, it's mine."

Then he let me go. I couldn't believe what had just happened. A jackpot, a hug, and a kiss all in one night. I was feelin' like I was on cloud nine.

After the attendant left to go get my pay, I turned to say how good it felt to win a jackpot. But my words were froze in midair because Handsome was gone.

I felt a little jilt in my stomach, the kind you get when you're coming down in an elevator.

"Oh wow."

I thought that I was going to share my winnings with him. It was because of him that I was playing the machine.

I wanted to do something for him, or offer to buy him a drink or something, because he gave me the machine that was for someone else.

I kept looking around for him, but he was gone.

So after looking around for him a little longer and not seeing him, I played the machine a little longer, but the machine wasn't doing anything so I decided to just take my winnings and go.

When I got home, I thought about calling my daughter and telling her about my winnings, and what happened after I hit; but I changed my mind and decided to call my sister. But not to tell her about my winnings but just to talk to her and see how things were going with her and her friend because I knew he was not feeling well.

When I talked to Denise, I asked her how was Mark doing. She said, "He's doing a lot better and back to his old self again. So what's going on with you?"

"Old same, same old."

"When was the last time that you talked to your brother?"

"Which one?"

"You know, Ralph."

"Oh, I heard about the conversation that the two of you had."

"What are you talking about?"

"You know, the one about me not having anybody or seeing anybody for a while. Damn, Denise, why is everybody trying to hook me up? I've been separated for only eight months."

"You mean more like a year, don't you?"

"Yeah, whatever."

"I mean, after all, you did put the man and all your children out of the house, didn't you, Ray? What is the problem? Are you on menopausal or what?"

"Denise, shut the fuck up because you did the same thing just a few years ago, and for the record, I did not put my children out. They got grown and left on their own."

"Anyway, what's going on with you? And don't say nothing because I can hear it in your voice that something is going on with you."

"What? What about my voice?"

"The tone that you get when something exciting is going on with you or about something or someone. Which one is it? Did something happen at work? What is it?"

"Oh, wait a minute, you mean to tell me that I just can't be happy without having a reason for it?"

"Why yes, you can. But I know you, and I know that something is going on, and don't forget that I am your big sister, and I know all your mood swings."

"Yeah, whatever."

"Damn, Ray, just come on out with it."

"Oh, all right already, okay? Well, a couple of days ago, I went across the water and caught a jackpot—well, not just one but two jackpots—and every time I think about it, I get happy at the thought."

"Why you dirty little bitch."

"What? See, I knew that you would be trippin' that's why I didn't say anything before now."

"Denise, you know doggone well that I would have went with you across the water, but do you say let's go? No, you just up and go all by yourself, or did someone else go with you?"

"No, I went by myself, and what are you getting all upset for when you know doggone well every time that you go play bingo you don't ask me if I want to go."

"Ray, you don't even like bingo, so why should I bother to ask you to go?"

"But that's not what I'm saying. What I'm saying is you up and go when you want to without asking anybody if they want to go with you now, don't you?"

"Yeah, but—"

"But my foot."

"See, that's my point exactly, so why are you trying to front on me for going to my new favorite place, huh?"

"Okay, okay, I'm just under a little pressure right now, and I took it out on you. Please forgive me."

"Well, let me think about it, okay? All's forgiven."

"Well, let me tell you right now Wanda and I are planning to go across the water sometime this weekend or Friday when I get off work. It all depends on how I'm feeling, but be ready for Friday anyway just in case. Okay?"

"Okay, we'll see you then." We hung up. When I finished talking to her, it was a big relief because she can always make something out of nothing. But then again, she can be a real sweetheart. Anyway, thinking about the casino made me think of Handsome.

I call him Handsome because I don't know his name yet. But just thinking about the joy I felt when he bent down and kissed me lightly on the lips and gave me that manly bear hug—damn—that felt good. Damn. I hope that I can hit a few more jackpots so that he will be right there to share my joy again and again. Just the thought of him makes me get all warm inside and puts a smile on my face. Boy, here I am taking things too far when I don't even know the man's name.

But I do know that I look forward to seeing him again at the casino. That's for sure.

Now I couldn't wait for Friday to get here and my workday to be over so that I could act like I was not looking for him when I knew that I would be.

Because just that fast I had gotten used to talking to him every time I go.

Funny how this same man who I thought was going to attack me in some kind of way is the same one that I look forward to seeing when I do go over the water.

Now here it is, Friday, and it's the end of the day. I'm looking forward to a relaxing, stressless day at the casino.

Trying not to look as though I'm rushing or in a big hurry, I took my time and showered and picked out some nice jeans and a low-cut blouse to wear. I was not trying to look like I was on the prowl even though I was once again.

After I got dressed, I poured myself a little glass of wine to calm my nerves a bit while waiting for my sisters to call. Finally, the phone rings; it seemed like it took forever, and then when I picked it up and said hello, it was my daughter. I looked at the caller ID after I said hello. She said, "Hey, Mom."

"Hi, little girl."

"What's wrong?"

"Why you ask that?"

"Because you sound all dry." She asked me what was I doing.

"Oh, nothing too much. I was supposed to be going out with your two aunts, but they are taking so long to call that I was thinking about just taking my clothes off and going to bed." I lied because I did not feel like hearing her telling me that I go to the casino too much, so I was glad that she didn't ask where we were going.

She thinks that I am getting a little out of hand with my gambling as though she's my mother.

I tried to perk up a little because she can act so damn spoiled at times—she and her brothers.

They are partly the reason that my second marriage didn't work; but that's all right, I thought, because now it's all about me being happy.

I had started thinking about my children when I started drifting off while listening to her talk. I just ignored her; then I heard her say, "Mom, Mom?"

"Huh," I said.

"You're falling asleep on the phone."

"Sorry, baby, what were you saying?"

"Never mind. Go ahead and go to sleep, and I will talk to you tomorrow, okay?"

"Yeah, all right. If your aunts don't call within the next ten minutes, I'm going to bed and catch up with them later."

"All right, Mom. I'll talk to you later."

"Okay, baby." Then we hung up the phone. Just as soon as we hung up the phone, it rang again. I thought that she had forgotten something, but it was Denise.

"Damn, Ray, why didn't you call me as soon as you got ready? Are we going tonight or what?"

"Yes, we are going. I just had some things to do that's all. So what? Are you all coming over here, or do I come over there?"

"Well, we are closer to the freeway than you are, so why don't you just come on over here?"

"Okay, I'm on my way."

Once again, we were on our way across the water when Wanda said again that she hoped she could find someone who would like to spend a little time with her because she was really horny.

I said, "Honey, you know damn well that tonight is not the only night that you are horny. The last time that we were all together, you met some little sweet thing that you wanted to give a little taste of you to."

"Yeah," Denise said. "Whatever happened to him? Did you talk to him?"

"Naw, he was a little too young. I gave him the wrong number because he might have tried to get me hooked on his sweet self."

"Don't tell me you got scared?"

"Hey, it wasn't that." Then she started laughing. "He was just too young, and I really didn't want him to get hooked on this sweet stuff that I carry around with me."

We all had a good laugh. I said, "Wanda, all you ever talk about is sex."

"But you know what? I think that I have really met my match this time in my own husband. That man keeps me on my back, knees, stomach, elbows, whatever, and whenever he feels like it. I don't get the chance to be the aggressor that often because that man be on a young girl."

We all laughed so hard.

Then Denise said, "Then why are you looking for another Mr. Good, bar girl?"

"I'm just kidding, I couldn't take a chance and fool around with someone else. It's too risky. So I talk a lot of shit. I've changed for real."

"Convince yourself that's good."

"Oh fuck both y'all." After laughing again, there was a moment of silence; then Wanda said, "So how is Mark doing?"

"Oh, he's truly blessed. Not to sound rude, but can we change the subject please?"

"Sure, we can." Then Wanda and I looked at each other because we knew that he was probably not doing as well as she wanted him to.

But we changed the subject quick so as not to put a cloud over the good mood that we were in because we were about to partake in the joy of pulling the handle on a slot machine, but I had another reason for being happy on the inside; I was about to get my flirt on.

I was looking forward to seeing Handsome.

Damn, I couldn't believe that I was acting like a kid with a bag of candy. *I could hardly wait to see my new handsome friend*, I thought to myself.

I was smiling to myself, and in my own world, when I heard Wanda say, "Isn't that right, Rachael?"

I said, "What?"

She said, "Didn't you hear me?"

"To be honest, no, I didn't. What were you saying? I was in a fantasy."

"Well, damn come back down to earth, would you?"

"Oh, what is it?"

"Wait a minute, what were you fantasizing about?"

"Girl, wouldn't you like to know?"

"Anyway, what were you saying?"

"We were talking about men in general. We were saying how, in the beginning of a relationship, we act toward each other. Then, as time goes on, things start to change. As though we take each other for granted, just knowing that we have each other. And that we aren't going anywhere because we're supposed to have everything that we want in each other. At least that's what we say in the beginning, isn't it?"

"Now did you hear me that time, or did you drift off again?"

"Hey, I heard you that time."

"You know, after you get all comfortable with each other and you get all the little things out of the way, your likes and dislikes—all that stuff is out of the way, and you really start to know one another, that's when the shit hits the fan."

I said, "Isn't that the truth? But you know, what if my husband and I don't make it this time around, then my third husband and I will, and from the looks of things, it looks as though there will be a number 3. And even if that doesn't work, then try number 4. Just keep going until you get it right." We laughed and gave each other a high five.

"Hey, we'll just wait and see what happens."

By now, we had reached our destination, and everybody was eager to get started.

I was ready to flirt a little with my nameless friend.

When we got inside, everyone was on a different path, so we agreed to meet up at 12:00 a.m.

With that agreement, we were all on our way.

I headed to the spot where my nameless friend usually hangs at. But when I got there, he was not there. So I began to play anyway, hoping that he would show up, but he didn't; so after about a half hour, I went to another area that he usually hangs out.

And once again, he was not there, so I tried to throw him out of my mind. But that soft little hug and kiss just wouldn't let me.

But as time went on, I continued to play. I wasn't really winning, just kind of breaking even.

So before I knew it, it was time to meet the girls.

So I left. We all met as planned, and as usual, they were not ready to leave. And I was not about to let them see the disappointment in me, so I agreed to just stay a little longer.

So once again, we agreed to meet up; but this time, it was going to be in one hour.

So off we went again. I was saying damn to myself for feeling so stupid over missing someone that I didn't really know, so I tried to cheer myself up and continued to play. This time, I was doing pretty good; and wouldn't you know it, it was time to meet up with the girls. This time, I wasn't ready; but if they were ready, then we would leave.

I was the first to get to our meeting place, so I just sat down and waited because I knew that they would be there soon. I sat there and looked around at all the different people.

Damn, they sure are taking a long time to get there. I wonder if they forgot to look at their watches or what. Before I could finish my thoughts, here they come; they were kind of half smiling, so I said, "What's up?"

They said that they had just began to warm up when it was time to leave. So I said, "Okay, it's up to you if you want to stay a little bit longer or we can go."

"Okay," Denise blurted out, "just one more hour." We agreed and off we went.

I was really just looking for my new friend, but he was nowhere to be found, so instead of losing any more money, I just watched the cards being played.

Saying to myself that the next time that I did come, I was going to play if just one hand of blackjack. Because it seemed like a lot of fun.

Well, again it was time to go, and we did just that. On the way home, Wanda was saying that she had talked to a couple of different guys, but nothing came of it.

"Good," I said, "because you already have a husband." So we all laughed.

Then Wanda said, "So I guess you have found you somebody?"

"No, I did not, and I am not looking."

So here we are, on our way back home; no one hit anything, but we still enjoyed the outing.

But I was hoping that I would see my handsome friend. Well now, I really couldn't call him friend, could I? Because we were not really that.

We really didn't even know each other.

After dropping them off and going home myself, I opened my door, and something hit me in the face: the loneliness. Sometimes it was okay; then again, it wasn't. Well, this time it wasn't.

A song came to mind: "Who Can I Run to?"

This was a night for male company. I was getting horny myself; then I decided to go take a hot bath while letting the water run in the tub.

A thought came to mind that maybe I should call my husband over for a touch-up.

Then I thought better of it because once he came over, I probably wouldn't want him to leave.

I knew that the good times would only last for a couple of days because of his drug habit that he kept on denying. His paycheck would come up short when it was time to pay a bill; then all his jewelry started to disappear. All that money that I spent buying him nice jewelry all disappeared, and I said that's quite all right. I'll just keep on doing what I had been doing, and that was thanking God for bringing Mr. Right, the real Mr. Right. Not someone still trying to play games. I needed someone who was ready to settle down and do some traveling and just enjoy each other. I won't give up on that dream.

I miss Robert, but he's no good for me. Sex every now and then was all right, but that had to stop soon.

After standing there and thinking about Robert, I decided to take a shower instead of a long hot bath. Because the way I was feeling, I would be there for a very long time.

The next morning, I woke up feeling really good, thanking God and singing, as I headed for the bathroom to get my day started.

As my last case ends, I find myself walking and talking to myself and cursing because my feet were killing me.

I think that I may have gained a pound or two. This last case has gotten me a little nervous even though I know that my client is guilty, but hell, who isn't?

It's not like they caught him with the goods; they have only circumstantial evidence against him.

I have got to find a way to discredit the prosecutors and witness; that won't be hard to do because you can look at her and see that she is seeing two many things at one time (ha-ha) with those cross-eyes.

Okay, okay, but that's not going to be enough. I think that my client told me that he knows the witness from years ago when they were sleeping together, so all I really got to do is let her hang her own ass. We'll see.

I don't even know why I'm sweatin' on this one because I know that I have won this case, and with a couple of more easy wins, I'll be promoted to president or some high shit (ha-ha). Girl, you are something else. I pat myself on the back. As I'm getting into my car, I hear someone calling my name.

"Hey, Rachael." I tried to ignore the voice because I knew who it was it was—that little annoying bitch from across the hall.

I shouldn't say that because she was really good to me when Shawn died and through the breakup with me and Robert.

She's still walking fast and calling my name. "Yeah, Lisa, I'm over here. What's up?"

"Damn, girl, I didn't think that you heard me calling you," she said as she's trying to catch her breath. "I'm so out of shape." *My mind says you look it too.*

"What's up? What's so important that you had to run to catch up with me?"

"Nothing really, I was just wondering if you were hanging out tonight because I have been getting bombarded with questions about you."

"What?" I said.

"Ray, you know the new guy down the hall?"

"No, I don't know the new guy down the hall."

"Well anyway, he keeps asking me to introduce him to you, but I know how you feel about that, so I thought that if we just show up where he's going to be tonight that, you know, I could hook you up."

"Girl, if you don't get out of my face with that schoolgirl shit… Anyway, why can't he introduce himself if he's that interested?"

"Well, he would, but he says that every time he sees you, you're in your office quite busy, or he's in a hurry to get back to court and can't stop himself. So he came up with the idea that maybe I could run interference."

"Thanks, but I'm not interested at this present time. But thanks again anyway."

"So what do I tell him?"

"Tell him that I have an early appointment in the morning and that I'm staying in."

"Well okay, but you don't know what you're missing."

"Well, if that's the case, then you are welcome to him. Hey, I've got to go, so I'll see you in the morning."

Lisa said, "Okay, if God is willing."

If God is willing and he is. If god is willing, I'm saying to myself as I get into my truck. As I'm driving, the thought that I have not eaten a thing all day hits me; then my stomach starts to growl. Damn, I'm going to give you something to eat. Calm down.

I'm starving but don't know what I want to eat—Taco Bell, Church's Chicken, what. Okay, I say churches it is and some hot peppers, a good movie, a good fuck, and I'm in heaven.

Then another thought hits me. Damn, there's nobody home to fuck. I should become a hooker by night and lawyer by day. Who would know?

Okay, okay, get real. So I go pick up my food and head home. As I'm lying there, watching TV, a casino commercial comes on.

I thought, *Damn, it's been weeks since I've been to the place.* If I wasn't so tired, I'd run over there right now, but I can wait until tomorrow since it will be Friday.

So it's on for tomorrow. Thinking about tomorrow, I wonder if Handsome will be there because a young girl such as myself would be trying to get her groove on. Just thinking about him made me want to go right away, but I'm strong; I can wait until tomorrow.

And I sure hope that Denise and Wanda don't want to go. Hell, it's been awhile since we all have been together, and they have not mentioned anything about going to play at the casino.

I know why; it's because their black asses must have been doing good at the bingo games that they love to play. They don't even bother to ask if I want to go with them but will curse me out if I say that I went and played at the casino.

Well, it really doesn't matter because three's a crowd anyway.

Tomorrow, I'll give Denise a call after I'm finished with my day; but right now, I'm just going to enjoy my quiet time, chill, eat, and sleep.

Before long, I was awakened by the alarm clock again. It seemed like I had just fallen asleep; I wanted to throw the clock straight out the window.

I just lay there for a minute before I got out of bed.

I thought today is going to be the day that the prosecutor's witness was going to hang herself in court.

I should be preparing for my next case because this one is over. The bitch has lied under oath.

I shouldn't call her a bitch, should I? After all, she has made me look good as a defense lawyer who wins case after case.

But anyway, this was going to be fun.

As I am entering the building to my office, Lisa was heading toward me. *Damn*, I'm thinking, *why do I let this girl get on my nerve so much?* She has been a good friend to me. But at times, I just can't stand the sight of her. Why I just don't know.

I'll never let her know that; I just don't care for her, so I play it off with a fake smile and a warm speech when I talk to her.

Anyway here she is.

"Hey, girl, I haven't seen you in a while."

"I've been pretty busy with a shitload of cases that I've been working on. So how have you been?"

"Who? Me?"

No, your blind ass twin, I'm thinking. "Yes, you."

"Oh, I've been just great, but I think that I might be pregnant."

"What?"

"That's right. You heard me right."

Not after all that talk about not wanting babies because they might ruin your figure and your lifestyle.

"Not meaning to be funny, but shit happens."

"Well, don't think that this next question is out of order, but you did say that you and your husband were separated and that you were thinking about divorcing him, didn't you? And then again, you have been hanging out quite a bit."

"Yeah, I know, but..."

"But what? Wait a minute. Could the father be the cute guy that you have been trying to introduce me to because you seem to like him?"

"Ray, I didn't really like him, okay, okay? I did, but he was not interested in me. He was always asking about you. As a matter of fact, he had to leave town for a week. But he had asked if I wouldn't mind trying to hook him up with you once again, and this time, if you decline, then he wouldn't bother you again. But then he paused then said, 'No, ask her to call me.' But, Ray, I haven't seen you or him lately. But anyway, he's probably back now, so if I see him, what shall I tell him?"

"Tell him I said no offense, but he's a little too old, I hope, to be using a middleman."

"Girl, isn't that the truth? But sometimes, all it takes is one introduction, and the middleman is gone."

"Well, the next time that you see him, tell him to give you his number, and I'll give him a call."

"Okay, Rachael, don't kill me, but he did give me his number, but I don't know what I did with it. I mean, I didn't see you for a while, and I was going through my own little thing."

"Lisa, what is wrong with you?"

"I told you that I am pregnant, and yes, it is my husband's baby. It's just that I don't know if I want this baby or not. I'm not sure if I would make a good mother or not. And I'm not sure if that lying, cheating husband of mine is going to clean up his act or not."

"Well, what is he saying about it?"

"Ray, he swears up and down that he has not been cheating since we've been back together, but I just don't know, Ray. He says, 'Please, baby, please let's have our baby. I want something that is all mine—well, okay, ours.' But you know what I mean."

Then I said, "Yeah, black ass, I know what you mean." Then we started to laugh.

"So anyway, what are you going to do?"

"I don't know."

"Well, how many months are you?"

"Between two or three."

"Lisa, please. In a minute, you won't have a choice."

"I know, and I m scared."

"Scared of what?"

"I don't know. But anyway, I'll talk to you later."

"All right."

"I'll give rather get Eugene's number again if I see him before you do, but you know what? I'm likely to walk right past him if I did see him because right now I'm in my own world."

You always are, I thought with a smile on my face.

I shut the door to my office. Damn, how time flies; it's almost eight thirty. And I'm due in court in a half hour. Okay, now let's see. Where do I begin? Okay, gather up all my paperwork for the case then head for the courtroom.

Okay, everything's in place. Now we wait for the judge.

"All rise, the honorable Judge Wilson is presiding."

First case on the docket resumes: *State v. Mr. Mathews*.

"Ms. Defense, are you ready to start?"

"Yes, Your Honor."

"You may call the prosecutor's witness back to the stand. Mrs. Wells, will you take the stand?" the judge said.

"Mrs. Wells, may I remind you that you are still under oath."

"Yes, Your Honor."

"Proceed."

"Mrs. Wells, you said that you were coming out of the store that was a few feet away when you saw my client as he was running and clutching something black up under his arm. Is that right?"

She hesitated for a minute, then said, "As a matter of fact, he almost knocked me down. He was running so fast."

"Is that right, Mrs. Wells?"

"Yes, it is," she said in a smug tone.

"Okay, for the record, Mrs. Wells, what was the name of the store that you were in again or did you say you were coming out of? Can you tell the court again the name and location of the store that my client was coming out of when you saw him?"

"It was called Little Greg's Fashions."

"And it was located where? And where were you?"

"It's in the mall."

"And again, what store were you in?"

"I was in Mansas Jewelry Store."

"Which is where again?"

"It's across from Little Greg's Fashions." At that moment, she paused and looked over at my client then over at her lawyer because she knew then that I had caught her up in a big fat lie, and I smiled.

"Objection, Your Honor. She is leading the witness."

"Overruled. Now again, Mrs. Wells, remember you are still under oath."

"I know that," she said again in a smug tone.

"And you still say that you have never seen my client before? Is that right?"

She hesitated and then said, "He may look a little familiar, but that name I've never heard before."

"Okay."

"Objection, Your Honor. What does this line of questioning has to do with my client?" the prosecutors yelled.

The judge said, "All right, order in the courtroom."

"Your Honor, I'm trying to give this witness a chance to come clean and tell the truth because she is lying about not knowing my client."

"Proceed."

"Mrs. Wells, can you please tell the court how my client could bump into you when the two stores are across the street from one another?" Everyone looked at Mrs. Wells in disbelief.

"Is that true, Mr. Prosecutor?"

"Your Honor, I have no idea what she is talking about. I mean, what the defense is talking about."

"Okay, let me rephrase the question so that you will understand."

"Mrs. Wells, what store was it that you were in again for the record?"

"It was Little Greg's Fashions."

"Located where again for the record?"

"In the strip mall."

"And where again was Mr. Mathews?"

She didn't answer.

"He was across from where you were at, wasn't he?"

The room was quiet while we waited for her to answer.

The defense said, "Your Honor, may I have a fifteen-minute recess to talk with my client?"

"The court will recess for one hour. We'll just take a lunch break. Be back in one hour."

I heard the prosecutor yelling at his key witness, asking her why didn't she tell him that she knew Mr. Mathews all along.

"Do you realize all the time and money spent? Even if he is guilty, I have no choice but to ask the judge to dismiss all the charges against

Mr. Mathews. I have to ask that all charges be dropped, and you better hope that they don't come after you for perjury.

"Damn, all the eyewitnesses and the cameras and you get up there and lie through your teeth. We had him. Now this why, you bitch."

"Yes," Mrs. Wells said.

"Nothing. I'll be back in a minute."

"Oh, Mrs. Brunson."

"Yes?"

"Can we talk for a minute? Even though my client is sorry for what she has done, she hopes that you won't come after her."

"What? You have got to be kidding. But that won't be up to me anyway. It will be in the hands of the judge."

"But maybe your client will say a word on her behalf if he will."

"You have got to be out of your mind. Your client tried to send my client to jail for God only knows how long, and you want him to turn around and get her freed of any charges that the judge may throw at her? Come on now, give me a break."

"But I'll tell you what. I'll run this with my client and see what she has to say about it. After all, we still have him on camera and other eyewitnesses."

"Well, we'll take our chances with a jury."

"Now I am willing to make a deal."

"No thanks, we'll take our chances with a jury, like I said, and go from there. But here is a word of advice for you so that you won't look totally stupid. I mean, so that you won't look so bad. If I were you, I'd just ask that all charges be dropped against Mr. Mathews, and I'll see what my client wants to do, but I'm not promising you anything."

"Well, let's get back into the courtroom."

The bailiff said, "Court is back in session."

The judge asked the prosecutor, "Do you wish to cross-examine your witness?"

"No, Your Honor. But, Your Honor, I would like to ask that all charges be dropped against Mr. Mathews," he mumbled.

The judge said, "We cannot hear you, Mr. Prosecutor."

"Your Honor, I would like to ask the court to drop all charges against Mrs. Brunson—I mean, the defense's client."

"On what grounds?"

"On the grounds that my client lied about knowing Mr. Mathews."

"Just how does your client know Mr. Mathews?"

"Mrs. Wells said that they used to date."

Then the defense said, "If I may offer just a little more to this, Your Honor. His client used to date Mr. Mathews. This is true, but she also told my client when he broke it off with her that she was going to get back at him for leaving her some kind of way. And this is how she thought to get back at him, through the courts."

"So ordered. Case dismissed. Ms. Defense, will you be filing charges against Mrs. Wells?"

"One minute, Your Honor, while I have a talk with my client."

"My client says that he does not wish to file any charges against Mrs. Wells."

"Okay, but let me say this to you, Mrs. Wells. If you ever come into my courtroom and look like you are about to tell a lie, even a hint of a lie, I'll throw you so far up under the jail that you won't see light for years to come. Because of your lies, you could have cost this man his freedom for the rest of his life. Do you understand? And let me say this too. It's really up to the defense to bring charges against you. That's my job, but this must be your lucky day. Take this as a warning. Case dismissed. But if I were him, you wouldn't be getting off so easy. Now get out of my courtroom." Then the judge said, "Next case."

My client hugged me once we finally made it outside the courtroom and said thank you.

I whispered in his ear and said, "I know why you didn't want to press charges against her."

He looked at me and said, "Why?"

"Because you wanted to get out of the courtroom as fast as you could before anybody had a chance to bring up the rest of the case about the cameras and the other eyewitnesses. The prosecutor didn't because his key witness messed up. And no one would believe anyone else that he would introduce as a witness. So watch yourself because the next time, you might not have me as your attorney."

He just hugged me, then said, "You know, you are all right, Mrs. Brunson." Then he said, "Off the record, I did mess up, but thank God she lied or got crossed up on what she was saying. I am through with that kind of life for real."

I just looked at him and said all right. We hugged, and he went on about his business.

I thought, *Well, now that that case is over, I think I'll go out and celebrate. Maybe I'll call Eugene and see what's up with him. See if he's free or not. After all, this is a last-minute call.* Then I thought about it. Lisa dumb ass never did give me his number. So I guess I'll celebrate by myself.

Naw, I'll just go home and chill for a while but then changed my mind and decided to go out and get something to eat because the hunger pains were beginning to kick in.

So I decided to go to Red Lobster before going home. I would kill two birds with one stone. I would celebrate and get something to eat at the same time.

I pulled up at the Red Lobster, got out, went inside. There was a little wait. So I told the hostess that I would be seated at the bar. When my table was ready, she said, "No problem."

I went in and ordered a Long Island iced tea.

I smiled to myself, knowing the effects that Long Island iced teas had on me.

But I thought, *I'm about to eat.*

But when the bartender asked what will it be, I started to change my mind and said, "Give me a Long Island iced tea please." What the hell, I'm celebrating, and I'm about to put some butter on my stomach, and that will eat up the alcohol in my stomach.

While sitting there, thinking about the case that I had just won—you know, not really thinking about anything—this guy walked up and asked if I mind if he sits next to me because he really didn't like being by himself in a restaurant because women always try to pick him up.

I just kinda looked at him, and he started laughing, then said, "I'm only kidding. It just seemed like a good way to break the ice." So I smiled. He was handsome, so I said, "You may have a seat."

Then the waiter comes over with my drink.

He asked me what I was drinking.

I said, "A Long Island iced tea."

So he told the bartender that he would have what the young lady was having.

Then he turned to me and asked if I was also having dinner or just enjoying.

I said, "A little of both. How about you?"

"Oh, I'm doing the same, but actually I'm on a late lunch. And what about you?"

"Well, officially I'm off the clock, so to speak, for the day. Anyway, I just decided to stop in here before going home."

At that moment, the waitress came over and said that my table was ready; so as I was getting ready to leave, I extended my hand to say bye and enjoy your meal.

He shook my hand a little too long, I thought. Then he said, "Since we are both alone. Oh, I'm sorry for assuming that you are alone, but are you?"

"Well, today I am."

"Well good, I mean, would you mind if we shared a table together? Since we are both alone."

I looked at him and said, "Well, why not? If it's all right with my waitress." She nodded her head with approval and left the bar.

We followed the waitress to our table; she seated us in a corner booth as if she knew that we wanted some privacy with no smoking, so I asked him if he smoked.

He said, "No, I don't smoke, Rachael. Do you?"

I answered him before I realized that he had called me by my name. "Wait a minute, I never mentioned my name nor do I remember anyone introducing us. So how do you know my name?"

"Well, I wasn't sure at first when I saw you sitting there. So I decided to come over and get a closer look before I just walked up to you and started talking."

"Wait a minute, what do you mean if it was me or not?"

"Well, your friend Lisa has been trying to do me a favor by trying to introduce us. But it never seems to be the right time for some reason or another. Because we both stay so busy, so I just kinda gave up on meeting you personally. I was getting the feeling that you didn't want to be bothered with me, so I stopped asking her what you said."

"So just who are you?"

"Well, let me introduce myself. My name is Eugene Michaels, and we work in the same office. Well, not in the same office but in the same building."

"Oh, so you're the one that she's been trying to get me to come out to meet?"

"Yes, I'm the one that she was trying to get you to come out to meet. Yes, I'm guilty. I'm the one unless there is someone else she was trying to introduce you to."

"No, I don't think that there was anybody else with the same name as you trying to meet me and at the same time." We kinda laughed a little.

"You know, I was wondering about you."

"Wondering about what?"

"Well, to be honest, I was wondering if something was wrong with you or what."

"Why you say that?"

"Well, you were trying to use a middleman when all you had to do was knock on my office door and ask if you could have a minute of my time. Would that have been so hard to do?"

"No, it would not have been so hard to do, but I know how it is when you are trying to get some work done and someone interrupts you. So that's why I asked Lisa to do me that little favor."

"You know, Lisa has a very strong crush on you herself. I'm surprised that I got the messages that you sent me. Anyway, I guess that she got over it or whatever, I don't know."

"Well, I don't know either, but I can tell you that there is nothing wrong with me. It's just like I said, every time I did see you, you were buried in paperwork. And with both of us in the same profession, I know how you can get caught up in what you're doing, and I just never seem to find the right time to talk to you. But you know what? That's not the only place that I have seen you."

"You've seen me someplace else before?"

"Yes, but I guess that you don't recognize me at all?"

"And why should I?"

"Because we were a little intimate together."

"What? Now I know that there is definitely something going on with you."

"Wait, wait, let me explain."

"Please do."

"Don't get upset."

"Well, start talking or I'm walking."

"Okay, okay, I'm a casino player."

"Yeah, and?"

"That's where I first saw you."

"Oh my goodness! Was that you that I accidently kissed?"

"Once again, I'm guilty. I go sometimes after a long day at work. To unwind a little, you know, take your mind off all the different cases that we have on a daily basis. You know, just not have to think about anything, but then one day, I spotted you. I thought that you looked a little familiar, but I wasn't sure because you were wearing different clothes than what I normally see you in. So I didn't want to say anything, but then I saw you in the building that we both work at. Then I knew that it was you. That's when I started to ask Lisa to introduce us. I wasn't trying to pick you up or anything like that. I just thought that I would get introduced and say hi to you. You know, let you know that we work and play at the same place. You know, something simple."

"Well, I am so embarrassed."

"Why?"

"Because you probably think that I am some kind of crazy person or something. Because—if I remember correctly—when that machine finally went off, I was so excited that when I did turn around, I practically jumped in your arms. I was just so excited. Damn, I feel so stupid, and here I am, thinking that you were losing it. We laughed then when I think about it. After the attendant returned, I turned around to tell you that I was sorry, but you were already gone. Why did you leave so abruptly like that?"

"I didn't. I stayed a minute."

"If you did, it was just a minute too."

"I even said I'll see you around, but I guess that you didn't hear me. But I didn't just run away."

"Okay."

"Oh, so now I do remember you."

"Oh, you do? Funny."

"Wait, you saw me over there plenty of times?"

"That's true, but like I said, I wasn't sure if it was you or not. And I was there to just enjoy myself, not really wanting to talk to anybody at that time. There were times when I would just happen to be standing around, and you would just show up."

"Well, I know one thing. When I first saw you there, you really scared the shit out of me."

"What?"

"Hey, I thought that you were following me, stalking me or something."

"Girl, please. I was thinking the same thing about you."

Then we both broke out laughing.

"Okay, okay, so now that we know that we were not stalking each other, let me formally introduce myself to you."

"But you already have."

"I know that. I just thought that I would do it again since we had bad feelings about each other at first because I even started to tell Lisa to just forget trying to introduce us, but later changed my mind. So let's act as though we are meeting for the first time. Is that okay with you?"

"Well, okay, if that will make you feel better."

"Okay, now let's see how do we do this."

"Do what?"

"Introduce myself."

"You just did it. What's the problem?"

"There's no problem, but it's just not that often that I do this."

"Do what?"

"Just walk up to someone and say, 'Hi, my name is Eugene Michaels. Do you mind if I sit next to you?' and then go as far as to ask you if you are alone. And if you say yes, then I'd ask you if I could buy you your next drink. Then I'd ask you your name. Now see there? I didn't do that right. I was supposed to ask you your name first then say all that other stuff."

We laughed.

I said, "You know what?"

"What?"

"For you to be an attorney, you sure are at a loss for words, and I would really have doubts about you defending me in a courtroom."

"Ouch, that hurt."

"Well, if you are having a hard time just introducing yourself to me, then how could you address a jury?"

"Now that's totally different."

"Why?"

"Because I wouldn't be trying to buy them a drink."

"Okay, so why are you having trouble now?"

"Well, don't take this the wrong way, but I am usually on the defensive side."

"What do you mean by that?"

"Well, women usually approach me before I have a chance to even say a word to anybody."

"Well, you did all right with me, so you don't have to worry because you are safe with me. I mean you no harm. Hey, I just might let you defend me after all in court if I had to." Then I laughed.

"Okay, now who's being funny?"

Then I looked down at my watch, and it was going on three p.m., and they had not brought our food yet. So I said, "Didn't you say that you had to be back at the office? That you were on a long lunch break?"

"Yeah, why?"

"Because you haven't eaten yet."

"It's okay. I'm actually done, but I did have some work to do before I go home tonight just so that it would be done, and I wouldn't have to worry about it or take it home. And do it there. I try to leave the job at the office unless I've got a tough case, and I have to take it home."

By this time, they had brought our food. I had ordered lobster and crab; Eugene ordered steak and lobster. After everything was set on the table, Eugene asked if I mind if he said grace before we start to eat.

"What?"

"You know, pray before eating."

"I know what you meant. It's just that it's such a rare thing for a guy to want to say grace before eating. Or even think about prayer. I'm usually the one that says the grace before eating, that's all."

"Oh, is that right?"

"Yeah, that's right." So while we were eating, he broke the silence and said, "So how often do you go out or date if I'm not being too personal?"

"No, you are not getting too personal, and I usually go out depending on how I'm feeling. And what about you?"

"Well, you know, I'm pretty much like you unless one of the fellas call and want to hang out. That's about it for me unless I go to the casino, and lately that's pretty often. I just go to get away."

Then Eugene ordered us both another drink.

We talked and talked until we were almost finished with dinner and our second drink. Then when we did finish, I said, "Well, Mr. Michaels, it was nice meeting you in person finally, and then look, we wind up meeting unexpectedly and having dinner together. I really did enjoy talking with you. And sharing a little laughter. Well, I guess now we can feel safe whenever we see each other at the casino again."

With that said, we both stood up, preparing to leave, when we noticed that there was only one check on the table.

When the waiter came over and asked if we wanted him to take the check up, Eugene already had his money in hand—handing it to the waiter—and said, "Please let me."

I didn't say a word, but when the waiter walked away, I said, "The next time that we meet accidently or run into each other out somewhere and we are both alone, the check's on me."

"Sounds good to me."

Then we headed for the parking lot.

As we were walking to our cars, we noticed that we were headed in the same direction. We looked at each other and said at the same time, "Are you following me?"

We started laughing again, then noticed that we were parked right next to each other when we reached our cars.

I looked over at him and said thanks.

"Thanks for what?"

"For not turning out to be a crazy man for one, then for not making me feel so stupid about what happened at the casino."

Eugene walked around to my car and said, "If it's all right with you, may I have a hug so that you will know for sure that it was all right and that there was no harm done?"

I was just a little hesitant.

Then he said, "Don't get shy on me now." We laughed; then I opened my arms to give him a big hug.

He put his long milk chocolate arms around me and held me so tight. It felt so good that I didn't want to let go.

The hug must have felt just as good to him as it did to me because he just held on to me as well.

We just held on to one another; it felt so good.

It seemed as though we were holding on to each other for half an hour, but it was only for a few seconds. We finally let go slowly and looked at each other for a few seconds.

Then we said our goodbyes. Eugene waited until I had climbed into my truck before he got into his Lincoln Town Car. Damn, I loved that car. And he made it look even better with him sitting in it.

He had a silver-on-silver Lincoln with just a hint of black. That baby was sharp.

As I'm sitting there, looking down at him sitting there with his handsome self, I thought to myself, *This can't be true. I must be dreaming.* This man was so good-looking and didn't realize it, or maybe he did but didn't act like he was God's gift to women.

And that was the good part. I rolled down my window and tapped on the horn. He rolled down his window.

And I said, "Do we live in the same building also?"

"You know what? We might have before I purchased my house."

"Because we seem to have a lot in common. But I guess that's where we differ."

"Okay, once again, it was nice meeting you, so I guess I'll see you at work. And don't let my head buried in paperwork stop you from speaking."

"Well, I won't, and you feel free to stop by when you have a free moment."

"Okay, I'll do just that."

Then I pulled off slowly, and he did the same. We went in different directions, but I kept my eye on him as he was driving away.

I was looking through my rearview mirror. He turned in the direction of where we both work. I was still in shock, thinking that this is truly a small world.

I could not believe that the guy that I was mysteriously attracted to from a distance was no longer at a distance but was right in arm's reach.

Speaking of arms, dammmmn, he felt so good; and I fit right into his arms perfectly.

I was relaxed and at ease right there in his arms. Dang, I wonder if he's married with kids. And a chick on the side.

But I still can't help holding on to the feeling of him holding me in his arms.

While driving along, Luther Vandross's "Other Side of the World" came on. And I thought, *Is this a hint or what?* I just kinda smiled to myself and said, "Yeah right."

When I got home, I was thinking about Eugene a little too much; I was letting my imagination run away. So I said, "Wait a minute, girl. Did he ask you for a home number, a pager number, a cell phone number, an address, anything that would constitute him wanting to get in touch with you outside of work? Duh, no, he didn't, so stop the silly thoughts right now."

Damn, I'm talking to myself just a little too much; so I said, "Girl, stop." And I kinda laughed at myself.

Oh, there was something that I noticed about Eugene when I was talking to him.

And that was he called me girl a lot as though we really had known each other for some time.

We really did have a nice time together, I thought.

Anyway, I do hope that he feels the same way too.

While I was deep in thought, the phone rang, and it snapped me back into reality.

I ran to the phone and looked at the caller ID; it was my baby girl, and Lord knows that I didn't feel like talking to her right now.

Not just her, but I didn't feel like talking to any female, no matter who it was, with the exception of my mother.

So I let the machine catch it. She said, "Hi, Mom, I haven't heard from you in a few days—okay, a day. You know you miss talking to me and your grandbabies. Oh well, call me when you get in. I love you. Talk to you later." Then she hung up the phone.

Boy oh boy, I was beginning to feel stressed like I needed a male body right here with me right now. We'd take a shower, and I'd light up some candles; the raspberry-scented ones were my favorite.

I was feeling a little scandless. I started to go down to the office and act like I had forgotten something, but then I said, "Naw, I'm not going to rush things."

I can't believe how I have changed since Shawn's death. It's as though I am a whole new person.

So I tossed that thought right out of my head as tempting as it was. I just headed for the bathroom, lit some candles, and started the shower.

Then I decided to have a bath instead, so I turned off the shower and let the water run into the tub to take a long relaxing bath and think about how my day went with the trial and then with Eugene.

Overall, it turned out to be a very good day.

I went and got my raspberry bubble bath and poured some in the tub. And watched the bubbles rise.

I checked to see how hot the water had gotten; it was fine, so I walked into the kitchen and got myself a wineglass out of the cabinet and then took the wind out of the fridge and poured myself a glass.

Then I wondered if mixing the wine and the Long Island iced tea that I had earlier would upset my stomach, but what the hell, I'm at home.

Anyway, if I get sick, I'll be okay right here at home; so I went ahead and poured the wine. I was headed back toward the bathroom when the doorbell rang. I turned around as if I was hearing things; then it rang again. I wondered who in the world this could be. Then I said, "Maybe it's Eugene," with a smile on my face; but then I thought he doesn't even know where I live.

So who could this be? And how did they get up here without the doorman calling up first?

So I looked out the peephole in the door to see that it was my husband. He was looking good, I thought; so what the hell could he want after all he did, just up and leave. Okay, I put his ass out, but he just doesn't want to stay out.

I have told him over and over that there won't be any more sex games played between us anymore, but this man is as hardheaded as they come. But even though we stay in touch, we would occasionally get our groove on. It was all that, but the thought of how he lied to me still comes back every time I see him.

Damn, I'm standing here, thinking about all of this, when Robert knocks on the door again and said, "Come on, Ray, let me in. I know that you are in there. I seen your car. And I know that you don't like riding with many people, so let me come in and talk to you for just a minute, will you? Then I'll be gone."

"Okay, but don't try anything, or I'm not opening the door for you again. You got that?"

"I hear you, Ray, and I won't try anything that you won't want me to."

I opened the door and said, "Hi, Robert, what are you doing here?"

"Oh, no real reason. Just thought that I would stop by since I was over in this area to say hello and see how you were doing."

Not realizing that I was wearing my bathrobe, I was looking at his eyes looking at me, so I followed his eyes looking down at my robe, which was standing wide-open. I quickly closed my robe.

He said, "Why'd you do that?"

"Because I felt a chill."

"Yeah right. I thought that maybe you didn't want me looking at those pretty thighs of yours and—"

"Stop, Robert."

"What? I was just complimenting you."

"Whatever." Then I thought about my bathwater running and said, "Come on in, Robert."

I walked back into the bathroom to turn off the water, then walked back into the living room.

Robert said, "It sure does smell good in here. It smells like you were about to have one of your long relaxing, I-need-to-think baths that smells so good."

"Oh, you remember that?"

"Yeah, and how I remember that."

"If you recall, you used to let me come in after you had been in there by yourself for a while. You would let me wash you from head to toe. Then you would stand, and I would rinse all the bubbles off you. Then I would hold you and tell you that whatever was bothering you would be all right. Then I would take your face in my hands. And kiss you on your cheeks, then your lips, your forehead, your eyes, your temples, down to your neck and shoulders. Then I'd cup your breast in my hands and kiss your big old nipples oh so softly and rub your ass until —"

"Okay, that's enough. I remember everything, even all the hurt that you caused also."

"You know I loved you so much, and we went through a lot together. I never thought in a million years that we would not be a couple, but you proved me wrong on that. So once again I had to dig deep inside of me and rid myself of all that pain that was in my heart, and now I'm doing good. That's why I'm able to talk to you with a clear peace of mind and not be angry anymore. Because I realized that we are all human and that we make mistakes from time to time. But some mistakes cause too much pain, and you have to just get over it and move on. So now that I have gotten that off my chest, I feel better. Look, Rachael, I didn't come over here to upset you. I came over here to make amends and be gone."

"What? What do you mean be gone?"

"I'm moving back to California because I realize all the pain that I have caused you. And I know that you could never trust me again, or can you?" he said with a little laugh. "But for real, I know that you won't do that or let me back in your life again. So rather than stay here and torture myself and you, I'd rather leave."

"Oh, you play too much. What is this? Another one of your tricks?"

"No, not this time. I am oh so serious."

"I don't believe you."

Then he reached behind his back and came back with an envelope and handed it to me. I flipped up the flap and saw a one-way ticket to California. I looked up in his face, and he looked so sad.

I turned my head and said, "I'll miss you." I tried hard to stop the tears from falling down my face by blinking and blinking, but that didn't help.

Because the tears rolled down my face uncontrollably, Robert walked up behind me, put his arms around my waist, and said, "See there, I have hurt you again. But this time, I really didn't mean to. I was just trying to show you that I'm growing up, just like you used to tell me to do. See, I'm going out on my own so that you won't have to be bothered with me. But I seem to have hurt you again. Rachael, please don't cry. You know I hate to see you in tears no matter what's going on with us."

I told him that I knew everything he said was true and that I thought it would be better if he did leave for his own sake.

I guess the tears came because of all the things that we had been through, and I still cared for him a lot. But it wasn't going to work because I knew that things would change after a while and we'd be right back where we started.

He whispered in my ear, "I will never ever stop loving you. That's why I have to go."

Then he slid his hands inside my bathrobe; one went to my breast, and the other went to my private place. My mind was saying, "Please stop."

But my body was saying, "Please don't stop."

He began kissing me behind the ear while rubbing my private spot, so soft and gentle that I thought I was going to pass out; it felt sooooo good. I was trying to say please don't do this, but my mouth wouldn't open to say a word. Because it had been awhile since we had had any contact.

I was really enjoying his touch, but I managed to say, "Please stop."

He let his tongue slide around to my temples and said, "Are you sure that you want me to stop?"

I didn't say a word for a minute, so he continued his rubbing. I got so wet and lost in the feeling. So Robert just continued until I said, "Yes, I'm sure that I want you to stop."

So he slowly began to move his hands off my body.

And I turned to face him.

He started saying, "I'm so sorry, baby. I'll leave now if you want me to."

I was thinking, *Lord, please don't let him leave without finishing what he started.*

But before I could say anything, he took my face in his hands and kissed me so passionately that my hands started to roam up and down his neck, his back, all over him—wherever I could reach. He was still kissing my neck, then started down to my breast. My hands went for his pants.

I was running my hands along the print of his joystick as he called it.

He was so erect that I thought that he was going to push through his pants.

So I reached for his zipper to try and release some of the pressure. But it would not bend, so I undid his belt, took his button a loose on his pants, and slowly pulled them down.

By then, we had backed up to the couch while he took off his pants. I looked at him, standing there with nothing on.

He looked down at me and said, "Are you sure, or do you want me stop now?"

And he got down on his knees and started kissing me without me saying one word.

His hand touched my stomach, my navel; he touched my weak spot. I moaned as his fingers slid inside of me. Dammmmn, why did he come here? Why didn't he just leave? "Ummmmm" was all I could say or do.

He slowly eased his way on top of me. And my legs began to open to let him have his way. Again, he asked before he entered me.

He said, "Are you sure?"

I couldn't answer him, so he ran his hands between my legs before he entered me. "Ummmmm," I moaned because he felt so good.

After we found a comfortable position—because he was not a small man when it came to his joystick—damn, we were going like rabbits.

When we were finally through, we just lay there with him on top of me.

I felt a teardrop on my face, and I looked up at him, and Robert actually had tears in his eyes that started rolling down his cheeks.

He said, "Rachael, I love you so much. I even hurt inside because of all the pain that I have caused you. But if I could take away the pain that I have caused you, I would in a second. And I'd be the best man that your heart could ever ask for. I'd never do anything to hurt you again."

But all I could do was rub his head because although I knew that he still loved me, I just could not find the words to say what he wanted me to say.

Even though he may have meant what he said, I couldn't get back with him because the thought would always be there when we were not together; I would be wondering what was he doing, who is he with, or if he is getting high. So I could not bring myself to go through that again. It's just not worth it.

So we just lay there in each other's arms quietly, without saying a word, until I broke the silence and asked him, "What did your family think about you going away?"

"Well, you know how they all are. They get upset at any little thing, but my mom cried, and my sisters wanted to cry but kept it together for Mom. And said if you think that you are going to do better for yourself, then go ahead and go with our blessings because we only want what you want for yourself, and hopefully, that's something a whole lot better than what you got going on right now in your life. Mom understood that I needed to get away and basically grow up. Get out from under her wings, but that's what you used to tell me too."

"Sure would."

Then we laughed like old times.

We both got up. He said, "Would you mind if we showered together like we used to? I know that you were about to take a bath before I got here, but will you take a shower with me? And tomorrow, we can have a bath."

I just looked at him and smiled without saying a word. I agreed, and we played in the shower just like old times; we had a lot of fun washing each other from head to toe over and over again.

When we finally finished, we got out and dried ourselves, and I headed for the bedroom with a towel wrapped around me.

While drying my hair with another towel, I sat down on the bed and looked at the clock; it was seven thirty. "My, how time flies." Then Robert stepped into the room and said, "Sure does when you're having fun."

Then he sat down next to me. He had gotten his clothes out of the living room and was putting on his socks and said, "So how's things going at the office?"

I said, "I just finished a case that was so—how can I put it without bragging? It was so cut-and-dry that a jury really wasn't needed. It went so smooth."

Then we lay back on the bed as Robert began talking about getting his old job back out in California.

I started laughing and said, "You must be losing it. I said do you think that after being away for three and a half years, they're just going to say, 'Oh good, you're back. Can you start on Monday?'"

Then we both laughed because he said, "I'm just going to walk up to my boss and say, 'Baby, I'm back.'"

Boy, we both laughed. Then the phone rang.

I had forgotten about everything and was just enjoying being with Robert, not thinking about any of the things that had caused us to split in the first place.

The phone kept on ringing and brought us back to reality. I picked up the receiver and said hello in such a cheery voice that my daughter said, "Mama, is that you?"

"No, it's not. In fact, this is the machine. Leave a message."

She said, "Quit playing." Then she asked, "What are you doing? You sound so happy."

"You know, you and your aunts act as though I'm not supposed to be happy. You all just think that I'm just supposed to be sad and down all the time."

"Hummmm, no, I didn't mean it like that. It's just that it's been awhile since I've heard such cheeriness in your voice, and you sound good. I'm happy that you're happy, and I hope that you stay that way."

At that moment, Robert began to kiss my belly.

I said, "Stop that."

She said, "Who are you talking to?"

"Robert," I said; then there was a pause on the phone because she knew all the pain that he had caused me and all the things that we had been through.

Then she asked the question that I knew was coming. "Are you two getting back together? Are you two kissing and making up, or what?"

"Or what," I said. "We're just having a little fun, and no to your second question."

"Stop," I said as he had begun to kiss my belly; his hands had begun to roam all over me again.

So she said, "Hey, don't the two of you make any babies? And I will talk to you later."

Then I hung up the phone and said, "Just what do you think you're doing? What are you trying to do to me, mister?"

He said, "I'm just enjoying myself for one last time. Is that all right?"

It really didn't matter what I was saying because he was setting me on fire. He continued to kiss me on my belly as he slowly began to head south. I began to moan and say his name until his mouth was right where he could have gotten me to say anything he wanted me to. My body had begun scooting upward; I don't know where I was going, but the top part of my body was hanging off the bed. And he kept at it for what seemed like forever until, I guess, he felt like he needed to be inside of me.

So he slowly began to rise, kissing his way up to my breast. He lingered there for a little bit because he knew how I loved the way he licked my breast. That was another one of my weak spots where he knew that he could get me to say just about anything, but I was cool and didn't say a word. I just let him continue. I reached between us, grabbing hold of his joystick. He was so erect and hard as I guided him inside of me while I licked his ears; he loved for me to do that.

He started saying again how much he loved me.

He just kept saying, "I love you, I love you very much, very much. Oooo, baby, you feel so good."

His movements were not too slow but not too fast either; it was perfect. Then I whispered in his ear, "I love you back."

At that moment, we both came together. He fell on top of me; then we both fell off to sleep. When we both woke up, it was four thirty in the morning. Good thing it was a weekend because I don't know if I would have made it to work that day; I was so weak. And I know he did that on purpose. He made love to me like that when we first got together; it was crazy,

Even lying down, I still felt drained. We both just lay there. Then I managed to say, "What time does your plane leave?"

"I have an open ticket, so I have a week. Rachael, it is a nonrefundable ticket, and I am leaving. But I wonder if I can spend this last week with you. And I promise that I won't bother you again. I'll just be on my merry way if you will let me stay."

"Robert, please don't start that."

"Look, I'm not going to beg you. I just want to spend this last week with you because it will be a long time before I'm coming back, and I'm going to miss you so much. And besides that, you're not going to be my wife for very much longer. So what do you say? Can I? Do you mind?"

"Yes, I mind." But I really didn't because I didn't know when the next time I was going to be with someone, so I thought that I had better make it last for as long as I could.

But I was not going to let him know that easily. I had to play with him for a while with the I don't think that would be a good idea.

But it had been awhile since he and I had been together, so I was willing to let him stay for one week.

It seemed like it had been so long since I had seen, let alone touched, a man's joystick that I didn't want to let go; but I went ahead and said, "One week, and at the end of that week, I'm taking you to the airport myself to make sure that you get on that plane. So that you won't be saying that you missed your flight and need one more day."

We laughed then made love all over again. But this time, I was the aggressor; we made love like the end of the world was coming in the next hour or so.

The next few days came and went so fast, but when I went to work, I didn't see Eugene, and I was glad that I didn't because Robert and I was having so much fun together that I almost got weak and asked him not to go.

But I was stronger than I thought I was. We did all the things that we should have been doing to keep us together in the first place.

He knew that I was having a good time with him.

It was the weekend, and we decided to go out to eat because it was his last day; he was to leave in the morning or before one in the afternoon the next day. And he had cooked all week.

So I said, "Let me take you out to dinner."

Robert said, "Why don't you cook me my last meal?"

"Like I said, let me take you out to dinner." So we showered and left.

We went to the movies then out to dinner.

And who do I run into? My coworker Mr. Michaels. I didn't see him, but I heard someone say, "Well, hello, Ms. Brunson, or is it Mrs. Brunson?"

I turned and saw him looking at me kind of funny. I didn't answer him about whether it was miss or missus. I just said, "Hello yourself, Mr. Michaels." We both looked at each other's company but didn't say a word nor did we introduce them to each other. We didn't say another word; we just kinda looked at each other like we were a couple caught cheatin' or something.

All the while, we were standing, waiting to be seated. Eugene and I kept staring at each other as though there was something going on between the two of us.

I couldn't believe that we were behaving like some school-age children, like we were a couple that had broken up but wasn't finished with each other.

All of a sudden, I heard a tapping on the table. I turned, and Robert was saying, "Who is that? Your new man?"

I said, "What? What are you talking about?"

Robert said, "Rachael, you know damn well what I'm talking about, and I'm pretty sure that the lady he's with feels the same way I do."

"What?"

"But I am not mad at you. But you know that this is our last night together, so could you please keep all your attention on me if you don't mind?"

"What?"

"Rachael, I don't know if you noticed it or not, but ever since we got here—well, ever since he called out your name—you have not taken your eyes off of him, and he's acting the same way that you are. So what's going on? Talk to me."

"There's nothing to talk about, and what do you mean we have not taken our eyes off each other? Because we do have food in front of us, so how could we have ordered if we could not stop looking at one another?"

"Girl, don't play. What's going on? Is he the reason that you have not asked me to stay or what?"

"Robert, don't start that bull with me. Not tonight, all right? We'll talk later because I can see that you are starting to trip."

So after dinner, we politely had a light conversation. I told him all about Eugene and who he was.

Robert said, "Well, if you think that Eugene can make you happy, then go for it."

I said, "Are you all right with that?"

Robert said, "Sure." And that was the end of that.

When Robert and I got back to the apartment, I was thinking about all the fun that he and I had had all week and how much I was going to miss him when he was gone.

It was times like these when I missed Robert and Shawn the most. When it was time to go to bed and there was no one there to say good night to.

I loved being married, whether we were happy or not, just knowing that there was always going to be someone there to lie down next to, to talk to, to hug while they slept.

But I know that I am going to have to go ahead and get my divorce so that I can move on with my life because I know that there is some mother's son out there looking for someone just like myself. And I'm looking for him also.

I know that that special someone is out there looking for me. *Can you hear me, love of my life, whoever you are and wherever you are?*

I started thinking to myself, *Hey, girl, watch out. You're beginning to talk to yourself.* But as long as I don't answer myself, I'll be all right, so I've heard.

But then again, I am answering myself, *Yeah, well, whatever.* Then I heard Robert say, "Hey, where are you?"

"What?" I had forgotten that I was with Robert and had drifted off into another world.

We were back in the apartment. I was looking around, then looked down at the phone; it had several messages on the machine. The light was flashing; it had seven calls waiting. *Damn*, I thought as I started to listen to the messages.

The first was from my daughter who didn't want anything.

The second call was from Lisa who only wanted me to know that she was feeling better and would see me tomorrow at work.

The third call was from a client, and so were the rest. So I just stored those calls until later because it was getting late, and I did have to get up in the morning.

And I still had to deal with Robert, and I knew that he was going to try to wear me out because it was his last night in town.

And I was really looking forward to it, to be honest about it. I walked into the bathroom, preparing for a shower and then for bed, when Robert walked up behind me. "Who is that?"

"Me."

"Me who?"

"You know who."

"Okay, okay." Then I turned around, and he was standing there, looking like new money; he was dressed in black and white.

I thought, *Damn for him to be on drugs. He sure does look good.* And he always kept himself together.

But I just could not deal with that part of his life or him being an occasional out all-nighter.

"Damn, girl, are you just going to continue to undress me with your eyes, or are you going to help me get out of all these clothes so that we can take our last shower together for a while?"

"Funny," I said, but he was right because if I didn't get with anyone before I saw him again, then we would be all in once again. Because he was good in bed, and I must give him that.

"Hey, Ray, what are you going to do, huh? Ray, the way you are looking at me, are you sure that you still want me to go?"

"Don't start with me, or I'll take you to the airport tonight."

We both started to laugh.

Robert put his arms around my neck, then started to kiss me lightly on the lips. I said, "You know, you really looked nice tonight."

"So did you." He continued to kiss me lightly. "I wanted to look my best for you tonight so that you would see just what you were letting go of."

"What? the outfit? It is nice, but I think that it's a little bit too big for me, so you can keep it."

We laughed; we could always make each other laugh.

"You know, Ray, I really did enjoy myself with you this past week, and it felt really good being all dressed up. It kinda makes a guy want to get his self together. It feels good to have on a suit every now and then. You know what I mean."

"Yeah, somewhat, and that's good for you. And I do hope that you keep yourself together."

"And when you see that I can keep myself together, can we be husband and wife again? Okay, don't answer now."

He said that kinda quick. I had begun to open my mouth to tell him no, but I guess the look on my face told him what I was thinking. He just started kissing me all over my face with little light kisses; then he started kissing me on my neck.

We began to walk back into the bedroom when I saw a light coming from the kitchen.

"Hold on a minute, Robert. I forgot that I had left the fridge door open when we came into the house. Let me close it."

He let me go to go close the refrigerator. I walked into the kitchen and opened the door up all the way just to take a look, and Robert was right behind me. He had a thing for coming up behind me because when we were together, I had told him that I loved the warmth and feel of his body up close on me—his body right next to mine with his arms around me.

I knew that that would make him hard as a rock every time he did that. So he did it every chance he got. I said, "You know, you always do that."

He turned me around and said, "I'm serious this time. If you will give me one more chance, you'll see that I have changed. I really have."

I could feel that the wine I had sipped was starting to make me feel all warm inside, along with the kisses that he was giving me. All I could do was look at him and say, "Why do you keep doing this to me?" But instead of him answering me, he kissed me, then stopped, looked at me, and said, "I'm sorry, Rachael. It's just that I love you so much."

"Robert, I'm sorry but—"

He said, "Get your *but* out of the way so that we can do this. I promise that I will change all the things that I used to do that made you so angry with me, I promise. Please say that you will take me back just one more time please, baby?"

"Robert, I'm sorry, but I just can't do that. Let's just enjoy this last night together before I have to take you to the airport in the morning."

"Robert," I said with tears in my eyes. "Please don't go there again because I just cannot go through all that pain again. Even though you might mean everything that you are saying, I just can't."

So he just held on to me, and we stood right in the kitchen, hugging for a few minutes. Then he looked at me and said, "Well, I won't ask you that question again, but will you let me stay for one more week?"

Then he started smiling and said, "I'm just messing with you." He kissed me on the lips and said, "I won't keep you up all night because I know that you have a lot of running to do in the morning, so I'll just savor every moment with you."

We walked into the bathroom and started to undress each other.

He reached in and turned the water on in the shower. We got in the water; it was cool at first, but I didn't care because Robert was heating us both up. He stopped kissing me, then said, "Let's bath each other."

We were enjoying soaping each other up; then he started to get aroused and began to swell.

He started kissing me again all over until the water started to go up his nose while he was on his knees, kissing me gently on my thighs, my belly, then back down to my kitty cat. Boy, that felt good.

We made our way out of the shower and into the bedroom where he thought that I was thirty-one flavors because he licked and kissed for quite some time until he needed to feel the warmth of my insides.

Damn, he felt good; we made love for hours until we both collapsed and fell off to sleep.

It seemed like we had just fallen to sleep when the alarm clock went off.

We dragged ourselves out of bed after hitting the Snooze button a couple of times.

We had a quick shower, and he didn't even try anything because he knew that that time, he had outdone himself and was just as drained as I was.

We dried ourselves; then Robert put on a pair of boxers, then went into the kitchen, and started breakfast. He always loved to cook for me, and I loved that. Hell, who wouldn't?

I went and got dressed for work.

While I was eating, he went and got dressed, came back into the kitchen, sat next to me, and then said, "Well, Ray, I guess this will be our last breakfast together for a while."

"Yeah, I guess that it will." I looked him in the eyes and said, "For what it's worth, I'm going to miss you a hell of lot, you know."

"Well, thanks, Ray. That really is going to make it a lot easier for me, knowing that you are going to miss me. But probably not half as much as I'm going to miss you. But I'll be all right. I know that I messed up with you big time, and no one could be more sorry than I am."

"Okay, now let's change the subject before you have me up in here crying."

"If you start crying, will that make you feel like keeping me for another week?"

"No." Then we started to laugh. We had finished eating and gathered up our things. He grabbed his luggage, and I got my briefcase. And we headed for the door.

On the way to the airport, we talked about his job. Well, the job that he was going to try and get back.

We laughed and talked all the way there. Before we knew it, we were there.

I parked the car; then Robert got his things out of the trunk of the car.

"Well, this is it for real. You don't have to wait and see me off you know."

"Yeah, I know but I want to stay and make sure that you get on that plane and not standing on the ground when the plane takes off."

He laughed and said, "You would say something like that, wouldn't you?"

We hugged, then walked inside so he could register for his flight.

We waited for about a half hour before they called his flight number. When they did call his number, we stood and hugged again. I could feel tears swelling up in my eyes.

Then Robert said, "See, there you go. You gonna make me stay right here if you start that booing."

I hit him on the arm and said, "Call me when you get settled in, okay?" With a light kiss, he said, "Okay, I will," and turned and walked away.

I watched him as far as I could until he was out of sight; then with tears rolling down my face, I turned and walked out of the airport and got into my car and headed for work even though I didn't feel much like working.

All I wanted to do at that moment was go home and have a good old-fashioned cry and feel sorry for myself.

Why I don't know because I knew that this had to happen sooner or later.

And I knew it, so I wiped my tears away and headed for work to keep my mind off Robert and Shawn.

When I got to the office, Lisa was already there. She came into my office, sat down, and started telling me about her husband and how she thought that he was cheating on her and that she was tired of him.

I said, "Good morning to you too."

She tried to laugh, then said, "Girl, I am so sorry. I just bust in here, then start telling you my problems."

I said, "You know, I thought that Shawn was cheating on me. But for once, I was wrong. I mean, the last time when I thought he was cheating, he wasn't. So what I'm saying, Lisa, is before you get all worked up, are you sure that he's cheating on you, or are you just guessing? Lisa, don't make waves if you don't have to."

"Rachael, I'm not just making up stuff." Lisa said that she had gotten a call from a lady, threatening to put Eric in jail for getting her daughter pregnant.

"What?"

"That's right, Ray. I told her that I would get back with her if she would give me her number so that I could have a talk with my husband. So that night, when Eric got home, I asked him all about what I had heard. I wasn't accusing, I was just asking to see just what was going on. And at first, he was in denial and started denying it until I said that the girl's mother called and said that she was thinking about putting his ass in jail. Then Eric said, 'Baby, I'm sorry. It happened one night that you and I were not together, and I was at the bar drinking and feeling lost when we just started talking.' I said, 'You son of a bitch, you did more than just talking. Anyway, how old is this girl?' He said, 'Baby, I'm so sorry.' 'How old is she?' 'Baby—' 'Baby my ass. How old is she?' 'She said that she was twenty-six.' 'Twenty-six? Then how could her mother be threatening to put you in jail?' 'Then she's just talking because that girl told me that she was old enough. I did tell her that I was married and that I loved my wife.' 'Yeah right, so she must have told her mother that she was pregnant by a married man.' 'Besides, it's probably not mine. I mean, I don't even remember sleeping with her. I was so drunk that I just don't know if I did or not.'

"Rachael, we really had it out. I told him not to open his mouth and say another word to me at that moment. Then I said, 'I'm leaving for one hour, and when I get back, I think that you should be gone.' Girl, that was on Saturday morning, and I have not talked to him since then."

"Oh, Lisa, I'm so sorry to hear that. Why didn't you call me?"

"Because I didn't want to bother you on the weekend with my problems. I knew that you would be there for me, but I couldn't talk about it
right then."

"Lisa, please, after all you did for me and the kids when Shawn died and when Robert and I split. You were my rock, Lisa. There was no way that you would have been bothering me. But I will forgive you for not contacting me because I know how, at times, you just want to be alone. I feel you, but always remember if you ever need me—I mean, for anything—I'm here for you. You got that? I love you just like one of my sisters, and yes, you get on my nerves just like they do. So feel free any hour of the day or night to get on my nerves, okay?"

"Yeah, okay."

"'Cause, girl, we could have cried together or something 'cause you know that I am always ready for a good cry for no reason at all. I'm good to go, Lisa, and now that Robert has left too. Girl, please call me crybaby for sure."

"You know, I feel better already just sharing that much with you."

"Lisa, you can't let this upset you too much because, after all, you're carrying your own little bundle of joy. And we don't want anything to happen to little him or her."

"I know. That's why I went for a walk to think things over, whether or not I'm going to forgive him or not."

"I think you will, but don't forget what he told you."

"What's that?"

"That the baby she says is his may not be his. After all, he said that he was drunk, right?"

"Right."

"And you know whether or not he can perform when he has been drinking, right?"

"Once again, you're right. You know exactly what to say to put a smile on my face or anybody else's that may need a lift. You're always right there. Thanks, Rachael." Then she gave me a hug.

I said, "Okay, Lisa, now get out of here so that I can get some work done. But, Lisa, really think about it when you see Eric. Don't be too hard but do tag that ass." We both laughed, then hugged again; then she left out of the office.

I do hope that she is feeling better because I know firsthand what cheating can do to a relationship. So I hope, for her sake, that the girl is lying. I shivered at the thought of Shawn sleeping with someone else. Even Robert for that matter.

But enough of that. I'm due in court.

As I left out of the office, I saw Lisa and said, "Hey, how about hanging out for a little while after work? My treat."

"That's cool, but can we go to the casino? I feel like doing a little bit of gambling."

"Sure, we can go to the casino, but I'm only treating to dinner. You are going to be on your own for the gambling."

"I know that. Maybe we both can lift up our spirits with a little gambling to take our minds off today's problems."

"Good." I hugged her, then said, "I'll see you after work." Then we both went our separate ways.

I thought, *Poor girl. I would have never thought that Eric would have cheated on her. They seem so happy together. But I guess he is no different from any other man who let the brains in his pants do all the thinking for him.*

But all I could think about was that whenever she needs me, I'll be right there for her. Because God knows she was there when I needed her.

I was lost and didn't feel like talking to my family.

But anyway, thinking of the casino, I was just there a few days ago.

But if that's what she wants to do, then that's fine with me. We'll do whatever she wants.

I was headed for the courtroom where my client was being accused of probation violation.

Boy, this girl I'm defending was straight out of the streets, always trying to see just how slick she could be.

If I wasn't her court-appointed lawyer for this case, I'd eat her ass up in legal fees because she doesn't think shit stinks, and she's a habitual criminal. I could eat for weeks off her ass alone.

But this time, I don't think that I'm going to be able to keep her out of jail.

She just might have to do a couple of days in the county.

Yeah, I think that I will let her sit and think about this one this time; or she'll be back again next week with the same dumb lie, talking about how the police keeps picking on her because she won't do them.

I smiled to myself when I saw her because this girl is a handful. But her parents keep taking up for her.

But this time, I think that I will fix up a deal where she can do a couple of days, maybe a week, in the big house.

Maybe this will teach her a lesson, and her poor parents won't have to worry about her for a few days; they'll know exactly where she is. Hopefully, this will stop her while she is still young, before she hit that age where she can become a hardened criminal.

Because I can see that's where she's headed.

I've seen it happen to a lot of young girls. They just get caught up with the wrong people, girls and boys. I'm so thankful that my own didn't stray and get caught up.

But this girl has a real mean streak in her.

But thinking of kids, I have not talked to my own children in a while. Well, I'll talk to them tomorrow.

As the day finally comes to a close and I go back to my office and sit down at my desk, I see a note from Lisa saying that she was going to meet with Eric because he needed to talk to her. He said that it was very important. *Well, that's good*, I thought. Oh well, I guess I'll just hang out by myself and relax a little bit.

By the time I left the office and returned home, it was five thirty. Just as I was about to go start my bathwater, the phone rang. It was Shawnda.

As usual, I knew that she didn't want anything.

But I picked up the phone anyway and said, "Hello, little girl."

"Hi, Ma, what are you doing? Did you get Robert off all right? Was he okay? Were you all right, or did you cry like a baby, like you do when one of us goes away for whatever reason?"

"Damn, girl, you didn't let me answer the first question. But yes and no to answer your question. First, I was about to run me some bathwater. Second, yes, Robert got off all right. And third, I only shed a few tears. So what? I can get a little emotional at times, but that's okay. Now what?"

"Nothing, Mama, I just wanted to make sure that you were all right."

"I'm fine, baby. After I get my bath, or maybe I'll take a shower, then go down to the casino for a little bit. So how are you and the kids?"

"Oh, we're fine. Ma, guess who's pregnant."

"Shawnda, please don't say you 'cause you know your baby daddy ain't." Then I just paused.

"Ma, please don't start on me, and no, it's not me."

"Thank God."

"Ma."

"Okay, okay. As long as it's not you, I can handle anything else."

"Well, it's Jaylen's girlfriend."

"What? Is he sure that it's his baby before his little happy ass start claiming shit that's not his?"

"Ma, you know that you are something else. I'm pretty sure that he thinks that it's his. He told me and Shawn that he was going to get married."

"Boy, that boy."

"Ma."

"What, girl?"

"Mama, can you not go off on him when he tries to talk to you about it? Ma, please just listen because he seem so happy, happier than I seen him in a long time. So be happy for him, will you?"

"You know what, I'm going to take your advice this time. I'm just glad that he's in a position to take care of her and the baby, so I will not put a cloud on his shining day.

"Well, anyway, it's about time that there was something to celebrate around here. Well, now that Jaylen's out of the way and I know what he's up to, what's going on with Shawn Jr.?"

"I haven't talked to him in a couple of days, and he didn't mention a word about Jaylen's good news, and neither did Jaylen when I talked to him as a matter of fact.

"Well, I guess they wanted to wait and be sure she was pregnant before they said anything because she had only taken one of those home pregnancy test. But since then, she has been to see a real doctor. So as of now, you're going to be another grandmother."

"Well, what can I say? Except that's great. So how is Shawn doing?"

"He's fine. He and Yvonne are doing okay. They say that they are happy for little Jay, better him than them. We were all together last weekend. I tried to get you to come over, but I kept getting your answering machine."

"Well, it's good that you guys stay close because Mama is about to make changes in her life too."

"Mama, just what are you talking about?"

"Nothing really. I'm just going to start getting out more."

"Who you and aunt Denise and Wanda?"

"Maybe, but I have no problem going places by myself. Because sometimes, it's good to be by yourself. You don't have to talk to anybody. You can just enjoy." I told Shawnda again that I was about to go to the casino.

She said, "You know that you spend a lot of time over there lately."

I said, "Girl, please. I'll talk to you later, all right?"

"Well, all right, but call me when you get back."

"We'll see." Then we hung up.

I was thinking about the casino, and Eugene crossed my mind. I hadn't seen him since that night that Robert and I were out having dinner. Matter of fact, I haven't even seen him at work either. I wondered if he will be at the casino.

A smile came across my face as I was thinking about the last time that I did see Eugene. It was kind of strange because we were acting like busted lovers.

I wonder what that was all about.

As luck would have it, it was the weekend, or I would make it my business to go to his office tomorrow.

But I'll do that first thing Monday morning. Okay, if not the first thing

Monday morning, then sometime that day.

I wonder if that was his wife or girlfriend that he was with.

I'm going to find out about that as soon as I see him. I was going to make it my business to see Mr. Eugene Michaels.

Just thinking about him made me more eager to get to the casino.

Because that's where he used to hang out.

I had forgotten about looking for him the last time that Denise, Wanda, and I were there.

It was probably because I was dealing with Robert's horny ass.

But if Mr. Michaels isn't married and he's available, maybe we can get to know each other a little better. Even if he is seeing someone, we can still hang out as friends. Well, now we'll see.

My feelings are going to be hurt if he is married or seeing someone on a regular basis.

Boy, I got a lot of nerves. I got a husband, but that's in name only. It's not like we're living together or anything. Damn, my mind was racing as I was getting dressed.

I was dressing in such a hurry that I put on two different shoes. "Dammmmn," I said. "Slow down. Get it together because you are really going to be hurt if he's heavily involved with someone."

Dang, I am going nuts with the thoughts of a man that I don't even know.

I really have changed. I would never have been like this if my life had not been through such dramatic changes. I told myself that I was going to go over there and act like I normally do when I'm over there and I didn't know who Eugene was.

I was going out the door when the phone rang. I ran back and looked at the caller ID only to see that it was Wanda's crazy ass. No way am I going to answer that phone now. I'll let the machine pick it up.

When it did pick it up, I listened to her talking about nothing that was interesting to me, so I turned to leave. As soon as I got to the door, the phone rang again.

This time I said that if it's her, then I'll pick it up and see what she wants, so I looked at the caller ID. This time, it was Lisa.

I thought about answering it, then thought against it because at that moment, I did not feel like listening to someone else's problems right then. But then I thought I could tell her that I met Eugene a few weeks ago, but I said never mind because the last time that I talked to her, she was feeling kinda low. And at that moment, I just wanted to do what I wanted to do, and that was to be on my way.

I decided that I would tell her at a later date. This time, I hurried out the door before her message even started playing so that it wouldn't distract me from my mission of enjoying the casino—alone, with no one to meet up with in a couple of hours. Not that it was such a bad thing. But I just wanted to be by myself and enjoy.

While riding over to the casino, I thought about Eugene and what I would say if he was there. Or just what he would say to me.

I tried hard to throw him out of my mind; but then Luther came on. It was the same song that had come on before, the last time that I saw him. I began to sing along with the song, not thinking about anything in particular.

And I was there before I knew it.

I started getting nervous; then I thought he might not even be here, so I stopped acting like a schoolgirl with a crush.

I valet parked and went inside and headed straight for the machine that I used to play before I even knew who Eugene was. When I got to the machine, he wasn't there, so I just sat down and got ready to play when I realized that I had not exchanged my money. So I put my jacket around my chair and went and exchanged the money. I came back and started to play my machine; it was hitting a little bit but not much, but I continued to play.

I tried looking around unnoticeably to see if Eugene was anywhere around, but I didn't see him. So I played for another fifteen or twenty minutes, then went to another one of my favorite machines, still trying not to look like I was looking for someone. But when I got to where my machine was, someone was sitting there; and from where I was coming from, it looked like it was Eugene.

But that was only wishful thinking because the closer that I got to the machine, the more I could see that it was not Eugene.

My heart had begun to beat fast at the thought of it being him because I thought that if it was him, would we pick up from where we left off? And that was staring at each other. Or would we just start a regular conversation and become good friends?

But when I got there, it was not him for real, and I was kind of relieved but a little disappointed because I just thought that he would be here tonight, so I just played a little longer, then left.

I went walking around, playing one machine after another, until I just decided to go home.

When I got home, I kicked off my shoes and sat down on the sofa and thought about Eugene and where in the world this man could be.

I haven't seen him in a while, not even at the job.

I thought, *Girl, you had better let the thoughts of being with this man go because he has got to be married or with someone.*

So I made up my mind not to let him into my head any longer and go on about my business. So I just kicked back and relaxed, cut the television on, and watched a movie. I looked over at the caller ID but didn't feel like listening to anybody right then.

I just wanted to get Eugene out of my head because I knew that he had to be married and happy. Besides, the lady that he was with that night was clinging to him pretty tightly. But whatever the case may be, I was going to find out just what was up with him.

If he was trying to have an affair or what, I was going to act just like one of our investigators that we sometimes used at the office.

Damn, girl, you are acting just like a loose canon over someone that you don't even know, so just let it go, I thought.

I was restless for the rest of the night and thought, well, I could call Lisa and find out what it was that she wanted. And then throw in a few questions about Eugene.

Then after talking to her for a while, I'll throw in that I had met Eugene a few weeks ago. After, I'll help her with whatever is brothering her because she was having some marital problems that she might want to talk about.

Damn, I know that I'm going to regret calling her, but she did look out for me.

Now see there, that's the problem with so-called friends. It's always one-sided when they have a problem and you have one at the same time; you only want to get yours solved, and the hell with theirs.

But I'm really going to try to help her if she needs me. I'll put mine on a shelf until I can walk her through with hers.

I'm really going to try to be a better friend no matter what it takes. Even though she can be worse, mum as hell sometimes, but that's all right.

I know that I am going to have to be there for her regardless of how I feel about it. She's my girl, and I'm going to be there for her. Okay, here goes.

Pick up the phone, girl, and dial it. Okay, the phone was ringing. I had begun to count: one ring, two rings, three rings. And just when I was about to hang up the phone, I heard her say hello.

"Damn, girl, I was just about to hang up when you said hello. Hi, Lisa, how are you? This is Rachael."

"Hey, Ray, I don't mean to be rude, but can I call you back tomorrow?"

I said, "Yeah."

"Ray, Eric is here."

"Oh, okay then. Call me tomorrow if you can find the time."

She said, "All right, girl." Then we hung up the phone.

Well, now she sounded pretty strong and happy. Hopefully she has forgiven him and has taken him back.

I really hope she did because even though she gets on my last nerve, she's still a little sweetheart and the best friend that anyone could ever ask for.

"Oh well, now what?"

It's the weekend, and I don't have anything to do. I've been to the casino, and he wasn't there.

I tried to talk to Lisa, but she wasn't having any conversation with me, so now what do I do?

It's times like this that I began to feel a longing, but not wanting to be with the kids.

So I'll just chill around the house for two days, see what's on cable, watch a movie, take a bath. I have lots to do to keep me busy until Monday morning when it's time to go back to work, only to complain about my clients.

First I'll take a long hot bubble bath and have a couple of glasses of wine, turn on the oldies station, and just relax.

So while relaxing in the tub and listening to the radio, I started thinking about how I wanted my next man to be, which was going to be a combination of men that I had been with over the years—even before I had any children.

If I could just have a man that was as handsome as Shawn or Robert, had style and class like Shawn or Robert, and was well-endowed like Shawn or Robert. Looks like I can't think of anybody but those two. But I'd have a dream come true. But this man would have to be God-fearing and love me and only me, not other women.

He would not be cheap, he wouldn't be an alcoholic or a drug user, and he wouldn't be violent or have a bad temper.

He would be loving and kind, wanting to spend all his time with me as long as we were not at work. He would want to travel and just enjoy being with me. Oh, one really important thing is he must not be a pervert.

And at least, he must like my children. Oh, and also be good in bed, knows what he's doing. Damn, just the thought of a mate that was well-endowed turned me on. To think about such a big piece of meat to play with whenever you wanted was great. Now if only it would come true, I'd be one happy woman.

It is said that good things come to those who wait. I hope that I don't have to wait too long before my wish comes true. Because right now, I need or could definitely use some male company. Taking another sip of wine, I sank deeper into the tub.

I thought just how happy we would be or could be. This is how I would like for things to go on occasions.

Now we both work days or whatever shift. It really doesn't matter. He phones me and leaves a message on my voice mail, saying to meet him at the casino in room 210. "I'm about to get off work a little early and head over there so that my little surprise will be ready when you get there, champagne and me."

Then there is a little giggle on the other end; then he says, "I'll see you around four thirty. The desk already knows that you are coming, so your card to enter the room will be waiting for you. So hurry up and get here. I won't start playing downstairs until you get here, and I have had a little taste of your sweetness. I know that you will be a little tired, so I'll have your favorite bubble bath run. It will still be hot if I time you right. Oh yeah, I'll have a little snack waiting for you too, and that will be me."

I could just hear him saying that.

Then saying, "Just kidding, honey. You know that I will have you something here for you to eat. Anyway, how are you feeling? Did you have a good day at work? Hey, baby, I'll see you in a little while, so be on your way as soon as you get this message, okay? Later, baby."

As I'm listening to the message, I get all smiley faced, feeling better instantly just with the thought of what was going to be waiting for me at the hotel inside the casino.

I still get excited at the thought of having someone that I really care about and he cares about me. But even after listening to the message, I still lay across the bed to gather my thoughts. I was thinking about my grandchildren and my children, thankful that they had someone special in their lives that they cared about.

And running the family business was going good for them. That was a big relief although I thought that Shawnda could do a little better in her choice of men, but that was going to change one day soon, I hoped.

As I lay across the bed thinking, I almost drifted off to sleep because of the medication that I had been taking for my cold and not knowing that he was going to have a surprise waiting for me. But I love it, but then suddenly I thought of what was waiting for me across that beautiful lake of water, someone very special. So I jumped up. I almost took a shower but remembered that he was going to have bathwater waiting for me. So instead, I called all my children and told them where I was going to be so that they would not be worried about me because they knew that I was not feeling very well due to the cold. And I also wanted to make sure that they didn't need anything.

After I had talked to the boys, I called Shawnda back because she could hear and not hear what I was saying to her unless it was something for her.

Then she could and understood very well, but I needed to remind her again that I was going to be gone for the whole weekend and to call or page me in case of emergency only because she would call for nothing, just to say hello and ask what are you all doing.

When I got her on the phone, I reminded her, then said, "Okay, goodbye for now."

But soon after I had hung up the phone, it rang. I picked it up and said, "What is it, little girl?" And the voice on the other end said, "I can assure you that I am not a little girl."

"Oh hi, baby."

"Are you all right?"

"Yeah, why do you ask?"

"Because I know that you were not feeling well for the last few days, but you sounded better. That's why I rented a room for the weekend."

"I'm fine. Well, feeling a little better anyway."

"Well, are you sure that you can make it over here?"

"Yeah, I'm sure."

"Then why are you not here? Wait, don't tell me now. Tell me when you get here and you are relaxing in the tub."

"Okay, I'm on my way. I just had to get everybody straight on my whereabouts for the weekend."

"Girl, if you don't be on your way—"

"Okay, I'm there. Just give me fifteen or twenty minutes. You know how the traffic can be."

"Yeah, but do hurry. I've got something special waiting for you."

"Oh yeah?"

"Yeah."

"Well, I'll bet that I can guess just what it is."

"No, it's not what you're thinking, so get your mind out of the gutter. And besides, I'll always have that for you. But I've got something else that I know that you are gonna like."

Now as I lay here enjoying my vision, I hate to get out and face reality, but sometimes dreams and visions do come true.

So I'll just continue to be patient; good things come to those who wait. So after soaking in the tub for hours, you can have the best daydreams if you want. They can be anything that you want them to be or anybody that you want it to be.

But enough of that now. I'll find a good movie to watch or watch something on cable, so I got all comfortable and checked the cable stations. There was a good movie on, a repeat as usual, but I watched it anyway.

After about an hour, I began to feel sleepy but didn't want to go to sleep just yet, so I moved around a little to keep myself from closing my eyes. But eventually, sleep got the best of me, and the movie began to watch me. So now it's Saturday morning.

And I get up, make myself breakfast and then clean the house, wash clothes, do all the things that needed to be done. Then after I finished, it was all most 11:00 p.m. My, how the time flies when you're having fun. So I showered and lay in bed and watched cable for the rest of the night until sleep took over.

When I woke up, it was early Sunday morning. I fiddled around, finding nothing to do, so I decided to go to church. I looked at the clock; it was 7:30 a.m., so I rushed to take a shower and eat breakfast. I got dressed and headed out to find a church that was not too far from where I lived.

I also didn't want a big church where everyone tried to outdress the other, where everyone stood out trying to be something that they weren't. It really doesn't matter so long as I get there and hear the word of the Lord because I surely could use it today.

So I guess I'll just ride around and see what happens.

So as I'm riding, I'm about two miles from where I live. I spotted this friendly looking church, so I pull in, got out and went inside, sat down, and listened to the preacher talk; he was talking about marriage and relationships.

I thought isn't this something he's talking about what's been on my mind for weeks now. He continued to preach.

He was doing a good job, then said, "Ladies and gentlemen, sisters and brothers, wait I say on the Lord, don't just jump in bed with anyone. Because nowadays, you can lie down with what you thought was a woman and wake up to find out that it was really a man and vice versa. So again, I say wait on the Lord."

He continued to preach until it was time for offering and the close of service. There was a nice-sized group of people that came to church that Sunday, I was thinking.

As I was preparing to leave, I was thinking this seems like a nice church. I think I might come back since it's not that far from where I live. Maybe I'll even join, but I'll see the next time that I come because I really did enjoy the service even though I felt like the preacher was talking about me.

As I was leaving, some of the members came over and was shaking my hand and asking if it was my first time visiting and, if it was, to please feel free to come again and that it was always nice to see new faces.

I was still headed for the door as the people were feeling good and friendly and still shaking my hand.

It was nice. But when I finally made my way out of the door and outside, headed toward my truck, I heard someone called out, "Mrs. Brunson! Mrs. Brunson!" I turned and looked. There he was, standing tall and looking good—Eugene in the flesh.

Boy, my heart started beating fast because I was looking for his wife to walk up right behind him at any minute.

I was so nervous, but I was not about to let him see me sweat, so to speak.

He came up and hugged me to my surprise.

Then he said, "How are you? I haven't seen you in a while. What? You haven't been working?"

Oh, I'm fine, and yes, I've been going to work. And I haven't seen you either." The man of my dreams all in one, I hope

He said, "Well, maybe we just keep missing each other coming in or going out. But it's nice to see you again."

"Anyway, what brings you this way?"

"What way is that?"

"Well, let me rephrase that statement and ask what brings you to this church this morning."

"Well, I wanted to go to church this morning, but I didn't feel like going to the one that I belong to because it's so far out. I just decided to find one a little closer, and this one stood out for me, so to speak."

We both kinda laughed.

Then he said, "Well, I'm glad that it did. Did you come alone?"

"Yes, I did. So what about you? Did you just happen to stop by yourself?"

"No, I belong to this church. I've been coming here for a while."

"Oh really?"

"Yes, ma'am."

"Eugene, please don't say 'yes, ma'am.'"

"Why not?"

"Because *ma'am* seems to me to fit an older person, at least that's the way I see it."

He said, "Well, okay, ma'am, as you wish." And we started to laugh, and I hit him on the arm. "Okay, okay, I won't call you ma'am again."

"So what are you getting ready to do now if you don't mind me asking?"

"Well, I have a date."

"A date?"

"Yeah."

"Well, why didn't you invite him to come to church with you?"

"Oh." I started laughing and said, "Not that kind of date."

"Well, what other kind of date is there?"

"I had a date with my television. There was a movie coming on, and I had planned to watch it. Lisa tells me that all I do is make dates with my television set."

This time, he laughed and looked kind of relieved. "Oh," he said, "I thought it was with the guy that I had seen you with a few weeks ago."

"Naw, that's a long story. And what about you and the lady that I saw you with? Was that your wife? Is she here?"

"Woah there. Now that's a long story too."

"Well, someday we'll discuss both of our long stories if we ever find the right time because we are both pretty busy."

"Well, we don't seem to be pretty busy now. Would you like to go and have lunch with me?"

"Right now?"

"Or would I be messing up your plans for the day?"

"No, you would not be messing up my plans, and lunch sounds good. Hey, I'll tell you what," I said. "I live about two, three miles from here. Would you mind following me? And that way, you could park your car at my house if you don't mind, and we could ride together, or we could just meet at whatever place it is that you want to go and have lunch at."

"That's okay with me. But can I make another suggestion and see if you like it."

"Sure."

"Now I only stay about five blocks from here, so you could follow me and park your truck in my driveway if you don't mind doing that."

"That's okay with me. Are you ready to lead the way?"

"Well, I have to run back inside for a minute, but it will only take a second, and I'll be right out."

"Okay, I'll just wait right here in my truck."

"Okay, be right back." And he took off.

I watched him go back inside the church. I got in my truck and sat there in disbelief, just thinking about the man I had been thinking about all along; and here he was, right in the palm of my hands, so to speak.

He came rushing out of the church and came up to my truck and said, "Okay, you can follow me."

I said, "Are you sure it's going to be safe?"

He looked at me and said, "What do you mean safe?"

"You know, the long story?"

"Oh, it's safe. I live there alone."

"Okay, lead the way."

He got in his car, and I followed him to his house. He pulled up into one of the most beautiful homes that looked like it had been pictured in a magazine or *Better Homes and Garden*.

His circular drive was larger than the ones you normally would see.

I wondered if the inside looked as elegant as the outside did or even as elegant as he looked and smelled.

I knew that if I had my way, I was going to see the inside plenty of times, but that would come in time. Right now, we were just going to park my truck and go out to lunch.

Looking at his house made me think of the house that Shawn and I had. Our house was a little bigger, but there was more of us living in it.

Suddenly I heard Eugene say, "Are you ready to go?"

"Sure." So I got out of my truck and got into Eugene's car. Boy, I love his town car, and I told him so.

He said, "I love that truck. I almost bought one but changed my mind at the last minute and bought the car instead."

Then he said, "What do you feel like eating?"

"Well, now since it was you who asked me out, I think that you knew ahead of time what you were going to do for lunch, or where you were going for lunch, so whatever you had planned is fine with me. I'm game for whatever."

He started laughing.

"Oh, what's funny? Let me rephrase that answer."

"No, I was just thinking. You see, I also had a date."

"You did?"

"Yeah." My heart started beating fast again, waiting for him to say who his date was.

"I had a date with my backyard and grill. But when I saw you, I thought that I might have a chance to let you buy lunch if you were going to be available."

Then he started to laugh and said, "So you see, now it's up to you. So whatever you want to do is fine with me."

So I said, "If you feel like cooking, then I'll help you if that's all right with you."

"Sure, let's go inside then. I already had a couple of shish kebobs made up so that when I got home, all I would have to do was put them on the grill and make a salad, pour myself a glass of wine, and chill for the rest of the day."

"Okay, but while you are getting the grill ready, I'll make the salad."

"Okay, everything that I was going to use is in the fridge."

"All right, just let me freshen up a bit, then I'll get started."

"Okay, but if you need anything else, just let me know."

"Well, since you asked, do you happen to have an apron?"

"No, but if you like, you can change into one of my jogging outfits, okay? Hold on, and I'll get it for you."

He came in, went into one of the bedrooms, and came out with a blue jogging outfit. I took it and went into the bathroom to change. It was well decorated to be a man's place.

I figured he had one of his lady friends decorate for him because everything was so neat and in place. I changed my clothes, and so did he.

He still looked even more sexier in his play clothes.

I was thinking after getting dressed. I went into the kitchen to make the salad. When I opened the refrigerator, I couldn't believe my eyes. He actually had food in there, so I decided to make a salad that was gonna be hard to forget. One that he would always remember. I used shrimp, onions, bell peppers, red peppers, crab meat, the greens, lettuce and tomatoes, crumbers. You name it, and I used it. He had everything; then I spotted a bottle of wine. So I walked to the sliding glass doors and asked if he would mind if I poured myself a glass of wine.

"No, help yourself, and would you mind pouring me one also?"

"Sure." As I was walking back into the house, he said, "The glasses are in the cabinet to your left."

So off I went and poured two glasses of wine. After pouring the wine, I took them outside to the patio and sat them down on the table and sat down.

I said, "You know, if it were a little warmer out here, I would take a dip in your pool."

He came back with, "It's okay. I keep the pool heated. Because sometimes, after a long stressful day at work and I've done all that I'm going to do for the day and I'm still feeling tensed, I'll just come out here and do a few laps—and I don't like freezing—so I had a heater put in."

"So now you don't have an excuse. You can swim all you like, be my guest."

"Well, it seems like you have forgotten the most important thing."

"What's that?"

"I don't have a swimming suit."

"Oh, that won't be a problem."

"Why is that?"

"Because I have plenty of ladies' swimsuits in the pool house."

"Oh, you do? I see you keep yourself well prepared."

"No, it's not like that. You see, I bought this house from a single man. And he has—or should I say, left—a lot of things here that a single man uses, and there are a lot of brand-new swimsuits in the pool house and in that spare closet that you might like. There are a variety of them, so you can take your pick."

"Well, let me think about it for a while and see how much time we have left before you'll be finished."

"Actually, I am finished."

"Well, that settles it. I don't think that I am going to be swimming."

"Why not?"

"Because if I swim, then the food is going to get cold."

"That's just an excuse that you want to use, but it's not a good one because the food can stay warm on the grill without drying out and keep warm. Now what?" he said with a smile.

"Okay, I'm hungry. So maybe if you invite me over again one day, then I can take a swim."

"Okay, then what are you doing tomorrow after work?"

"I don't know about tomorrow."

"Why?"

"Because I don't know what the day is going to hold for me."

"But you have to go home at sometime."

"I know that. That's why I said I don't know about tomorrow."

"Well, you can come here instead of going home, take a swim, then let me fix dinner for you."

"Oh, that sounds so tempting, but I still have to think about it."

"Well, let me know whatever you decide. Hey, what's the matter? You don't know how to swim? Because you keep trying to get out of taking a swim when I have everything that you may need, so what is it? You don't know how to swim, do you?"

"As a matter of fact, I don't, but I like playing in the water. We used to have a pool, but I never had the time to learn how to swim. But I do like standing on the side and playing in the water."

"That seems like it was a long time ago, so now would you like for me to teach you how to swim someday?"

"That would be nice."

"So would you like another glass of wine?"

I looked down at my glass and didn't realize that I had just about drank all my wine, so I said, "Sure, I'll have another glass if you will."

Eugene drank the last that was in his glass and stood up to go get some more. He brought the whole bottle out in an ice bucket. I poured us both another glass.

Then Eugene said, "These babies are ready to go." He took the steaks off the grill, sat them on a tray, and closed the lid of the grill. Then he sat back down and said, "We can eat whenever you are ready."

I was feeling relaxed, so I said, "Hey, you never said how I look in your jogging clothes."

He was sitting in a lounge chair that was overlooking the pool, which looked as though it would be a beautiful place to sit and look at the stars at night.

Robert said, "Hey, you look just fine. Your pants are a little too big, but your dress hides that."

"Oh, I look terrible, don't I?"

"Sure you do." Then he started laughing. "But for real, you look great. You are at home when you are over here, so don't ever worry how you look because I'm sure that I'll see worst." Then he laughed again and said, "I'm only kidding. I like looking at you no matter what you have on, so what can I say?"

Then I asked, "What is it you want? If I knew you better."

"Why'd you say that?"

"Because with a compliment like that, there's always something behind it that someone wants."

"You know what, that's true because my girls are always up to something when they call and say, 'Hey, handsome,' or 'Hi, love of my life.' Then I'd say, 'What do you want?' They'll laugh and say, 'Dang, my handsome dad.' Can't I just talk sweet things without you thinking that I want something? So you see, you are right and wrong because I don't want anything. I'm not like my girls. Oh wait, yes, I do."

"I knew it, so what is it?"

"I want to be your best friend if you don't have one already, and I want… Never mind."

"Hey, don't let the cat get your tongue now."

"I won't. I'll just save that one for later."

"Oh no. You don't out with it."

"If I say what I almost said, then I don't want you to take it the wrong way. Because it's so soon and you don't know me yet."

"Good excuse, but out with it anyway."

"Okay, here goes. If you don't have a best friend, I want to be it, and if you don't have a lover, I'd like to be that in your life too—all in one day if you don't mind. Now what do you have to say?"

"Well, what can I say except let me think about it for a while, and I'll let you know later. But back to my question—we'll skip my question because I forgot what I was saying anyway."

"Okay, now that that is out of the way, I have got everything ready, the table is set. Are you ready to eat?"

"Sure."

"Then let's eat. I'll say grace."

"Hold it."

"What's wrong?"

"Nothing. It's just that it's my turn to say grace this time."

"Well, look at you. Be my guest. And the next time and anytime after that, we'll just say grace together, okay? Now how does that sound?"

"Sounds good to me. Now can we please eat?"

He looked at the salad and said, "It looks good and smells great. Looks like you put everything in it that I was going to put in it."

"That way, you get really full of something light. Hey, you know what?"

"What?"

"You really fooled me."

"How's that? Hey, don't get tight-lipped on me now."

"Oh, I'm not. It's just that your refrigerator is so full of everything."

"Well, I love cooking, and when something out of the ordinary comes to mind to cook, I like to be ready to fix it so that I don't have to go and get something when I'm in the mood to cook something different. So I like to be prepared."

"Okay, these shish kebobs taste delicious."

"Thanks, and so does this salad. It tastes much better than I would have made it, and you put much more in it than I would have."

"So is that good or bad?"

"It's excellent." As he was pouring more wine, I said, "Hey, don't forget that I have to drive myself home."

"You don't have to you know. How about I take you home and pick you up for work in the morning and bring you back here after work tomorrow?"

"Sounds good, but I won't have a change of clothes."

"That can be solved easily by bring extra clothes when I pick you up in the morning."

"You mean that you want me to spend the night with you tomorrow?"

"Well yeah."

"I don't know you like that."

"I don't mean sleep with me. Not yet anyway."

"You sure don't bite your tongue, do you?"

"Baby girl, if I don't put it out there like that, then you would never know how I feel about you."

"That's why I wanted to talk to you a long time ago."

"But you weren't having any conversation with me. You remember I tried to get Lisa to run interference, but that didn't work. So now that I got the chance to tell you what I wanted to say before, I'm just saying it. But I probably would not have been so bold as I am now, but I just want to be a part of your life if at all possible."

"Dammmn, I like that but—"

"Get your *but* out of the way."

"Cute. But for real, it all sounds good. But by us both being lawyers, you know that we are both going to need our cars because you know, at any minute, things could go haywire, and you gotta make a move fast."

"Okay, that's all true, but you can still come over and spend the night. I do have a few extra bedrooms. We can just chill and get to know each other better, but you are right about the wine. You don't need any more. I was just enjoying your company so much that I just didn't want you to leave because there's no telling when I'll see you again if I don't invite you to come back over."

"Well, I was enjoying your company also, but you know that there is no getting around not having your car at work. You know that. But thanks for the offer."

"Well, let me follow you home to make sure that you get there all right."

"Hey, there's no need for that."

"Are you sure?"

"Yeah, I'm sure."

"Well, at least take my number and call me when you get there. So that I'll know that you are all right."

"Okay." He gave me his number.

And I said, "I'll be fine. I'll call you when I get in."

"You know what, it seems like you are rushing me out."

"No, I'm not. Why would you say something like that?"

"Because it just seems that way."

"Well, you should know better than that when I'm trying to get you to spend the night. So why would I be trying to rush you out?"

"I don't know. I guess it's the wine making me say things, and look at me, I'm still wearing your clothes. The dishes are dirty, and you are ready to walk me to my car."

"Well, Ms. Brunson, that's not the case at all. I just didn't want you out so late, driving around by yourself. But if it will make you feel any better, then lets go in and wash the dishes as you wish."

We laughed and walked into the kitchen.

"Okay, I'll dry and you wash."

"No, I want to dry," I told him.

"That's fine with me, okay? The dishwasher is all ready to go, then you can knock yourself out drying them." He started to laugh.

I said, "That's not fair."

"Oh, all right, crybaby. I'll help you dry the dishes and put them away."

"Okay, while you load the dishwasher, I'll pick up around the backyard."

"Fair enough."

So I walked out into the backyard as he began to put the dishes into the dishwasher.

As I was putting napkins into the trash, I was thinking can this really be happening? I mean, can this man really be real? I mean, we have a good time every time that we are together. So far, he's what every woman want in a man.

He's tall, dark, and handsome; has good job; owns his own home. He's kind, gentle, has good sense of humor, friendly. I mean, is this too good to be true? I've heard that anything that seems too good to be true is too good to be true.

Is there something wrong with this man? I mean, he has it going on. I wonder if he's gay or has a very small penis. Oh, Lord, I hope not either one of those ugly thoughts that I just had.

Just then, he walked into the backyard as I was standing there, looking into the water, with my thoughts running wild.

He said, "Is there something wrong?"

"Oh no, I was just thinking about a case that I'm working on or about to start working on."

He said, "Look, I know that you are a good lawyer and your clients come first, but today is Sunday and tomorrow will be here soon enough. So can we change the subject, or can I change your thoughts to something else?"

"Okay, you're right. So have you finished putting all the dishes into the dishwasher?"

"Yeah, that's all taken care of."

"Well, you know what, Mr. Michaels, I have really enjoyed myself. Going to church and running into you, then spending the day with you. I really had a good time. And to think that I was going to go home and watch whatever was on television or cable. But I truly thank you for saving me from such a boring day. And showing me such a wonderful time."

"Well, I thank you for accepting my invitation on such a short notice."

"And I enjoyed you just as much, I really did."

"And I hope that we can do this again tomorrow and the next day and the day after that." Then he laughed. "But for real, I will come and pick you up, take you out. We can do whatever you want to do. Just let a guy know."

"Hey, I will, but right now, I'm going to go into the room and change clothes."

"Why don't you just keep them on and bring them back another day?"

"Oh, okay then. I'll just get my things and be on my way."

"Hey, Ray—oh, you don't mind me calling you Ray, do you?"

"No, that's fine. It sounds much better than you calling me ma'am."

He just smiled and said, "Okay, I won't call you ma'am again. Anyway, how about we make a date for next Saturday? I'll cook, or we can go out to eat. It'll be your choice."

"Well, I'll let you know when I see you at work, or if I don't see you at work, then I'll give you a call or you can call me. Let me give you my number."

"Oh, that's okay. I've already got it."

"How?"

"After we first met at Red Lobster, I decided to do some investigating, and I got your name and address."

"How did you do that?"

"Did you forget that we are lawyers? But I didn't use it, hoping that one day you would give it to me, and you did. Well, you offered it to me anyway. You are not mad at me for doing that, are you?"

"No, because at one point, I thought about doing the same to you but thought against it. Because I didn't want to find out that you were married."

"Well, now we both know. So how about a date next weekend?"

"But in the meantime, let me cook something for you until we go out or do whatever you want to do. What do you say to that?"

"I say that you have a date. I'll call you when I get home, Mr. Michaels. I really did enjoy myself with you."

He kissed me on my cheek and walked me to the door where he kissed me again. Damn, he had some soft lips, and I thought this is going to be fun for how ever long we last because I do believe that he is going to surprise me with a hidden girlfriend or something unreal.

Not that I don't believe that good things can happen. It's just that— well, we'll see. I'll just wait and see as time goes on. Damn, I'm running away with things, aren't I?

So again I said, "I'll see you tomorrow, Mr. Michaels." He walked me to my truck and gave my hand a light squeeze and kiss, then said, "I'll see you tomorrow."

I got in my truck, and he kissed me goodbye. I pulled off before I decided to take him up on his offer to spend the night because it seemed as though we didn't want to leave each other.

While driving home, I thought about what's happening to me. I think that I'm falling in love with someone that I really don't even know. What is it? Has it been that long since I felt love, or was it his smooth way of reeling me in and putting a notch on his headboard? Well, I don't really know, but what I do know is that I could fall head over heels if I don't watch myself.

I was pulling up into my parking structure before I knew it. I couldn't explain it, but I was unbelievably happy once again.

It felt just like when Shawn and I first started dating. Those were the days. "Hey, Shawn, what do you think? Do you approve? Sure you do," I said, smiling, as I walked into my apartment building.

I was still smiling and thinking about how Shawn would feel about my dating someone else.

I was thinking and still smiling to myself when I opened the door; then I remembered that I was supposed to call Eugene and let him know that I had made it home.

I started looking around the apartment. I said, "Dang, I have been gone all day it seems."

Just as I shut the door, the phone rang. I thought it was Eugene, but when I got to the phone and looked at the caller ID, it was my son Jaylen. I picked up the phone and said, "Hey, my baby."

He said, "Hi, Ma."

"Jaylen, yeah, it's me. Are you all right?"

"Yeah."

"What's up?"

"Oh, nothing much. I was just calling because I had not talked to you in a few days, and I wanted to see how you were doing."

"Well, I'm fine, sweetheart. How are you?"

"Ma, I'm all right I guess."

"What do you mean you guess? Because if you don't know, then nobody knows."

"Well, Ma, you know the girl that I have been seeing?"

"Yeah." I thought, *Oh boy, here we go.* But I would be cool just like

Shawnda said. "Well, Ma, she's going to have a baby."
Silence.
Then I said, "Oh really?"
"Yeah, Ma, but this chick…"
"Who?"
"I mean, the girl who says I'm her baby's daddy."
"Well, what is her name again?"
"Belinda."
"Oh yeah, now I remember because you call her BB."
"Yeah, Ma."

"Jay, what's wrong?"

"Ma, can I come over?"

"Jaylen, you know that you don't have to ask if you can come over. What's bothering you? Jay, do you still have your keys?"

"Yeah."

"Okay, then I'll see you shortly. I love you."

"Mama, I love you too."

"Jay, so be on your way, all right?"

When we hung up, I was a little worried. I thought if this bitch has done something to hurt my baby, God help her.

I was boiling because he didn't sound like his happy little self, and I did not like that not one little bit, so I basically paced the floor until he got there. When he got to the door, he knocked. I said, "Jay?"

He said, "Yeah, Ma, it's me."

I rushed to open the door. Looking at him standing there, looking like his dad, all I could do was hug him.

"Come in, my baby."

"Ma, I'm not bothering you?"

"Jay, please. You are never a bother to me. You are my baby. Okay, okay, sometimes all of you get on my nerves. But that's okay. But you know what, that's children's job to worry their parents, but we love it. So what's up? Because if you're hurting, I'm hurting. Jay, I'm going to start crying if you don't tell me the truth about what's going on with you. So sit down and tell me what's wrong with you."

I was trying with all my strength not to just bust out and say, "Did that bitch do anything to hurt you?" But I didn't say a word; I just looked at him.

"Jaylen, what's wrong?"

He had tears in his eyes.

"Jaylen." Now I was crying with him.

"Jay," I hollered, "what is it, my baby? What?"

"Ma, I'm scared."

"Scared?"

"Yeah, Ma."

"Wait, I do not understand what you're saying. Just what are you talking about? You're scared? What could you possibly be scared of?"

"Ma, you know that I have dated a lot of girls, and well, Ma, when I look back at how at times you and Dad were so happy."

"Yeah."

"Well, this is how I feel about her, and it scares me. We get along so good that at times it seems unreal. I begin to think that I might lose her, and I'm scared to get any closer to her because something might happen to her. I'm afraid that she might die or leave me knowing how I feel about her."

"Jay, why would you think something like that?"

"Because, Ma, when you and Dad seem to be the happiest, then I've seen you be in such a long time. From what I could remember. Then he was taken away from us. He was gone."

All I could do was hold him and let the tears roll down my cheeks and his.

"Then after getting on with your life, after what seemed like forever, you married Robert, and then once again you were happy, and then that ended. I don't want to be so happy enjoying my life, Ma, when you have no one but us. And if I do marry Belinda, she'll take away some of the time that I do get to spend with you."

"Oh my goodness, Jaylen, I didn't realize that you paid any attention to my life once you got older and started dating. But, baby, my baby, I don't want you to worry about me. I'll be fine. And all I want for you, your brother, and sister is to experience the joy and happiness of sharing your life with someone so special. Your mama is a strong woman and will always bounce back stronger than before. My baby, please don't worry about your mama. Oh, my baby."

As I wiped the tears from his eyes, I said, "So you are going to make me another grandmother, huh?"

"Yeah, Mama, and it looks like she might be having twins."

"Oh my! I always wanted two sets of twins in the family, and it looks like we just might be getting that second set after all. Jaylen, why did you hold all this inside you for so long? When I told you children that— whenever anything was bothering you—to always come to me no matter what it was, you should have come to me and shared your feelings with me instead of struggling with this by yourself for all these years. Baby, I'm so sorry. Because I even had to talk to someone myself. My family and coworkers helped, and even you children helped me. Because when your father was killed, I still had a part of him, which was you kids. So you see, we all need to talk to somebody at sometime or another. I just wish now that I would have paid closer attention to you all, and then I would have known that something was going on with you. And I would have known that something was wrong.”

“Ma, if you got any closer, you have been smothering us.”

I smiled and said, “I still didn’t pick up on your feelings.”

“That’s because I’m just like you. I hide my feelings well.”

I couldn’t say a word, but I just hugged him because he was right. I always held my feelings in when Shawn and I argued because I didn’t want the children to worry, so I would just stop talking. “So how does Shawn and Shawnda feel about this?”

“I haven’t really talked to them about my feelings because they would have called me a mama’s boy like they always do.”

“Do they? I didn’t know that either. Well, sweetheart, let me tell you something. You are my baby and will always be, so don’t worry about what they call you. They’re just jealous.”

Then we both laughed. He smiled and looked at me and said, “Thanks, Ma.”

“For what, my baby?”

“For just listening to me. Ma, I couldn’t really tell you how I felt because I hurt for you. But, Ma, I love Belinda so much. She’s not at all like the other girls that I have dated before. She actually reminds me of you. She works at the hospital, and she’s going to school to become a nurse, but she says that she is not going to stop there. She’s going on to become a pediatrician. She wanted to do this even before she got pregnant.”

“Jay, I have to ask you this. Are you sure that she’s carrying your baby?”

“You know, at first, I thought about it, but we’re always together. And if we are not together, then we’re either at work or she’s at school or we’re on the phone. So yes, Ma, you’re going to be another grandmother, and like I said, she’s a lot like you.”

I hugged him again and said, “If you love her, then I love her too.”

"Tell me, does she know how you feel about what's been going on in my life?"

"Well, she is the only one that I could tell my true feelings to without sounding like a spoiled brat. She also had said that I should tell you how I was feeling. I knew that I could have talked to you about my feelings, but my heart was hurting for you too much. I wanted so much for you to be truly happy before I said anything, but I couldn't hold it any longer."

"Well, my baby, don't you worry about me because as a matter of fact, I was out on a date today myself."

"What?"

"That's right."

"Ma, who is he? Mama, you know that you have got to be careful. Ma, you know I'm working in the construction business, I meet a lot of people, and I could hook you up with someone that I know."

"Look, my child, even if you did find someone that you thought that I might like, you would only know him from the outside. He would probably be a whole different person once you got to know the real him. I truly thank you, but I think that I'm going to stick with the one that I'm already seeing."

"Well, Ma, how long has this been going on?"

"It actually just got started today. I went to church, and there he was."

"Ma, you mean that you just met this man and you went out with him?"

"No no, it's not like that. I haven't turned into a hooker." Then we laughed. "As a matter of fact, Lisa, the paralegal where I work... You know her, right?"

"Yeah."

"Well, she had been trying to hook us up for the longest, as you all say. But we could never find the right time to meet. But the first time that I actually met him, it was by accident. We met at a restaurant, and we started talking, and one thing led to another. We found out that we work in the same building, and both of us are lawyers. It's a long story, so you see, we are not strangers so to speak. And you are the only one who knows about this because this was our first date. Well, not really a date, but the first time that we found time to get together and talk by ourselves. But we are supposed to get together this weekend. So you see, my child, Mama will be all right. I'm going to let the other two know later. There's no need to rush things. As a matter of fact, I was supposed to call him when I got in so that he would know that I made it home safe. We had dinner over at his place. He has a beautiful house, and he's single. And I think that he is a pretty decent guy. Oh well, you'll see one day soon."

"One day soon. When will that be?"

"Let me get to know him a little before I bring you guys in the picture. How does that sound?"

"Good, I can't wait to tell BB. She'll be happy for the both of us. I say that because she'll be glad that I finally talked to you, and we both will be glad for you because you won't be alone like I thought. Okay, Mama, now that I know that you are all right, I'll be going."

"Wait a minute, let me say this to you. Don't be afraid to live, be happy, love BB, love life. Take things one day at a time. And be happy, not afraid of what might happen, because it just might not happen for a thousand years. You know what I'm saying, my baby."

"Yeah, Ma." He hugged me and kissed me, then said, "I'm out."

"Okay, one more thing."

"Huh?"

"What about this wedding?"

"Well, we haven't really talked about it because of the way that I was feelin' about you being alone."

"So now that you know that I'm going to be all right, what are you going to do?"

"I don't know, Ma. I've got some money saved, but not much."

"Well, I'll tell you what. Is Belinda's parents alive?"

"Yeah."

"Well, how about one day, when you and Belinda have had a chance to talk about what the two of you want to do, we all get together and discuss the wedding plans and go from there?"

"Well, we have already kind of set a date, but it's not in stone yet."

"You have?"

"Yeah, it's supposedly set for Christmas."

"Christmas holidays. Why then?"

"Because no matter what's going on, you are always happiest then. Even with all the tragedies, you still enjoy Christmas."

"Jaylen, I can't believe you. Oh, my baby." All I could do was hug him and cry all over again. "I love you, Jaylen Brunson."

"I love you too, Ma." Then he said, "I'll tell you what. When I get home, I'll talk to Belinda and see just when would be a good time for all of us to get together and make this happen. Thanks, Ma, thanks." He hugs me, then said, "I'll call you tomorrow. What time do you get home?"

"Jaylen, I really don't know because I'm getting myself together. I'm getting a life like you kids used to tell me. With Eugene."

"Oh, that's his name?"

"Yeah, that's his name. If he wants to go out to dinner, it doesn't matter. You can always reach me on my cell phone. And if I'm in the middle of a conversation, then leave a message on the voice mail. The answering machine will pick it up. And I'll call you back, all right?"

"Okay, Ma. I love you, and I'll talk to you tomorrow, all right?"

"My baby, call me when you get in."

"I will. Bye now." We hugged and he left.

I looked at my watch; it was ten thirty. "Dang, Eugene is probably in bed. I'll just call and leave a message on his machine. Just to let him know that I did call even though it's much later."

So I sat down on the bed and waited for the machine to pick up, but on the third ring, he picked up and said hello in such a sexy voice. I said, "Eugene."

"Yeah."

"This is Rachael."

"Oh, I wondered what happened to you. I started to call your place, but I didn't. I just decided to wait and see just when you were going to call. I didn't want you to think I was being to pushy, if that's even the right thing to say. But I am glad you called. Now I know that you are all right."

"Oh, I'm fine. I'm sorry that I didn't call you as soon as I got in. But my son called and was so upset."

"So is he all right?"

"Yeah. He's fine now."

"That's good, and I'm glad that the both of you are all right."

"I'll explain."

"Hey, you don't have to explain. I mean, it's not that I don't care about your son, but everything's okay, right?"

"Right, but I still want to tell you all about what happened."

"But we can talk tomorrow."

"I promise that I will find time tomorrow to talk to you. I'll tell you what. Let's exchange cell phone numbers so that we can keep track of one another. And if we are both free at lunch, we'll go out to eat."

"That sounds good."

"We can even leave a message so that we'll know for sure where we stand."

"Okay then, so I'll talk to you in the morning."

"All right. Good night, sleep tight."

"You too." Then we hung up the phone. I thought, *Damn, I feel like I have died and gone to heaven.* I can't believe that God has seen it fit to answer my prayers. But I knew he would one day. Thank you, Jesus, for my new husband being someone that you approved of and so do I. Thank you again. I know that I will have to get my divorce soon. I'll make sure to do that this week for sure. I'll go right upstairs and talk to Roselyn. All I need is a simple divorce. That shouldn't cost too much or take a long time.

Robert has already left town, but that won't be a problem. I've got to move on with my life. Life doesn't stop because of someone else's fuckups, so on I go with life. And a very happy one at that.

Oh well, I went and turned on the shower, then took off my clothes, looked down at the clothes lying on the floor, and thought about whose clothes they were. I just wonder what's up his sleeve. I hope nothing. But this man has got it going on, and he's not with anybody that I know of anyway. But tomorrow, I'll get straight to the point, and there will be no beating around the bush with him. I'll find out just what's going on with him. I'll find out if he's married, single, widowed, or divorced. Or is he like me—needs to get a divorce? I'll find out if we're going to get married or what?

I started laughing and thought if I say that to that man, he will think that I have lost my last ounce of sense. I'll just wait and see.

What the hell. Nobody's here but me anyway. The joys of living alone, with no children. It felt good to wake up with the covers clinging to me and sleeping in the nude.

I haven't done that in a while except when there was a man around to spend the night; but from now on, if it's nice out, I'll be sleeping the very same way.

I just lay there for a while, then looked over at the clock; it was six thirty. Let me get up from here and get myself together. I'll eat a piece of toast and drink a glass of juice. Then be on my way shortly.

By the time I got dressed, it was seven thirty.

I like to look through the paper before I go to work. So I poured myself another glass of juice, then walked over, and opened the door to see if my paper was going to be there or not because my neighbors across the hall were good at taking my paper, then say that they didn't get it.

I had been meaning to tell the paperboy to ring my buzzer when he brings my paper so that there won't be any more confusion about it.

Well, what do you know; it's there. I bent down to get the paper and looked up and saw Sabrina's husband shutting their door. I heard him say, "Damn, she beat."

I thought, *Ain't that a bitch.*

Let me get inside, it's too early for an argument. I'll save that for the courtroom. But just think, they both have good jobs but are too cheap to buy their own newspaper and keep stealing mine. A thirty-five-cent paper.

Boy, was I angry early in the morning over some old bullshit. They act worse than their own grandchildren, stupid son of a bitch.

I have let them get me all riled up even before my day can get started. Let me get out of this house before I just knock on their door and get started with them. It ain't worth it.

But one day, I am going to confront them because they have got to stop. I should put a hidden camera in the hall and show it to the manager. But I won't because that could get them kicked out for stealing a little old newspaper.

I just sat down at the bar in the kitchen, drank my juice, and ate my toast.

I left still cursing to myself. The nerve of some people.

I got in my car and drove to work with my jaws tight until I got closer to work. The closer I got, the more relaxed I got.

Now I thought about my coworker, and a big smile came over my face. I thought I'm not going to let those people steal my joy from me today. Today was going to be the day that I find out a lot about my Eugene.

As soon as I got into my office and sat down, in comes Lisa.

"Hey, girl, what's up?"

"You know, I am so messed up."

"Messed up about what?"

"Girl, Eric is trying so hard to please me. He's trying to make up for all his damn cheating. He's being so attentive until he is getting on my last nerve."

"Oh." I was smiling. "Lisa, what is he doing?"

"He comes straight home from work, and he stays."

"So what's wrong with that?"

"Nothing. It's just that he's always asking, 'Honey, are you all right?' 'Can I get anything for you?' 'Are you feeling okay?' 'Honey, are you getting sleepy?' Honey, honey, honey. All night long, he's driving me crazy."

"Well, have you said anything to him about how you are feeling?"

"No, not yet."

See what I mean? She is not too bright at times, I thought.

"Well, why not?"

"I don't know. I mean, I like the attention, but then again, it gets to be too much."

"Well, Lisa, you need to tell him exactly what you just told me. He should understand."

"I mean, after all, he wasn't doing that before he got caught cheating, Ray."

"Just talk to him. Lisa, you have got to let him know. Say something, girl, because a lot of relationships break up over little things that could be nicked in the butt before it gets blown out of proportion. Stop it now."

I looked at my watch; it said eight forty-five already. "Dammmn, I've got to go. I'm running late. We'll talk later because there is something that I have to tell you anyway. Today I'm defending a lady accused of child abuse. But after researching, the baby has a condition that causes weeps. It's pretty much an open-and-shut case once I get the experts on the witness stand. But anyway, girl, I've got to go. I'll talk to you later."

As I was walking out of the door, Lisa said, "Hey, have you met Gene yet?"

"Excuse me?"

"I mean, have you met Eugene yet, or have you run into him yet with his fine ass?"

"Oh yeah, that's what I was going to talk to you about, but I don't have the time now." Again I said, "I will talk to you later."

She looked at me with a strange smile on her face.

"What? What? Girl, I have got to go. We'll talk, I promise, okay?"

"Ray, I am not going to let you get out without telling me what happened or how you met him."

I just left her standing there, looking crazy. I was smiling to myself as I thought about how I was going to tell her. I'll just invite her over. We'll have a few drinks. Oh, but she can't drink. But she can have some juice or something. We'll have a little girl talk. I'll tell my sisters to come by, and we'll just make a day of it.

But it won't be this weekend because I already have plans that I refuse to break even though I haven't told him okay yet. But I'm going to.

Oh boy, this new relationship is going to be a lot of fun; and if I have my way, it's always going to be fun.

As I entered the courtroom, I saw that the prosecutor was already there, so I signed in.

Then he walked over and asked if I was ready to make a plea bargain.

"Of course not. Are you willing, or are you ready to drop all charges?" We kinda smiled at each other and walked back to our tables.

This shouldn't take long at all.

After my client and I talked a little, I heard the bailiff say, "All rise."

I never understood why we all had to rise when a judge came into the room. Why?

Court is now in session; the court secretary called another case before mine. Damn, they won't be finished by noon, and then I'll have to cancel my lunch date. But then again, maybe not.

I sat and listened to the case, and I knew that there was going to be no getting in and out on this one. But I had to wait just in case something got postponed and they called my case next. These things always happen unexpectedly because this kind of case could go either way. Maybe they will settle.

It's going on twelve, and they are still picking a jury, so if Eugene is free, I'll be able to make lunch. So I stepped into the hall to call Gene. As his phone rang, I thought, *Oh well, it looks as though I might be having lunch with some of the other lawyers.*

Then his voice mail came on. I said, "Hi, Eugene. This is Rachael. I'm calling about our lunch date to let you know where I stand. But I can see that you are tied up, so I'll give you a call later."

Then I heard someone say, "What time later?" I turned around, and he was standing right there, right behind me.

"Oh you."

Then I said, "Oh, you almost scared me."

"Oh, you mean I didn't from the way you jumped?"

I hit him on the arm and said, "Okay, you got me."

I thought that I was going to have to do it all over again.

"But anyway, I was just about to call you when I looked down this way and saw you standing here. I thought that you might have seen me too. Until you turned around. That's when I decided to just walk down here. I was in the courtroom down the hall."

"Oh, so what were you going to tell me about lunch?"

"I was going to tell you that I could make lunch around one if you were going to be available."

"Well, it looks like we will be coming out at around the same time because this judge always calls lunch at the same time."

"So I'll see you around one."

"Okay, so where do we meet?"

"Well, since we both will be coming out at the same time, why not right here?"

"All right, one it is." We shook hands; then we both went our separate ways.

He looked back, and I said, "One it is."

Then we went back into the courtroom.

As I entered the room, they were still trying to pick a jury.

I just wondered how could they have gotten the cases mixed up because I know the secretary said that I'd be the first case this morning.

But I'm okay with it.

I just sat and listened to the lawyers argue about dismissing certain jurors. They continued to discuss juror after juror right up until the one-o'clock lunch hour.

The judge called for recess, then said court will resume at two thirty. I didn't realize that the time had moved so fast; it was twelve fifty.

I walked out of the courtroom and saw Eugene standing there, talking to a lady. They were just standing there talking. When I walked up, I did a double look at the lady he was talking to, only to notice that she was the same lady that I had seen him with at the restaurant the night that Robert and I were there. Oh boy, this is going to be interesting.

So at first, I was a little hesitant about walking up to him, but I did it anyway.

I walked up and said, "Hi."

He turned and said, "Hi, sweetheart," and gave me a light kiss on the lips.

Then he introduced the lady that he was talking to.

He put his arms around my waist and said, "Honey, this is Veronica."

"Hi, Veronica," I said.

Then Eugene said, "Hey, Veronica, I'll see you later." And we walked away.

I didn't say anything until we were out of the building. Then I looked up at him.

He said, "I'll explain in the car." We walked to the lot where he had parked. When we got into his car, he turned and looked at me and said, "I'm sorry about that." Then he started the car and said, "So where would you like to go eat?"

I told him that it really didn't matter.

Then I asked him what he has a taste for.

He said, "I'll tell you what. Can we go to the park, eat hot dogs, and talk? Then after work, I'll cook you a nice, healthy meal."

"Okay."

"We can do that."

"That's fine with me." Then my cell phone rang. I said excuse me. I answered the phone; the voice on the other end said, "Hey, Ma."

"Hi, my baby."

"You said to call you and let you know just what was going on with Belinda's parents. Well, Ma, they are just as excited as we are, and they too want to know when we can all get together and make these plans. So, Ma, how about Saturday?"

"I don't know about Saturday because I already have plans for Saturday. Can I call you later tonight, and we'll talk?"

"All right, Ma. I love you."

"I love you too. So we'll talk tonight when you call."

"Okay. Later, Ma. I mean, I'll talk to you later."

Some of the excitement had left his voice, I could tell.

Jaylen was puzzled, but I assured him that I would call him later, and we'd talk. I hung up.

I looked at Eugene and said, "That was my baby boy."

"Oh, is everything all right?"

"Yeah, everything's fine, but that's a long story too."

"We sure have a lot of long stories to tell."

"Yes, we do, and someday we'll get them all out of our system."

Eugene looked pleased to hear that.

"But until then, tell me what was that little scene all about, not that I didn't enjoy the kiss."

He looked at me and smiled. As we were pulling up into a parking spot in the park, he said, "Well, I really don't know where to start."

"Well, just start."

"All right, Veronica used to work for me for about three years. She was my paralegal. Then I gave her a little promotion, and she took it the wrong way. She started making advances toward me, but I told her that it was flattering but 'no thanks, so back off.' She backed off for a while, then she quit working for me and went upstairs to work. So about a month or so later, I saw Veronica in a hardware store. We started talking, and she asked me if I was busy and, if not, could I do her a favor and follow her to her house. I said what for, and she said to put up a ceiling fan for her. So not really thinking, I agreed. When we got to her place, she asked if I would like a drink. And I said sure, so she made the drinks, and we sat and talked for a while. Then I asked her about the ceiling fan. She said oh yeah, then we went into her bedroom where she had a ladder in the place, where she wanted the fan to go, which was over her bed. She said that it was kind of awkward for her, that's why she didn't have it put up yet. She was hoping to get someone to do it for her. But anyway, I climbed up on the ladder and was looking up at the wires when the ladder moved. I was trying to balance myself by holding on to the wires and the ladder at the same time, but that was not gonna work, so I let go of the wires to keep from pulling them out of the ceiling. The ladder tilted, and I fell on her bed. She headed for the bed, asking if I was all right. I told her that I was. So she sat on the bed while I was trying to get up. She grabbed my face and said, 'Are you sure you are all right?' I said, 'Yeah, I'm fine, but I'm a little shocked because the ladder was sitting steady.' She said, 'I'm sorry, I bumped it by mistake. Oh, that's what it was. But I didn't think that you were going to fall, and it was a mistake.' Then she started kissing me. I told her to stop, but she just continued."

"So why didn't you just get up?"

"I don't know. Maybe I needed that."

"Needed what?"

"To feel needed at the time, but that was a bad move because now I can't get rid of her."

"So what you're saying is that you went ahead and slept with her? So is that what you do every time you think that you feel needed? You just go out and sleep with someone? Oh wait, is that what you want to do with me now? Sleep with me because you are feeling needed?"

"Wow, wait a minute, Rachael. Let me stop you because you are headed in the wrong direction. First, let me say no, that's not what I do when I feel like I need to be needed. Second, we are all entitled to make a mistake. And third, I am not feeling needed. That's not why I am trying to get next to you."

"Get next to me?"

"Yes, I would like to be the man in your life if you are not involved with anyone. And this is not how I had planned on asking you again, but I had no choice."

"So what now? She still wants you."

"Yes, she does, and I have told her no on several occasions, but she doesn't seem to get the message. So I had to be outright rude to her. But I didn't know what else to do."

"So let me ask you this. How many times have you slept with her?"

"Did I say that I slept with her?"

"Okay then, funny man, then how many times did you make love to her, to make her keep coming back like she does?"

"We had sex one night all night. The next morning, I got up and left. I'm being blunt because I don't want her to be able to say anything different to you."

"To me?"

"Yeah, she might ask you a question or two. Like she questioned me that night at the restaurant about you."

"Why did she ask you about me?"

"You know why."

"No, I don't."

"You know that you and I both couldn't keep our eyes off each other. Your date, or whoever he was, was probably saying the same thing about me. Who was he anyway?"

"Well, you're right, and he did ask who you were. But anyway, did you have safe sex?"

"Yes, we did. She had plenty of jackets. Know what I mean? Now what, Ms. Lawyer?"

"So you say that that was the first and last time? Or did you say that that was the last of a few times? Are you being totally honest with me, or are you still having sex with her?"

"Wait a minute, I can see why you are such a great lawyer."

"Why would you say that?"

"Because you don't give a person a chance to answer the first question before you are off and running with the next questions. That's not fair."

"What do you mean not fair? I'm just trying to find out what's going on with you before I get involved with you."

"Oh, so you are going to give us a chance? See, you didn't give me a chance to tell you my whole story as to why I was feeling the way I was feeling."

"Okay, go ahead, and I'll pull out the violin."

We both laughed.

"Okay, now let me explain. I was going through a divorce, and I told you that she worked for me, so she knew all the things that I was going through. She knew all the times that I had to go home."

"And just where is home?"

"I'm from Atlanta, and a lot of times when I got back home, I would be kinda distant, and she would always try to cheer me up. But I didn't want to be bothered."

"So that's what you meant when you said she was making sexual advances to you."

"Yeah. That's why she quit working for me. And she knew that I wasn't seeing anyone, so she kept tabs on me, so to speak. Hoping that I would change my mind. But the time that I ran into her at the hardware store, I think that that was an accident. But I'm not really sure now because she will pop up at some of the other places that I be at. But anyway, we talked, and she asked me if I would help her out at her house, and one thing led to another that one time."

"Sure? One time?"

"Honestly, it was only one time because at that point in my life, I didn't want to be bothered with anyone. My wife was messing me up mentally, and that was another reason that I was at the casino a lot. Just to get away from everything. But then I started seeing you there. But my feelings were still against all women. But you seemed different for some reason. But anyway, I told her that I didn't want a relationship, that it was to soon after my divorce. But she still kept coming around. Even now she still keeps coming around, making people think that we are a couple. Every chance she gets, she's in my face. She got in close with my secretary to find out my plans for the day or for the week for that matter. That's why you saw her at the restaurant standing next to me. We were not together, she just happen to find out what my plans were for the day. And I always have my secretary phone in ahead for me, but sometimes it doesn't matter, and you still have to wait. So you see, I didn't invite her to dinner. She just showed up at the same time."

"Oh, how convenient. So in other words, you're saying she's stalking you?"

"Well, we'll see after today."

"What do you mean after today?"

"Well, she saw me and you together, and she saw me kiss you, so maybe she has gotten the hint now that I have someone. And she sees me with you, so now maybe she will leave me alone."

"Oh, so you were just using me as a decoy, right?"

"No, woman, you are something else. You were just in the right place at the right time, that's all."

"Well, I'll be damned. Was that the only reason that you kissed me?"

"Once again, no. Woman, that was something that I wanted to do for a long time. And anyway, what goes around comes back around. Haven't you heard of that?"

"Yes, but what are you talking about?"

"I'm talking about the time that machine went off and you kissed me."

"Huh? But we were both caught off guard."

"I was there for you, and you were there for me. A kiss for a kiss. We both gave each other that fake smile." Then he leaned over and kissed me.

"Now what do you have to say, Ms. Lawyer?"

"Payback, that's all." I looked at my watch and said, "You know what?"

"No. What?"

"It's time for us to be back at work."

"You're kidding?"

"No, I'm not."

He looked at his watch and said, "You're right. We have been sitting in the car talking so much that we didn't get a chance to have lunch."

As he was starting up the car, he said, "Let me cook dinner for you."

"When?" I said.

"Tonight."

"Tonight?"

"Yes. Do you have something else to do? But even if you do, you still have to eat, right?"

"Right."

"So then come by my place after work. But if you have something to do, that's cool because I have a run to make. So just give me a call when you are ready to come over."

"Sure will."

"Or if you don't think about calling, then let's make it around six thirty. If that's good for you."

"Okay, if anything comes up before then, I'll give you a call."

By now, we were pulling back up into the parking garage. We parked and got out; he paid the parking attendant, and we walked on toward the building. As soon as we reached the door of the building and got a few steps inside, Eugene put his arms around my waist. I looked up at him, and his eyes kind of told me that something was going on. So I just played it off. I was looking up at him and smiling until we got to the elevator.

At the elevator, he bent his head down and kissed me a little more passionately than before.

When we got inside the elevator and turned to the front, I saw the reason Eugene did what he did. All the lovey-dovey stuff. Veronica was standing across the entryway, so he had seen her before she saw us, which was good because we looked like a real couple, not like a new couple trying to get started.

So once the doors closed, I beat him to the punch by saying, "I saw the reason you were being so kissey-kissey, so just what did you say to that girl Veronica? Did you tell her that you would contact her when you were ready for a relationship and now she's trying to see where you are coming from? Is she trying to see if you are ready or what? Or otherwise, just what did you do to that woman in bed for her to keep stalking you like this?"

Eugene looked at me, getting ready to open his mouth and answer me, when the elevator door opened up. He just said, "We'll talk about this later."

We were still standing just outside the elevator when another door opened up and Veronica stepped out. She saw us standing there and said, "Hmm, Eugene, can I speak to you for a minute?"

He looked at me, then said, "Do you mind if I see what it is she wants?" He then said, "Can you wait here for just one more minute while I see what she wants?"

I looked at my watch and said, "Okay, I have a few more minutes."

He kissed me on the cheek and walked a few feet away.

I could hear her asking him just what was going on with him and me.

"First, let me say that this is not the type of place for this kind of conversation, and second of all, I don't owe you any explanation about who I'm with. And to sum it all up, it's none of your dammmn business. I told you that night at the restaurant that she and I had had a little quarrel, and that was the reason that she and I kept looking at each other. But I also told you that I love that woman and hoped that she would consider marrying me soon. Now would you please leave me alone? Don't you remember me telling you that I had asked someone awhile back to marry me?"

"Yes, but you also told me that you were not ready for a relationship. Or ready to get involved with anybody because it was too soon after your divorce."

"Veronica, how long has that been? Six months ago."

"But…"

"But nothing. Didn't I tell you that night in the restaurant that I had met someone special and that we had a falling-out? I even showed her to you."

By chance, she was standing with a client, I thought.

"Yes, but…"

"I have to go, Veronica." He walked away, came over to me, and said, "Baby, I'll see you later for dinner." He kissed me; then we went our separate ways.

As he was walking past her, I heard her call out his name.

I heard him say, "Veronica, you can't keep following me, calling me, or showing up at places that you know that I'm going to be at. But I have put a stop to you finding anything else from my secretary. She won't be giving you any more information."

She looked at him as if to say, "How did you know that that's where I was getting all my information?"

So he said, "If you would excuse me, I have got a case waiting for me."

I saw him walk away, shaking his head.

I walked on into the courtroom but hurried right back out and called out Eugene's name.

He turned, and I said, "Hey, I love you."

"And I love you back."

We smiled at each other, then went back into our courtrooms.

I could see Veronica still standing there, looking like a wounded puppy in a daze just standing there.

When I entered the courtroom, the jury was just coming back in—at least the ones who were chosen before recess.

After everyone was seated, the bailiff said, "All rise. Court is now back in session."

The judge came back into the courtroom.

I was in the courtroom, but my mind was still in the hallway, looking at Veronica make a fool of herself.

Dammmn, I thought, just what did he do to her in bed to make her act the way that she was acting? I was shocked at the way Eugene talked to her and the things that he said to her.

If I had not been there to see and hear it for myself, I would not have believed it was true.

But I guess he had to say what he said to her to prove to me that he was telling me the truth.

Boy, I couldn't wait to tell my sisters about this man. This was a good one, but I wasn't going to say anything until we finished talking.

Then I heard the gavel hitting the desk, and it snapped me back into the courtroom.

The judge said there will be a ten-minute recess while I talk with the other lawyers in the courtroom.

The prosecutor and I walked into the judge's chambers. He said, "Have a seat." He then began to explain that his secretary had made a mistake in changing the dockets this morning and asked if we wanted to be reassigned to another courtroom, and he would grant it with no problem.

But if we stayed with him until this case was over, we would definitely be next whenever the case was over.

The prosecutor and I looked at each other; then he asked me what I wanted to do. I told him that as long as my client remained out of jail and on bond, I could wait because I had another case that I could be working on. So he agreed also.

The judge said, "I'm sorry about the mix-up. But you would be contacted as soon as this case is over."

I asked the judge if he knew how long this trial was going to last.

He said, "Unless they settle, it could take up to at least two weeks. That's why I wanted to let you know because there's no reason for you to hang around the courtroom today. So we'll let you know as soon as this trial is over, and again, I am truly sorry."

"Thank you, Your Honor," we both said at the same time; then we all got up to leave.

The judge tapped on the door, and I heard the bailiff say, "All rise. Court is now in session." We both gathered our things and prepared to leave the courtroom.

I motioned to my client to meet me in the hallway so that I could let her know what was going on.

When I entered into the hallway, there was Eugene standing, talking to Veronica.

I acted as though they were not there and continued on to talk to my client.

She said, "You know, Ms. Brunson, I have been a nervous wreck. And I know that you said that everything was going to be all right, but I still am a little nervous. But as bad as I want this case to be over, I'm glad that it has been postponed for a while."

"All right, Rochell, just remember if anything happens to the baby and she has to go to the hospital, make sure that you give me a call so that I can meet you there. Okay?"

"I sure will, Ms. Brunson." Then she picked up the baby and walked away.

Eugene and Veronica were still standing there, talking, so I walked up to them and put my arm around Eugene's waist and said, "What's up?"

"Veronica told the security in the courtroom that there was an urgent matter in the hall that needed my attention and asked if he would give me the message right away, so when I came out into the hallway, I thought that something had happened to you. But instead, she was out here crying. I asked her if she was all right. Then she said how could I do this to her, that she loved me, and that I lied to her. I'm trying to tell her right now that this is not the place for this kind of behavior. She said that she doesn't believe that I asked you to marry me. I don't know what else to do."

So I said, "Veronica, I'm sorry that you don't believe him, but he's telling you the truth about us. We have not set a date yet, but we will soon. Would you like to see my engagement ring?" I held my hand out real fast so that she could see the ring. It could pass for an engagement ring.

I looked up at Eugene and stretched my eyes at him and mouthed, "Now you got me lying for you."

He looked at me and mouthed, "I'm sorry."

While Veronica was looking at my ring, she looked up at Eugene and said, "I'm sorry for bothering you, Eugene, and you too, miss. I won't bother you again." Then she turned and walked away.

I felt so sorry for her.

But before I could say a word, he hugged me and said, "Thanks, you saved the day for me again. Once again, you came to my rescue."

"Yeah, well, we'll find a way for you to repay the favor."

"All right, but let me ask you. Was that a real engagement ring? Because I have not found out anything about you. But you know a lot about me."

"Well, if it were a real engagement ring, do you think that I would be accepting your offer to come over and let you cook for me?"

"Oh, so you will be able to make it this evening?"

"It looks like it anyway."

"So what are you doing out here anyway?"

"There was a mix-up in the dockets, and the judge postponed our date with him until later when the trial that he's working on is over."

"Why didn't you get reassigned?"

"Well, the judge did offer, but the prosecutor and I both like this judge. And I needed to get started on another case because this one will be over real soon after it gets started."

"Oh, I see. Well, sweetheart, thanks again for your help, and I gotta get back into the courtroom. So I'll see you later."

He turned to go back into the courtroom but came back and kissed me lightly on the lips and said, "Just in case she's looking."

"Yeah right." We both laughed.

Then he said, "After all, we are engaged, don't forget."

"Get out of here."

"Hey, I'll call you when I get home," he said.

Then he asked me what was I about to do.

"Nothing really. Check on a few things and then head home."

"Okay, so I'll see you later." He waved, then walked back into the courtroom.

I walked over to the elevators and pushed the Down button on the elevator and waited for the doors to open.

When it finally did come and I made my way inside, I thought boy he sure does owe me big time.

As I was walking toward the doors to go out, I heard someone say, "Hey, miss! Miss!" I kept walking, then the voice got closer. I turned to see if the person that was calling out miss's was actually calling me.

And sure enough, it was for me. It was Veronica.

She said, "Could I talk to you for a minute?"

"Well, Veronica, I'm in somewhat of a hurry."

"Just a minute of your time."

"Sure, what is it?"

She said, "Can we sit and talk for a minute? I'm sorry, but I don't remember Eugene saying your name. That's why I was calling you miss."

"Well, what did you want to talk about?"

"Can we talk woman to woman for a minute?"

"Veronica, I really don't have time for this."

"Oh, it won't take long. I just have a few questions to ask you."

"Please be quick about it, or I'm going to leave."

"Okay. Did Eugene really ask you to marry him? And if he did, are you sure that he really meant it?"

I just looked at her for a moment.

Then she said, "Because he told me that he didn't want to get involved with anybody in a serious relationship, that's why I asked. Because he said that it was too soon after his divorce, and if he did get involved with anyone, it would be for sex and sex only."

"Well, Veronica, how long has that been? And he does have the right to change his mind as time goes on, doesn't he?"

"Yes, but you don't understand. He said that he was never getting married again because his wife really hurt his heart."

"Well, Veronica, I can only tell you again that people and situations do change all the time. We can be angry one minute about one thing, but the next minute, we say or do something else."

"So you're saying that he might change his mind about marrying you?"

"That's right, but I hope that he doesn't. But if he does or if I change my mind about him, we have that right. You see, I was divorced also, and I said that I would never get married again. But he proposed, and I accepted. So again, you see we all change our minds all the time."

"I know. That's why I wanted to know if he was sure that he was getting married or just saying something so that I would stop bothering him."

"Well, I don't know what else to tell you."

"Can you tell me if the two of you have set a wedding day yet?"

"We have not set a date yet, but I'm sure that when we do, you'll hear about it."

"Well, when you guys do set the date, can I come to the wedding? I mean, would you mind if I came?"

"Well, Veronica, I wouldn't mind, but I would have to talk to Eugene first."

"All right. That sounds fair enough. I bet he thinks that I'm a nutcase.

But I'm really not. I just enjoyed his company so much, and when he said that he couldn't date me because we worked together, I just thought that that was a clue for me. So that's why I quit working for him, thinking that we might get together. But I was wrong. I fell in love with the wrong man, that's all."

"Well, did Eugene give you the impression that he wanted to be with you?"

"No, he didn't. He kept saying no, but I wasn't listening. He never treated me mean when I would show up at some of the places that he was going to be at. Maybe that's why I'm so crazy about him. Because he's never mean to me. He treats me with nothing but kindness."

"Well, maybe so, but are you going to be all right?"

"Yeah, I'll be fine."

Then I stood up to leave, and she said, "Can I ask you one more question?"

"What's that?"

"Well, it's kind of personal—real personal, to be frank. But first, can I ask you your name? I won't bother you, I promise. But the next question is personal. But I am going to ask it anyway."

"All right, what is it?"

"Well, have you slept with Eugene yet?"

"Well, now you were right, and I won't answer that one. But the first question I will answer. My name is Rachael."

"Well, Rachael, it was nice to meet you. And I thank you for talking to me. One more thing, Rachael."

"What's that?"

"I guess that Eugene really does care about you."

"Why'd you say that?"

"Because when I asked him your name, he told me that your name shouldn't be mixed up with his and my conversation. He said that this was between him and I. He doesn't know this, but I saw you and him at the casino before. I saw you kiss him in public. I got mad and left. So he never knew that I knew that he was already seeing someone. But I didn't know that it was you until I saw you again at the restaurant."

"You mean that night that you were with him?"

"No, not then. I saw the two of you at Red Lobster."

"What? So you are stalking him?"

"Hey, now I wouldn't say that."

"Well, what would you say then?"

"I don't really know. But I know that when he told me that he was seeing someone, I already knew. I just needed more proof."

"For what? He still doesn't want you. I hate to be so blunt, but dammmn, you need to get on with your life. I'm sure that there is someone out there for you if you will only let go of Eugene."

"I am, but the last thing that I have to say is… Well, you might not like this, but…"

Oh, here it comes. The condom broke, and now she's going to have his baby. But it wasn't that at all.

She said, "If you have not slept with him yet, then you are in for a treat. And if you have slept with him, then you know why I'm still trying to see if he's still available."

"Well, like I said, that part of our life is personal. Now let me ask you a question."

"Go ahead. And ask away. I'll answer anything you want. But I'll bet that you want to know how many times Eugene and I slept together. Well, it was only once, when I ran into him at the hardware store, and I really did need the help. We had drinks and sex. Then afterward, he said that he was sorry for taking advantage of me and that it would not happen again. But it was actually me taking advantage of him because I wanted him so bad, but I do hope that you will forgive me for that. Now, is there any more questions that you would like to ask?"

"Actually, I didn't get to ask you a question. You just assumed that I wanted to know about you and Eugene sleeping together. But he had already told me about the time he slept with you. I wanted to ask you how old you were. Because you seem to be… Well, you look kind of young."

"Well, I am thirty-two. I'll be thirty-three in a couple of months."

Oh, she does have a screw loose because she is too old to be acting this way.

"Well, Veronica, can I give you a word of advice?"

"Sure."

"When someone tells you and shows that they are not interested, then maybe you should back off. Then maybe they will eventually have a change of heart about you."

"I will next time."

"Well, Veronica, I'm glad that we had this little talk, and I'll let you know about the wedding if someone doesn't beat me to it. But remember, that's not an invitation, and remember that I told you that I have to talk to Eugene first about you coming to the wedding."

"Okay, okay, Rachael. Thanks for talking to me."

"Well, you are welcome, and I really do have to go now. So I'll see you around." Then I got up and left.

Man, that girl has got Eugene on the brain, and she's going to be a problem. I can tell. I can't wait to see Eugene for dinner so that I can tell him all the stuff that she told me.

Well, he did tell me the truth about him and her sleeping together and that it was only the one time that they did do it. But that's all a part of his past. I'm a part of his present.

Now old things have passed away.

Damn, I couldn't get to my car fast enough. This chick was a loose firecracker ready to go off at anytime. I had to stay calm or at least act calm anyway. She had me nervous as hell with all that rocking back and forth. Shit, I wanted to tell her to keep her ass still, but I didn't want to upset her anymore than she already was.

I was so nervous that if I had to pee, I would have done it on myself. Boy, I think she is really going to be a problem. I've got to warn Eugene to be extra careful because she has got more than just a crush on him. Something is boiling inside that girl, and if we slip and don't keep an eye on her, she just might hurt somebody or herself.

I was halfway home when my phone rang. I put my headset on and said, "Hello."

"Hi, sweetheart. What are you doing? Relaxing? Did you have time to talk to your son yet? Is everything straight?"

"Eugene."

"Baby, Rachael, what's wrong?"

"I'm not even at home and haven't been there yet."

"Why? Did you have extra errands or what? What's wrong? You

sound as if something has happened, and you are trying not to tell me."

"Eugene, I just left the building."

"What? Did you decide to take on another case before you left?"

"No, honey, but there needs to be some paperwork on that Veronica."

"Why? Did she do something to you? Did she say something out of the way to you? What, baby? Baby, what's going on? Did she do something to your car? Rachael, what's going on?"

I was pulling up into my parking spot. I parked the car and then told Eugene to hold on for a minute while I change headsets, so I did that real quick. "Okay, I'm back."

"So what happened?"

"When I left you and got downstairs, Veronica came up behind me and asked me if she could talk to me for a minute, and I agreed."

"No, you didn't."

"Yes, I did, and I am glad that I did. Because I learned a lot. That girl has more than a crush on you."

"What?"

"That girl has nothing but Eugene on the brain."

"Are you kidding?"

"No."

"Are you all right? Do you need me to come over to your place and get you, or are you all right to drive?"

"I'm fine."

"Do you still feel up to coming over for dinner? Because I can cook at your place. It doesn't matter so long as you are all right."

"I'm fine, and I'll be over to your place. Well, I was gonna take a shower here, but I think I'll just grab a few things and take a shower at your house. You don't mind, do you?"

"No, I don't, and I'll see you in a few minutes."

"Yeah, I'll be on my way in a minute."

"Okay, I'll meet you there. I was gonna stop at the store and get another bottle of that wine that you like. But I'll just go straight home."

"Okay, then I'll see you in a few."

By now, as I was hanging up, I heard Eugene calling out my name.

"Hey, honey, I just wanted to remind you to bring over your work clothes so that you won't have to worry about going home tonight. Just in case."

"Just in case what?"

"Hey, woman, get your mind out of the gutter. I've got plenty of extra bedrooms, and if you like, I'll sleep in one of them, and you can sleep in my bed. I just thought that you might not want to drive back home tonight. That's all, nothing more."

"Well, I'll think about it."

"All right. Later, baby."

We hung up the phone, and I smiled to myself because I already had planned on spending the night, but not sleeping with him. While walking around my apartment, I thought about the day that I had just had. I was thinking about Veronica. I thought, *Damn, a girl like that really makes you think and take a look at your life. And I have had one heck of a life.*

Just when I thought that things were going to be all right, here comes this bitch. But she only caught me off guard for a minute. I won't let this be another Sharon. I've got my eyes open this time, and I'm ready.

I'll act just as nutty as she is. I'm going to be ready for whatever bag that this bitch can come out of because I can see straight through her little obsession.

I knew that something had to go wrong being with a man like Eugene. He has got a stalker on his hands and doesn't even realize it. But I do, and girlfriend is going to have to step the fuck off. I sat down on the bed and kinda just laughed to myself and thought, *There is always something going on with a man. Why? Why? Why?*

I lay back across the bed, and sleep came before I knew it.

But before I could get to sleep real good, the phone woke me up.

"Hey, baby, are you all right?"

"Oh yeah. I was lying across the bed, thinking about the day, and I guess I was about to fall asleep."

"Well, I was not going to let you go for a long time this time without hearing from you. After the kind of day that you had."

"Okay, I'll be on my way."

We hung up the phone, and just as soon as I hung up the phone, it rang again. "Yes, sweetheart, I'm on my way."

"Hey, Ma, did I wake you because you sound like you were sleeping?"

"Well, I was, but Eugene called right before you did. And I'm supposed to be on my way over to his house because he's cooking dinner for me. But what's up, Jay? Is everything okay?"

"Well, you did say to call you so that we could make plans for the wedding."

"Well, I'll tell you what. Let me get myself up from here, and as soon as I get myself together at Eugene's house, I'll give you a call, and we'll see just where we go from there. Okay? But I know that we had plans for this weekend. But who knows we'll get it together before it's too late."

"Okay then, Ma. Call me when you get there."

"I will, baby. Bye now."

And then we hung up. As soon as I hung up the phone, it rang again.

"Hey, sleepyhead, what are you doing answering the phone at the house? You're supposed to be on your way."

"Well, I was when I hung up talking to you the first time. But the phone rang, and I thought it was you. But it was Jaylen."

"Is he all right?"

"Yeah, I told him that I would call him when I got settled at your house. So you see, I'm on my way for real this time. Hey, you know what? I think that I'm just gonna stay here after all."

"Yeah, that's okay. I'll be on my way over there just as soon as we hang up the phone."

"I'm only kidding. I'm on my way."

"Hey, don't forget that you are leaving from here to go to work tomorrow."

"Oh I am?"

"Yes, you are. I just thought that I would remind you, that's all."

"I'll see you in a minute." Then we hung up the phone. I hurried up and grabbed my things before the phone had a chance to ring again.

The day's events came creeping back. But I just continued to get my things and left. As I was driving, I could see a car following behind me, but I wasn't really paying that much attention until the car got right up on me and made me notice it.

I couldn't really see who it was because the car had its bright lights on.

But as I got about two blocks away from Eugene's house, the car that I thought was following me turned, and I felt a little bit better. I'll bet that that was old girl following me.

I'm not going to let that girl control my life and keep her on my mind all the time. As I was pulling up into Eugene's driveway, I called him.

Eugene answered the phone, and I said, "Hey there."

He said, "Where are you? You should be here by now."

"Well, if you will open the door, then you will see where I am."

Then the door opened. "Oh, funny. how are you?"

"I'm fine."

As he was getting my bags out of the car, I said, "You know, for a minute, I thought that I was being followed."

"Oh yeah? Well, what changed your mind?"

"The car that I thought was following me turned off two blocks away."

"Well, what person did you help put behind bars because now they're coming after you?" We both laughed.

Then I said, "Now who's being funny? But for real, I couldn't see who it was nor could I tell what kind of car they were driving because when I did notice the car, it was right up behind me with its bright lights shining right in my face."

"Well, you're safe now. So relax. What would you like to drink? A sloe gin or a Long Island?"

"Oh, they both sound good. But I'll tell you what. You make the choice after you show me where to shower and put my things away."

"Fine, follow me."

Eugene pointed the way, then said, "Shower wherever you feel the most comfortable."

"Oh, you are funny."

"I just want you to feel at home."

"All right then."

"Are you all right with that?"

"Yes, I am." Then I headed for one of his spare rooms. I decided on the one that was closest to the bathroom. I did notice his bedroom and the shower that was in it, but I passed it up. I was just about to call out and ask where the towels were, but then I opened up a closet door in the bathroom and saw everything that I might need.

I heard him holler, "Do you need any help?"

"No, thanks," I said, then stepped out to see if I could see what Eugene was doing.

He was standing at the front door. He had it open.

"Hey, what are you doing?"

"I'm just getting the mail."

"Mail my foot. You think that she might be out there, don't you?"

"I don't know, but I just wanted to make sure that everything was okay. I'm just about to mix those drinks, and I decided to make the gin fizz."

"That sounds good. I haven't had one of those in a long time."

"Now you know what is said about drinking gin, don't you?"

"Yeah, I know, and I also know just what it says and that it's just a miff, a saying that you can't prove to me."

"Well, all right then, Ms. Brunson."

I turned and headed for the shower. "I was gonna ask you where the towels were, but I found them."

"Whatever you need, just open up the cabinets and drawers until you find what you are looking for. You should find whatever you are looking for. I have nothing to hide."

"Okay, now you know by saying that, it gives me the right to pull out drawers, turn mattresses upside down."

"Feel free to do whatever you like," he said, then laughed.

I went into the bathroom, turned on the shower, took off my clothes, stepped into the water, and let the water hit my face. The water was not quite warm yet, but it still felt good.

I was thinking about his linen closet and thought about mine. He had plenty of stuff in his, much more than I did in mine. I was gonna have to make a list of things to pick up before I invite him over to my place.

The water was beginning to warm up and was feeling great.

I was just enjoying the water when I heard a knock on the door.

"Would you like your drink now?"

"Sure, you can sit it on the little vanity table and keep your eyes closed."

"Yes, m—"

"You better not say ma'am."

"I was gonna say 'yes, my love.'"

"Yeah right."

"Do you need me to wash your back? I can do that with my eyes closed, you know."

"Wait a minute, let me think. Hmm, no, thank you."

He started laughing and said, "After all, we are engaged."

"Get away from here, or the engagement is off."

"Oh, all right. I'm leaving. I'm leaving. I'll go finish fixing dinner."

"Give me about fifteen more minutes, and I'll be out."

When I heard him shut the door, I opened the shower doors and stepped out to taste the drink that he had made for me. "Hmm, this is good." I sipped some more, then jumped back into the water.

Hey, that was good. He is a man of many talents, I see. There is no way that I'm going to give this man up to that sick bitch.

I was beginning to feel at ease, then thought I should have been taking a bath. But then, he would have a problem getting me out of the water. He would think that I drowned between the water and the drink. I was feeling no pain. I had jumped in and out of the shower so much that I finished off my drink.

I was really just enjoying myself; then I said, "Let me get out of here before he comes back." But he was already knocking at the door just like I thought.

"Hey, are you all right?"

"Yeah, I'll be out in a minute." Now just what would he think if I was having one of my I-need-to-think baths. But I've got yet to find out. Oh well, let me get out.

I got out and wiped off some of the water, but not all of it because I liked to mix the water left on my body with the lotion that I was going to put on my body. And this time, it was going to be raspberry. I loved the smell of raspberry. But I could only use it sparingly because of my sensitive skin. After putting on my lotion, I put on one of my teddies and thought, *You are such a tease.*

But I also put on a long bathrobe so that he wouldn't know just what I had on. Finally finished, I walked out of the bathroom and into the room that I was going to sleep in.

I put my personal things back into my bag and went into the living room. But Eugene was not in there; he had made a fire in the den even though it was warm outside, but it made for a cozier setting. He had Anita Baker's rhythm and blues playing softly in the background. I called out his name.

He said, "I'm out here."

He had the grill all ready to go. With Anita Baker's sounds coming softly out of the speakers on his patio. He said that he was waiting for me to get out of the shower before he put the steaks on because the steaks didn't take long to cook. He said, "How would you like a steak? Or would you like to taste my famous spaghetti sauce?"

"Famous? I haven't seen you on the television set pushing your sauce."

"That's because I'm still perfecting it. You know, good things come to those who wait, so I'm taking my time so that when I'm ready to bring it out to the world, they'll appreciate it."

"Okay, then I want to taste your famous spaghetti sauce so that when you make the commercials, I can say that I tasted it before anyone else did."

"But would you like a steak as well?"

"Yes, I would like a steak also. I'll watch the meat while you make your famous sauce. Oh, you haven't put them on the grill yet, have you?"

"No, I haven't."

"Okay, then give me a minute while I go call my son before you put them on. I told my son that I was gonna give him a call when I got settled in over here. And I want to help you."

"That's fine. Is everything all right?"

"Yeah, it's just that the girl that he has been dating for two years is going to have a baby, and he wants… Well, I want for her parents and I to get together. And help them make plans for their wedding. I had told him to set a date so that all of us could sit down and discuss just what we were going to do to help out. But he made plans for this Saturday. But I told him that you and I had already made plans for this weekend."

"You know I told you that whatever you wanted to do was going to be fine with me. So that's your call. I mean, is that going to take all day? Because if not, then you and I could hang out later that evening."

"Okay."

"Because what I wanted to do, we can do that later in the evening anyway."

"So it's okay with you that I won't be with you in the earlier part of the day."

"It's going to break my heart, but I'll have you for the rest of the night and from then on. I mean, we are engaged. Right?"

"That was only for Veronica's ears."

"I know that we were supposed to talk about her, but that can wait for another day. I really don't want her name mentioned right now because we are having a good time."

"Okay, but we do have to talk about her. But right now, I'm about to call my son and see just where it is they want to meet and talk about this wedding."

"Hey, if you want, you can tell him that if they have not set up a meeting place, then they can meet right here if you don't mind."

I looked at Eugene and smiled. I was about to pick up the phone and call Jaylen.

But I put the phone down and walked over to Eugene, put my arms around his waist, and kissed him.

He picked me up and sat me down on the kitchen counter.

I put my arms around his neck and kissed him again. First lightly then with a little passion. And then with a little more passion. And a little tongue.

He started rubbing his hands up and down my back then around to the front of my robe.

He started taking my belt a loose, and his hands slipped inside of my robe. He started rubbing my breast.

He stopped and said, "Woman, we better stop because we won't get anything done. And we'll wind up ordering take-out food."

"You're right. My mistake."

"What do you have on under that big robe anyway?"

"None of your business," I said as he helped me off the counter. While he was holding me in the air, he kissed me again.

I said, "You are such a tease." And we laughed.

I went on and picked up the phone. And Eugene was saying that he would pick up some steak ribs, make shish kebabs, the works; and that we could kill two birds at once.

"I'll get to meet my other set of children, or do you only have one?"

"No, I have a set of twins and two grandbabies. And a daughter-in-law in the making. What about you?"

"Oh, I have five."

"Oh, you do?"

"Yeah, but for now, you'll only get to meet four of them. The baby is in Atlanta with her mother. So you'll get to meet her even later than the others. So if he agrees, then I'll get to meet your side. Then some other weekend, you can meet my children."

"Okay, okay, but I still have a small problem."

"What's that?"

"You call my children your other set when you and I are only coworkers."

"See, now that's not true because earlier you and I were supposed to be engaged." We laughed. Then he said, "Oh, I see you want me to ask you to officially be my woman?"

"Yes."

"Well, I'm asking. Will you share the rest of your life with me?"

"Well, since you said it like that, I can't refuse. Yes, I will share your life with you. And I want the same thing, I want you in my life forever."

Then we kissed. I had to grab his hands because they had begun to roam. "That's what I wanted to talk to you about after I talked to Jaylen. But now, that part is out of the way." We laughed.

I picked up the phone and called Jaylen, and Belinda answered.

"Hi, Belinda. This is Rachael."

"Oh hi, Ms. Brunson."

"Belinda, you can call me Ray or Rachael. You don't have to call me Ms. Brunson. Is Jaylen in?"

"Yes, he is, but he's taking a shower."

"I called because we were going to set a time and place so that we could get together. Have you all set a meeting place yet? Because I'm sure that his sister and brother will want to be there also. Belinda, do you have any sisters and brothers?"

"Yes, I do. I have two sisters and two brothers. None are twins though."

"And I'm pretty sure that they would like to be a part of this planning also."

"Yes, ma'am, they would."

"Belinda, would you do me a favor?"

"Sure, what is it?"

"Would you not call me ma'am?"

"Okay, my mother doesn't like to be called ma'am either."

"Well, Belinda, my friend has offered his house for all of us to meet. If that's all right with you and Jaylen?"

"Here comes Jay now."

I could hear her telling Jaylen what I had said. He was saying really. Then he got on the phone. "Hi, Ma."

"Hey, baby."

"Belinda told me what you had said. And if it's really all right with him, then it's okay with us. We'll just let everyone know. And it will give us a chance to meet him."

"It sure will." Then I looked over at Eugene who was busy making his famous spaghetti sauce.

"Okay, sweetheart, give me a call and let me know just how many people will be coming so that we can pick up enough food for everyone."

"Mama, you all don't have to do that. We can pick up something."

"Look, Jay, I know that we don't have to do that, but I want to. Hold on a minute while I get you some directions and the address so you'll know how to get here. Then you can pass it on."

"Hey, Eugene! Hey, Eugene, can you give Jaylen directions on how to get over here?"

Eugene came and got the phone.

"Hi, Jay." I heard him say. Then I heard him give Jaylen the address and all the how-tos.

I ran into the kitchen and poured myself another drink. I looked at Eugene's glass and poured him some, then took his glass and gave it to him. He put his arms around my waist as he continued to talk to Jaylen. I heard him say, "Okay, I'll see you on Saturday," and hung up the phone.

He looked down at me and said, "Jaylen sounds like a very intelligent young man."

"He is. Now that we got that out of the way, what's up with your sauce?"

"I can tell you that my sauce will be ready before the steaks are. Let me put them on the grill, and you can keep flipping them until I come out there, okay?"

"You know what, I am really not that hungry since I drank all that gin. So what do you say we skip the steaks and just eat your famous spaghetti, and I'll make a salad if you want?"

"You really don't have to do that."

"No, I'll do the salad, and let me hurry up with that."

"Don't worry, I'll help you cut up whatever you are going to put in the salad."

"No thanks, I can handle it. When you finish, just go have a seat, and I'll do the rest."

When he did finish, Eugene walked outside and said, "It really does feel nice out here. Do you want to eat out here?"

"I don't mind."

He walked back in and checked on his spaghetti. "Almost ready."

"Hey, I thought you were finished?" He sat down at the bar in the kitchen where I was making my salad and said, "So how many people do you think will be here? And do you think that all your children will be here? Do you think that they will be all right with me?"

"I can only say that I hope so. But I'm pretty sure that they will like you as much as I do. And all my children will be here with their other half except Shawnda. She's alone now thank God. So you have five kids?"

"Sure do."

"Are they all by five different women or just one woman?"

"Oh, now that's cold."

"What?"

"You said five different ladies. I'm not a playboy if that's what you think of me."

"Well, you know." Then his phone rang. He said excuse me and went to answer the phone. He picked it up and said, "Hello? Hello?" Then he hung it up, came back, and said it was for me.

"Yeah right. Nobody even knows where I'm at except for Jay, and I didn't give him your number."

"But I did, but I was only kidding. I don't know who that was on the phone, but I did give Jay my number because you'll be here a lot."

"You are really sure of yourself, aren't you?"

"I sure am, and I hope that I'm right."

"Well, you are." We laughed; then I said, "Does Veronica have your house number?"

"Yes, she does."

"Then it was probably her. That girl has it bad for you, and that's no joke."

He started pouring his spaghetti into a strainer and said, "You really think so?"

"No, I don't think so. I know so."

"I just don't see it."

"Well, you had better start opening up your eyes."

"I will. But enough of her. Now back to what we were talking about before. So you think that I am a playboy with five children from five different women?”

“Honestly, I do.”

“Well, sweetheart, I’m going to have to disappoint you. My five children are by two different women. My first wife, and I had four. Then she passed away two years after our last baby was born. It took me awhile to get myself together, but with the help of the children and family, we made it. Then years later, I met my second wife. She has the fifth kid. That’s why I said for now, you’ll only get to meet my oldest four. My baby girl lives with her mother in Atlanta. She’s the reason that I have to keep running back and forth to Atlanta. My wife is insecure of herself. That’s why she always accused me of cheating if I worked late, then I was out fucking no matter what. Excuse my French. If she called the office and it was late, even if I answered the phone, then she’d say, ‘So who are you fucking at the office now?’ You wouldn’t believe how she changed after we were married. She became another person.”

Now we were eating out by the pool still with Anita playing in the background.

“Really, you just wouldn’t believe how she started acting even if I was at home and got a call from one of our friends. Hear me when I say ‘our friends’ mind you. She would say, ‘Who are you sweet-talking on the phone now?’ But after five years, I couldn’t take it anymore, so I told her that I was going away and work on this case and would be gone for six months. I was really just trying to give her a chance to see that nothing was going on with me and that I loved her. I told her, while I was away, to think about us. Whether or not we were going to continue to be husband and wife. It was going to be her choice. But if we stayed together, she would have to change her jealous ways. I wasn’t really going to be gone for six months. I just wanted her reaction.”

“So how did she react?”

“She didn’t. It was as if she didn’t believe that I meant what I had said. She just looked at me as if I were crazy. Anyway, two months after I was gone, she filed for divorce. I was sure glad that she did. But the problem now is she won’t let me see my baby until the courts set the visitations or if she feels like letting me see her.”

"How old is the baby?"

"She's four. But you know what, enough about me. I have been talking and talking all about myself. Now you tell me about you. Because all I know about you is that you have three kids and you gamble a lot." We laughed.

I took a sip of water and said, "Well, where do I start?"

He said, "How about starting with the guy you were with the night I saw you at the restaurant?"

"All right then. That was my husband."

"Husband? Wait. You didn't say ex-husband, or did I speak too fast?"

"Well, he's not my ex yet, but I am filing for divorce."

"Why? The two of you seemed to get along pretty good. But don't get me wrong. I'm glad that you are here. I just don't want any surprises. I just don't want my heart broken, so is it really over? Or are you… ?" Then he stopped talking.

"Am I what? Don't stop now. We're grown. I can handle your next question."

"You can?"

"Yes, I can."

"All right then. Are the two of you still intimate? And I want the truth."

"Okay, the truth. Not anymore."

"What does that mean? Anymore. Does that mean since yesterday, today, or what? Because anymore could mean all of the above."

"You're right. It could mean anything. But not in this case. Because not anymore means not since the time that we saw each other with someone else that weekend at the restaurant."

"Okay, now that was about two months ago."

"Three to be exact."

"Ummm humm, so nothing since then. I mean, because after all, he was—I mean, is—your husband."

"I know that, but we weren't together anyway. But we would get together once in a while, but I had put a stop to that. It's just that at the time, he was moving out of town, and he asked me if we could spend his last week here together for the last time. He was trying to see if I would give him another chance and let him back into my life. But I told him no way. A little sex here and there, and that was it."

"But if he comes back?"

"He might come back, but that has nothing to do with me. I'm filing for divorce. I should have done that a long time ago, but I just didn't. I really didn't see any hurry for it. We weren't living together. But I'm engaged now anyway, or have you forgotten that you asked me to spend the rest of your life with you? Wait, don't tell me that you have changed your mind about me?"

"No, I have not forgotten nor have I changed my mind. Rachael, it's just that when I love someone, I love only that one person, and I don't care what else may be out there. I'm not that kind of guy. I made a mistake with Veronica and haven't been with anyone since then."

"Well, what about your wife?"

"Ex-wife. Well, for a while, I was still sleeping with her when I was running back and forth home. But that was the only way that she was gonna let me see my baby."

"So what's going to happen now when you go back again?"

"I've been back, and nothing happened. The sex stopped from the time she filed for divorce, and we haven't slept together since. My feelings have changed for her after all the bullshit she put me through. Excuse my choice of words, but I get angry every time I think of her. But enough of her and him. Can I get serious with you for a minute?"

"Sure can, but let's take the dishes in the house while we talk."

We finished putting the dishes in the dishwasher. He poured us another drink.

I said, "Hey, you just might get your spot on television with that sauce," even though neither one of us had eaten much. We were too busy talking.

I had begun to feel like I had known him for a long time, and he felt the same.

"That's why I want to talk to you on a serious note."

We were sipping our drinks as we headed for the den where he had a fire going, and the smooth sounds of Anita Baker was still playing. The fire was feeling good because it had begun to get pretty cool outside. I guess because of the breeze coming off the water and the coolness of the night.

We sat down on the love seat where Eugene laid his head back and said as he was sitting up, "Rachael, I hope that I don't scare you with what I'm about to say."

He took my hand in his, and my heart started beating fast now because I didn't know what he was about to say.

Then he said, "Rachael, I've loved you from the first moment that I saw you. Okay, maybe the second"—he chuckled—"but for real."

He then got down on one knee and said, "I know that this may sound strange, or maybe even a little corny, but it's the truth. And I'm glad that I had the chance to say this in front of Veronica and with her being a witness because you might not have believed me. I know that it's really soon to be saying this, but I love you. I really do, and I told my mother because I would talk to her a lot about my relationships with my wives, and she always gave me good advice even when I was dating a lot when I was younger. She told me that I shouldn't date more than one girl at a time because somebody was going to get hurt, and eventually I found out that she was right. That's why, thanks to my mother, I'm a one-woman man. But anyway, with all the problems that my last wife and I had, I talked to my mother and told her that my feelings had changed for my wife. She told me to treat her with the same respect and to continue to be good to her, treat her no different even when it was all over. One day, when my heart was able to stand love again, it would happen, and I would know real love and not just something to play with. That's why I've asked you to spend the rest of your life with me. You wanna know something funny? When my mother first met my second wife, she said that she wasn't the one for me, but I didn't listen and I married her anyway, and see what happened. But anyway, I have found the right person now that I hope to spend the rest of my life with, and I hope that you will feel the same way one day. Do you believe in love at first sight?"

"No."

"I don't either." Then we both laughed. "But for real, I do love you. Very much."

"Well, Eugene, tell me what your mother had to say when you told her about me? That you had met someone."

"Well, at first she said, 'Take it slow, baby.' Then I would feed her a little about you every day until she said, 'I want to meet her. Then I can tell for myself if she's right for you or not.'"

"Oh no, now I'm going to be a nervous wreck when I do meet her. And what if I don't pass the test with her?"

"Don't worry, you will do just fine because I know that I have found the right woman. I feel the same way about you that I did about my first wife, and God knows that my mother loved her, and she's gonna love you too."

"To be honest with you, I can relate with what you're saying because I felt the same way you did the first time that I kissed you at the casino until we met accidently at Red Lobster. You were all that I thought about. I thought I was going to go crazy because I had feelings for a man that I didn't even know. I didn't know if you were married or not, but I was going to find out on that following Monday when I got back to work. But then, there you were in church. What a coincidence. I thought that you were about to introduce me to a wife or a girlfriend at any minute while we were standing there talking. I just knew that someone was going to walk up and put her arms around you. Then I was going to be heart broken even though I had a husband in name only at times."

"Really? You felt like that?"

"Yeah."

"Well, now we both know how we really feel about each other, so once again, will you marry me? Again, I say will you marry me?"

"Wait, let me think. Humm mmmmm, yes, I will marry you. But let me say this, and I should have said this before I agreed to marry you. There is one thing—no, two things—that I believe will tear up a relationship, married or not, and that is lying and cheating. I can't deal with it. That's why I told you the truth about my husband. I want no secrets between us. None. If I find out one time you did either, then it's over because I believe that if I can pass up temptation, then I believe you can too."

"Baby, I already told you that I learned my lesson a long time ago, and I feel the same way that you do about that."

"So don't you cheat or lie to me, and we'll be all right."

"So will you marry me, Ms. Brunson?"

"Yes, I will, but I'm not playing with you because I have been through a lot with the men in my life. And I have had enough."

"Your life has not been too different from mine, and I told you that my mother schooled me a long time ago about women. And I listen to her, so you won't ever have to worry about me doing anything behind your back. I promise."

"Well, you know that I was married twice, and my first husband was murdered by a crazy lady just like Veronica."

"Are you kidding?"

"No, I'm not. That's why she worries me. Well, Sharon didn't actually kill him. She hired someone to do it for her. This woman also worked for Shawn. And like you, he couldn't see the love that she held for him. Shawn just thought that it was a great friendship with someone that he had no interest in. But he was wrong. I even tried to warn him about her, but he wouldn't listen. He just thought that I was being a jealous wife. But now we know about a woman's instinct. But to make a long story short, he didn't want her, and Sharon felt if she couldn't have him, then I couldn't either. So she hired two young boys to kill my husband. Sharon tricked them by saying that she was gonna put blanks in the gun that she was going to give them to use, and they didn't realize it until it was too late—when they saw it on the news. The owner of a construction company and his secretary were shot, and the owner died at the scene. But the secretary was doing fine and would be released. Then after seeing that on the news, the guys turned themselves in because they never would have agreed to murder anyone. They said that they were hired just to scare the supposed husband by shooting him and then her to make it look good. But she changed the whole thing by putting real bullets in the gun."

Tears started running down my eyes as I remembered that day in court. "I learned about all this information a second time because his friends Kirt and Wendal, who were also police friends of mine, had already told me what had happened when the guys came in to confess."

"Oh, baby, I'm so sorry to hear that. Was Shawn the father of your children?"

"Yes, he was."

"I'm sorry, baby."

I was lying in his arms crying, and Eugene was rubbing my head and apologizing to me as if he knew him.

But Eugene said that he did remember hearing about the murder when it was on the news.

As I was drying my eyes after talking about Shawn, I started talking about my second husband.

He said, "Are you sure that you can talk about him right now?"

"Yeah, I'm all right."

"Well, why are you divorcing him?"

"That's a long story."

"Baby, I want to hear any and everything that's bothering you."

"Well, years ago—before Shawn and I had any children—Shawn was doing drugs, and we broke up over it. So after a few months, he swore that he would never do that again if I came back to him. I told him that before I would come back, he had to go get help. He did, and we got back together. But then years later, he started doing it again. We split again. But this time, we had the twins. He went and got help again. But this time, he told me all the signs to look for if he started doing drugs again. But he did stay clean. Then as his business progressed, he needed someone to do the paperwork, so he hired Sharon. But what he didn't know was that Sharon was a drug user. He found out by going to the meetings that he was going to and later became a counselor at those meetings. And he tried to help her. But anyway, getting back to my second husband, things started changing. The things that my first husband had told me to look for in him I saw in Robert. But I ignored it for a long time because we were getting along great, and we had talked, and I had told him how I felt about drugs and what had happened with my first husband. So I guess I was just in denial. But anyway, he turned out to be a drug user, and I couldn't take it anymore. I tell you for years I blocked out all the signs. Until it became too much. I told him that I loved him, but I was not going to sit around and watch him kill himself. He tried the old 'I'm gonna get help.' But I told him that that still was not going to work because I had been there before, and he knew that. So he had no choice but to leave. Oh, and he also started cheating on me. It was as though the drugs make you want to have sex every time you blink your eyes, and I'm not lying. That's why I said to you no cheating. I'd rather be alone than be with someone who's going to cheat and lie to me. I'll be 100 percent in your corner and also 100 percent against you if you try to hurt me."

"Oh, my baby, no one would ever think that you have been through so much. But I make a promise to you that as long as God keeps me in my right mind, I will not cheat on you. It will always be you and I. You can check my background. I have never used drugs. I don't smoke, but I do drink sometimes, and it's not something that I must have. But when I feel like it, I will make myself a drink or drink a beer. I don't have any bad habits that I know of."

"Well, we'll see as time goes on."

"So, baby, are you all right? Do you need me to do anything for you right now?"

"No, I'm fine. Just thinking about that situation brought back memories. That's all. But I'm all right now."

"Are you sure?"

"Yes."

"Okay then since we are official now."

"No no no."

"You don't even know what it was that I was going to ask you."

"No, I don't, but I bet that I can guess what it is that you were going to say."

"Okay then, go ahead and guess what it was that I was going to say."

"I'll just say one word, and if I'm right, then tell the truth, okay? Sex huh?"

"Okay, you're right, but why not?"

"Because this is our first real date, and it's not really a date, and I'm old-fashioned."

"Well, can I have a real kiss then?"

"Sure." He leaned forward and kissed me very lightly and tenderly on the lips and said, "I'm old-fashioned too. That's all you get."

Then we started to laugh. He said, "Come on, let's get the dishes out of the dishwasher and pick up around the backyard so that we can get ready for bed. We do have to go to work in the morning."

"You're right."

We both got up feeling a little stiff from sitting so long and just talking.

Eugene said, "You know, we found out a lot about each other in one sitting than a lot of people find out years down the road."

"You're right," I said as we were walking into the kitchen to put the dishes away. I started putting the dishes away while he brought in the candles from outside.

When he came in, he said, "It's getting pretty chilly outside. You might need to get another blanket. And if you do need one, then I want you to look until you find one. That way you'll get to know where everything is or where you want them to go."

I said, "Yes, sir."

Gene came around the bar and put his arms around my neck and said, "I promise that I'll do my best to make you forget about all the pain that's been going on in your life."

I looked up at him and put my arms around his waist and said, "I promise to do my best to do the same for you."

He kissed me on the nose, then lightly on my cheeks, then lightly on my lips; then he slowly started kissing my neck as he whispered, "I love you, Mrs. Michaels."

Then he came back to my lips. This time, his warm tongue was slowly licking all around my lips; he found his way inside my mouth.

I was moaning and began to feel him rising. But I was not going to go back on my word. So I pulled myself away from him and said, "All right, buddy, that's enough kissing for the night."

"What time do you have your clocks set for?"

"Six thirty."

"Why so early?"

"Well, I usually get up and do a few sit-ups, make myself some breakfast, take a shower or take a swim, then flip through the paperwork for the day, then just chill out for a while, then get ready to go."

"So what time do you usually get up?"

"Well, my clock goes off around that time, but I hit the Snooze button a couple of times before I hit the shower, then make a little breakfast.”

So he put his arms around my waist and said, “Will you sleep with me?”

“One of these days, I will, but not tonight.”

“I don’t mean have sex or let me make love to you. I just want you in the same bed with me. I promise that I won’t touch you.”

“Mister, please. So you’re saying that if I sleep with you, you won’t try your old smooth kiss on me and then try not to make a move?”

“I promise.”

“Gene, if I lie in bed with you, then you won’t have to touch me because after lying there for a few minutes, I’ll be all over you. And I really don’t want to sleep with you right now. So for tonight at least, let’s just sleep in separate rooms. Then the next time that I spend the night, we’ll try it your way. Same bed but hands off, okay?”

“Okay, but I must tell you this. I sleepwalk.”

“Oh yeah, and I throw things.”

We had a hearty laughed.

We kissed a little, and I could still feel his slight erection. But I didn’t let that bother me. There would be plenty of time for that.

I said, “Okay, baby, good night.” I turned and walked away and went into the room where I was going to be sleeping. I grabbed a pillow off the bed and put it on the floor and got down on my knees and said my prayers. When I had finished, I got up and pulled the covers back, but then I wondered if the sheets were clean. So I opened the door and called out his name.

But there was no answer, so I looked out the room and called out his name. Again, still no answer. Then I looked and saw him on his knees. I smiled and went back into my room.

I had just turned over when a knock came on the door.

“Yes,” I said.

He said, “Did you call me?”

“You can open the door.”

“I thought that I heard you call my name.”

“Well, I did. I wanted to see if these sheets were safe to sleep on.”

“So what made you decide that they were safe?”

“I don’t know. I guess I just thought I’d take a chance.”

"Well, you can relax because they are. I put fresh sheets on after I talked to you at your place."

"But how did you know which room I was going to choose to sleep in?"

"I took a good guess."

"Thanks and good night." Gene had on a bathrobe, but I could see his legs; they looked real strong, and he had plenty of muscles in them. "Okay, thanks again for the info. Now good night."

He bent his head down and kissed me, then said, "Are you sure that you don't want me to join you since you won't join me?"

"I'm sure. Now get out of here."

He left, saying, "You don't have to close the door. I won't bother you. I'm not going to sleepwalk tonight."

I bent down and grabbed my house shoe and said, "But I am going to throw this shoe if you don't get out of here."

I looked at the clock. It was twelve forty-five. "We've got six hours to sleep—well, five and a half. So go away." And he did.

Dammmmn, I thought I must be strong. I've got to hold out for a few more days at least. Well, until this weekend anyway.

I didn't want to appear to be to easy, but Lord knows that if I hadn't pulled myself away from him, we would have been on that kitchen floor, making out like a couple of teenagers.

Oh boy, let me go to sleep before I get up and take him up on his offer to just sleep together with no sex.

Well, that was my last thought for the night that I remembered right before my clock went off.

I woke up to the smell of fresh coffee brewing and bacon frying.

Before I realized what I was doing or where I was at, I was out of bed and headed for the kitchen.

But I turned around and headed back to the room and grabbed my bag, got my toothbrush out of the bag, went into the bathroom, and brushed my teeth and washed my face with cold water so that I could see.

When I finished, I walked out into the kitchen. Eugene was standing there in his shorts and a T-shirt. He had a nice build—not too big, not too small. He was the perfect size.

He looked up and saw me standing there and said, "Are you ready to eat? I saw you when you first came in here partway, then turned around. I thought that you were going to put on your robe?"

"Huh?" Then I looked down and saw that I was standing there in my teddy.

He looked and kept looking and then said, "If you don't go and cover yourself up, then I won't be responsible for my action."

I just smiled, then turned around, and went to cover myself.

I put my bathrobe on and then went back into the kitchen and said, "Now that I am covered up, what about you?"

"What about me?"

"You're wearing only your shorts and a T-shirt."

"But I'm covered up more than you were."

"Yeah right."

"Hey, you know I'm right. Now how would you like your omelet?"

"You can just scramble me a couple of eggs very lightly but not runny."

"Coming right up."

"Hey, you didn't get much sleep, did you?"

"As a matter of fact, no, I didn't. But I'm good with just a couple of hours under my belt. What's on your agenda after work?"

"Well, I'm going home and soak in the tub, then I'm going to do absolutely nothing. But I'll probably stay in the tub for a couple of hours and have a glass of wine and just soak."

"Why not come over here and do just that?"

"Because I'm going to let you get some rest."

"I did get some rest, so now what?"

"Nothing, I think I'll just go to my place for the night."

"Well, can I come over there with you?"

"Huh? No."

"Why not?"

"Because I only have one bed."

"So where's the problem?"

"Standing there in those shorts."

"What do you mean?"

I got up, walked over to him, and said, "Now you wouldn't want to sleep on the floor when you have a big king-sized bed to sleep in."

"What you mean on the floor?"

"Okay, then on the sofa."

I kissed him, then said, "You know, after all the conversation we have had so far this morning, we still have not said good morning."

He held me close and said, "Girl, girl, girl, why do you want to tease me first thing in the morning?"

"I'm not trying to tease you. I just wanted a good-morning kiss and a big hug to start the day off right. Because God only knows what lies ahead."

"Girl, you know that you have basically nothing on up under that robe, then gone get all close up on me like that."

"Oh please." Then I went and got some plates out of the cabinet. "And you standing there fully dressed I suppose."

"Girl, I'm still wearing more than you are."

We started laughing.

Then I asked him what kind of day he in for.

He said that he was handling a harassment suit, which was funny because the boss and the lady that's bringing this suit against him used to date at one time. But now, she's tired of his advances because she has found herself an unmarried younger man. The man's not younger than she is, but he is younger than the man she was fooling around with. She's twenty-six, and he's fifty-seven. But she now has a man half his age. So now, she's getting her groove on with someone she can better relate with. I said, "You go, girl."

"Anyway, what's on your agenda for the day?"

"Well, I had put everything on hold, thinking that I was going to be in court for a while. So now I'll just be working on paperwork of some of the other cases that I got to get ready for anyway. Until the case is over with my favorite judge."

We finished eating, and I got up to start putting the dishes in the dishwasher.

As I was leaning over to put the dishes into the dishwasher, Eugene came up behind me, leaned over, and said, "I love you, Mrs. Michaels." Then he stood up.

I stood up and just looked at him for a minute and then said, "You know, love is a very powerful word, and when I say I love you, I'll mean it. So I won't say it until I know for sure that I mean what I say."

"Well, you must have meant it because you have already said it."

"Well, I probably did say something like I love you too."

"You know, something like that. But I won't say it again until I know for sure. I mean, I know now, but you know, I just want to be sure."

"Do you know what I'm saying?"

"Somewhat, but I do know for sure, and I don't care who knows."

Then we kissed, and his hands started roaming, and I had to stop him.

"Hey, I'm going to get in the shower."

"Yeah, me too."

I looked at him.

Then he said, "I'm going in my room to take a shower."

"Oh, so you give me the room without the shower?"

"No, I didn't. You chose the room across the hall."

"All right, you got me there."

"Hey, girl, don't forget that I asked you to sleep with me, but you chose not to. Now see, we could be taking a shower together. You wash yourself and I wash you too."

"Funny, but I'll find a way to pay you back."

"Pay me back?"

"Yes."

"For what?"

"I don't know yet, but I'll come up with something."

After that, we laughed, then headed for our rooms to get dressed for work. Twenty minutes later, when I came out of the room, Eugene was already outside.

He was wiping my truck windows. I said, "Hey, what are you doing?"

"Well, you must have been right."

"Right about what?"

"Someone following you."

"Why'd you say that?"

"Because someone wrote *bitch* on your windows."

"What?"

"I'm sorry, baby. I should have put your truck inside the garage with mine. But I park out here all the time, and no one bothers my car. Ever. But I'll make sure that I park your truck inside the garage tonight."

"Tonight?"

"That's right."

"I would park in the garage if I was going to stay at your house tonight, but I think I'll just go home like I told you last night."

"Why, sweetheart?"

"Because I need to stay at my house sometimes, or I'll be paying rent for no reason."

"But you could move over here with me," he said as he was walking up to put his arms around my waist, kissing my nose and then my cheeks. Then he went down to my neck.

I said, "And you call me a tease."

I just pulled away from him and walked back inside the house to make sure that I didn't leave anything.

Eugene came back into the house and said, "How about one quickie for the road?"

"Get away from me. We have got to get out of here, and you know that."

"Hey, are you going to be all right?"

"All right about what?"

"The writing on your windows."

"Oh sure, I'll be fine. Hey, I had my eyes closed once before, but not this time. But I know that I can't just confront her about something that I'm not sure that she did. But I can let it be known that if I catch anybody messing with anything that belongs to me, then it's going to be hell to pay. And I do mean just that, and when I say anything that belongs to me, that includes you, my sweets." Then I kissed him this time. Then I said, "We have got to go." We walked out of the house hand in hand.

I got into my truck, and Eugene shut my door. Then he went and got into his car.

He blew his horn, then said, "Wait a minute."

I said, "What's wrong?"

"Nothing." He jumped out of his car, came over, kissed me, and then said, "I love you, and I'll see you at the job, baby."

I smiled and said, "I'll see you there."

Eugene followed me to the job. We parked our cars across from the building we work at.

Eugene walked me to my office and then said, "I'll talk to you later," after touching my nose.

He was walking away, and I said, "Hey, I'm going to tell Lisa about us."

He said, "You mean that she doesn't know?"

"Not unless you told her. But you'll know when I tell her because she'll probably be looking at you all crazy."

"Well, you can also let her know that I truly thank her for trying to bring us together. But I did it my way."

Eugene left and went down to his office, and I went into mine.

I sat down, then thought, *Where do I start?*

Well, I've got the one trial that I'm waiting on. So I guess I'll head over to the jail and talk to one of my other clients.

After that, I've got to prepare for another court-appointed case.

And I know that I have another important case, but where is the paperwork on it, and where is my notepad? Oh, there it is. I picked it up and flipped through the pages and saw that some had been scratched out. I got on the intercom and called my secretary, Janel.

"Yes, Ms. Brunson?"

"Janel, have you seen anyone come into my office?"

"No, I haven't."

"Well, I want you to keep an eye out for me."

"Okay, but is something wrong, Rachael?"

"Naw, I just don't want anyone in my office from now on. I want you to lock it whenever you walk away. You do have your keys, right?"

"Yes, I do, but what's wrong?"

"I hope nothing. Anyway, it's nothing for you to worry about. I'm about to go over to the precinct to talk to a client, so I'll be gone for a while."

When I got in the hallway, I was headed for the elevator when I heard my name being called. I looked around but didn't see anyone.

Then I heard it again. This time, it was a little closer. I looked again and saw that it was Lisa. She said, "Girl, I have been calling you all day—well, yesterday anyway. Where were you?"

"Would you believe it if I told you that I spent the night at Eugene's house?"

"Girl, please."

"I'm not kidding." She was standing there, looking like someone had just given her an electrical shock treatment. "Well, Lisa, don't look like that. Anyway, I've got an appointment, but how about you come by my place tonight and we'll talk?"

"What time 'cause I'll be there with bells on?"

"How about between five thirty and six. I'm going to call Wanda and Denise over. We'll just make it a girl thing."

"Oh, come on, five thirty. I'll be waiting in your parking spot when you get home."

"That's fine. I gotta go."

So I finally got into the elevator, pressed the First Floor button, and thought that someone has been waiting for the elevator. And I've been standing in it with the door open.

When I got to the first floor, walked out the elevator, and was walking toward the front door, I saw Veronica. She said, "Hi, Rachael."

"Hi, Veronica."

Then she said, "What are you doing leaving the building this time of the morning?"

"What? Look, Veronica, my leaving the building or coming into the building or going anywhere is my business. But I will say this for your sake. I'm a lawyer and can come and go as I please."

"Excuse me."

"You are excused."

"What's wrong with you? Didn't you get enough last night?"

"I beg your pardon? What did you say?"

"I was only saying that maybe you didn't get enough sleep last night."

"And what would make you say that?"

"I just asked because I didn't get much sleep myself last night, and I know that Eugene likes to stay up late and get up early."

"How would you know that, Veronica?"

"Well, don't forget that I used to work for him. And I learned some of his habits."

"But what would make you ask me if I got enough sleep then throw Eugene's name in at the same time? Were you following me or something?"

I started walking toward her, then said, "Well, his habits have changed since I've come into his life, so you can forget everything that you memorized about him."

She just stared at me.

And I turned and walked away. While I was walking away, I wondered if she had done anything to my car like scratching it up. But she probably did nothing because it was in a public place, and there are cameras in all the parking structures.

I thought, *Anyway someone would see her.*

When I got to my truck, I looked all around to see if she had done anything to it, but she hadn't.

So I walked around Eugene's car to see if she had done anything to his, and she hadn't done anything to his car either, but I did notice that she left a note on his windshield. So I picked it up and read it.

It said, "I don't see what you see in a stuck-up bitch like her. You know that I'm the one that you really want, but I believe in time you'll come to your senses and see that."

Well, I'll be damned. I'll show this to Eugene when I get back and if he's still here. He should know what her handwriting looks like, and if it is hers, then that sick bitch is mine because I'm not about to start playing these little head games with her and neither is he.

I got into my truck and headed down to the jail.

When I got there, my client asked me, "What is wrong, Ms. Brunson? Is something wrong with my case?"

"Oh no," I said. "Toya, someone left a note on my fiancé's car, confessing that he really loved her but didn't realize it."

"Ms. Brunson, when you get me out of here, I'll find out who it was and take care of it for you. If it's one thing that I can't stand, that's some bitch trying to steal someone else's man."

We looked at each other, then started laughing because that was part of the reason that she was in jail now.

She had jumped on some girl about her old man.

But I said, "Thanks, but no thanks. I can handle it. I came here to talk about you. Not about what's going on with me."

She said, "Could I call you Rachael when we're alone?"

"You sure can."

"Well, Rachael, I really like you, and this is the first time that I really feel like changing my life."

"But first, I've got to get you out of here."

"I know that. You know, while I was sitting in my jail cell, I thought about where my life was headed, and it really looks like I'm headed nowhere. But when I get out of here, I'm going to enroll back in school. I finished high school, you know?"

"Toya, you did?"

"Yes, ma'am, I did. But I know if you look at me you'd probably think that I was just a country bumpkin, but you know, Rachael, I only act tough. But I'll admit I can be sometimes, but I have to because that's the way that I grew up. You see, I basically grew up on my own and in the streets. But I've always wanted to work in the hospitals, and there was even one time that I actually thought about becoming a doctor. But I don't know about that anymore."

"Why not, Toya?"

"Because I don't think that my nerves could take all that classroom work."

"How would you know if you didn't give it a try?"

"I don't know."

"Well, tomorrow we go to court, and hopefully the girl won't show up. And I'll ask that all charges be dropped against you. And if they are, then that will be a fresh start, a new beginning of a new life for you. I've got some friends that work in the hospital, and one does owe me a favor. So I'll see if they are doing any hiring. And if they are, I'll see if she can get you in. Now I don't even know if they are hiring, and if they are hiring, what they are hiring for. But we'll see. Is there anything in particular that you are looking for?"

"Well, yeah."

"What's that?"

"A job."

We laughed.

Then Toya said, "I don't care what it is. I just want to work, go to school, do something to change my life. I'm twenty-five."

"Twenty-five? Girl, I thought you were about eighteen. I really had not paid that much attention to the paperwork on you just yet. But anyway, Toya, I've got to go. I'll see you first thing in the morning."

"But what if she does show up?"

"Then the most that can happen is probation." She looked surprised, then said, "Really."

I stood up to go, and Toya stood up too, then she said, "Rachael." Then she paused.

I said, "Yes?" as I was putting my papers back in my briefcase.

She said, "Can I have a hug?"

I looked at her, and she looked so sad.

So I said, "Now let me ask you what's wrong?"

"It's just that I can't remember the last time that anyone treated me with such kindness. People always look at me as if I'm nothing because I live in the streets all the time. So I have to act tough. But since you've been coming to see me, I see a change in myself already, and I just want to thank you for that. You know, all I really needed was for someone to say that I needed to change my lifestyle and mean it. And you really did mean it. You did that for me without you even knowing it."

"Well, thanks, Toya."

"Rachael, I am so happy but also so unhappy and sad."

"Why are you sad, Toya?" She didn't say anything for a minute; then I asked again, "Why are you sad, Toya?"

"Where I live, all they do is drink, smoke, play cards, and screw around. And that's what I really want to get away from."

"Toya, do you realize that because they do that, you don't have to do that too?"

"I know, so when I get out of here tomorrow and you give me that good news about the job, I'm going to scrape up some money and move into a hotel room all by myself. That way, I won't be around all that bullshit. Oh, I'm sorry. I mean, all that stuff that goes on where I live."

"Well, good for you." I hugged her again and said, "I'll see you in the morning."

She had such a big smile on her face as she went back into lockup. That was such a nice thing to hear, someone wanting to change her life because of a few words spoken; that makes my day. When I got back outside, I just thought that being here for even just a short period of time, even I would want to change my life too. Because this is no place to be unless you're just an ice-hearted person, and that was the best place for you.

Damn, I sure hope that Elizabeth can find Toya a job; but if she doesn't have one there, then I'll call Lanet. Between the two of them, they'll come up with something. I'm pretty sure.

When I got back to my office, my secretary told me that Mr. Michaels had stopped by. And she told him that I was out of the building.

"He said that he would get back with you later."

"Okay, thanks. Did anybody else stop by?"

"Not before I left to go to lunch. Oh yeah, Lisa stopped by right after you left. Did she catch you? I almost forgot about her."

"Yeah, she did." I went into my office and started reviewing paperwork for an upcoming trial.

I had gotten well into my paperwork when my phone rang. "Yes, Janel?"

"Ms. Brunson, Mr. Michaels is on line 1?"

"I'll take it, thanks. Hello."

"Hey, baby, are you free for lunch?"

"Sure, I didn't realize that it was that late. Where are you?"

"I'm over at the court. Where would you like to meet me, and what do you feel like eating?"

"How about some Chinese?"

"Okay, where should we meet?"

"I'll tell you what. Since you're closer, I'll pick you up in front of the building."

"Sounds good."

"Okay, I'll be on my way." We hung up. I grabbed my keys and left.

When I pulled up in front of the building, I saw Eugene standing there and talking to a lady. She was a pretty, decent-looking lady.

But seeing him standing there talking remind me of the note that was left on his car. I couldn't wait to tell him about the note that I had found on his car. Hell, it could be anybody.

He looked up and saw me. He waved and said, "Hi, honey." I could tell that he was saying bye to the lady.

I wasn't jealous because in our profession, we have to be in contact with the opposite sex all the time.

He stepped into the truck, then leaned over, and kissed me.

Then he said, "She's also an attorney."

"Eugene, you didn't have to tell me who she was. I'm not that jealous. It comes with the territory, and the same goes for me. Just as long as we remember that we have each other, nothing is going to come between us."

He kissed me again as we were riding along.

Then Eugene said, "I know. It's just that I can't help thinking about every time I talked to some other woman. When I was married and my wife saw me, I always had to explain who that person was; so I guess old habits are kind of hard to get rid of, but I will."

"I know that you will. But that doesn't mean that I don't get jealous or that I won't break your neck." We laughed.

He said, "So how was your day so far?"

"It's just fine. How about yours?"

"Great now that I am with my baby."

I just looked over at him and smiled. "Oh, look at this." I handed him the note sitting on top of a cup. "It's yours." He unfold it, then started reading it.

He looked up at me and said, "Where in the world did you get this?"

"It was on your car this morning when I left the office. I saw Veronica and wondered if she had done anything to my car, but she hadn't, so I walked around your car and found this note on your windshield. Does the handwriting look familiar to you?"

He looked at it, then said, "Not really. Baby, I'm sorry that this is happening to us. But if I see Veronica today, I'll ask in an unsuspecting kind of way a few good questions about what she's been up to and how was her day. I'll think of something. Anyway, don't you worry about her. I won't let her or anyone else hurt you."

"Well, that's sweet, but I'm still going to keep a close eye out for both of us."

He leaned over and kissed me again.

As we were pulling up into the valet parking to go eat, he said, "I'm starving."

And I said, "I'm starving too."

"Well, let's go eat."

When we got inside and was seated, we picked up the menu.

But Eugene asked, "What do you like most?"

"Let's see. I like almost everything. But I'll have the shrimp fried rice and the boneless almond chicken."

"I like that also."

Before the waiter came back to take our order, Eugene asked if it would be all right if he ordered for both of us.

"Sure you can. Just don't forget that we are on our lunch hour. So don't order everything on the menu."

He laughed and said, "I'm glad that you reminded me because as hungry as I am, I could have eaten everything on the menu."

"I'll bet. But why are you so hungry anyway? We had breakfast."

"I know, but I've been chewing gum, and it empties my stomach every time. And it makes me feel like I haven't eaten anything."

I started to laugh.

"What?"

"Nothing really. It's just that I feel the same way. Gum does the same for me."

"Well, we've got a lot in common, don't we?"

Just then, the waiter came over, and Eugene told him that we were ready to order. So he pulled out his order pad, and Eugene started talking in Chinese. The waiter looked at Eugene and smiled, then started writing.

When he was done ordering and the waiter walked away, I said, "When did you have time to learn Chinese?"

He said, "I knew that that would surprise you. I had a roommate in college, and we helped each other learn the other's language."

"Well, I'm impressed, and so was the waiter."

"Thank you," he said. "So what time are you coming over tonight?"

"I'm not."

"What?"

"I told you this morning that I was going to stay at home tonight."

"That's right. So can I come over there and stay with you?"

"Sure, you can stay with me anytime you like, but I hope that you don't feel uncomfortable tonight."

"Why is that?"

Then the waiter walked up with our food. He thanked him in Chinese.

The waiter smiled and walked away.

I said, "Everything looks good." Then I started to taste different things on the platter. "Hmm, what is this?"

"Oh, that's pressed duck."

"Well, you are full of surprises because this is something that I have not had before. And it's pretty good."

"Okay, now back to our conversation. Why wouldn't I be comfortable?"

"Because I have invited Lisa and my sisters over to talk about you."

"Me? Why?"

"Because I want them to know that I have someone in my life now, and they can stop trying to hook me up with their friends."

"Is that so? Well, in that case, you let them know that you are hooked up for life, and they don't have to look out for you anymore, all right?"

"Yeah, and you know Lisa."

"Yeah, that's my girl. And since you put it like that, you girls enjoy yourselves, and don't let them bash me too much."

"Don't worry, I won't." Then I leaned over and kissed him and said, "I'll see you on Saturday."

"Oh, that's right."

"What? You forgot."

"No, I just wanted to know if it would be all right if I invited my family over. After all, we could kill two birds with one stone."

"Mr. Michaels, isn't that what I said when we first talked about it?"

"Yeah, but now I think that it will be a lot of fun."

"Hey, it sounds like a party to me."

"So you won't mind?"

"No, I'll get to meet my other children, and you'll meet mine."

"Oh, my mother and father will be there too."

"Okay, no problem."

"Are your parents living?"

"My mother and father are both living, and they'll both be there. I can't wait."

"Oh, let me remind you now to bring your church clothes so that we can get up and go to church the next day."

"Okay. Now eat up so that we can get back to work."

Eugene suddenly said, "What do you mean you'll see me on Saturday? I know that you're going to come over on Friday so that we can prepare. And I want you to go shopping with me."

"Well, I was gonna come over on Friday, but when you didn't say anything, I figure that you could handle everything yourself."

"Don't think that I couldn't, but I don't have to do anything alone anymore since we are together."

"That was cute."

"Cute? What do you mean by cute?"

"Eugene, I know that you have said that line to plenty of other women, and you want me to believe that you have been with only two or three women?"

"Yeah."

Then we both laughed.

"But for real, we'll talk about this on Friday while we're getting ready for Saturday, all right?"

We finished eating and left.

I pulled up in front of the courthouse and let Eugene out.

He got out and said, "Thanks for lunch, sweetheart." Then he walked around the truck and said, "Here."

So I let the window all the way down.

He said, "Stick your head out a little bit."

And I did. He put his hands on my face and held my head while trying to push his tongue down my throat.

Then he laughed.

I said, "Get out of here."

"Well, I'll let that hold me for a day and a half."

"Yeah right. I'll call you later, all right?"

Eugene turned and walked away. I watched him for a minute, then pulled away with a smile on my face, thinking about what lies ahead for the rest of the night.

When I got back to the office, I thought about Toya.

Oh yeah, I've got to call Liz. So as soon as I got settled in, I called Liz.

She picked up and said, "Hello."

I said, "Hey, Liz, this is Rachael."

"Hey, Ray, what's up?"

"Hey, I need a favor from you if you can."

"What is it and I'll see what I can do."

"I've got this client who's in need of a job."

"Ray, you're a lawyer, and your clients are all crooks."

"Girl, please. Some are innocent sometimes."

She laughed and said, "Girl, we're on a budget, and one of your clients would rob us blind."

We both laughed; then I said, "This one is different."

"How's that? Is this person in jail or going to jail or what?"

We laughed again; then I said, "Well, this person is in jail and for some reason." Elizabeth burst out laughing while trying to say I knew it.

After a minute of getting herself back together, she said, "Girl, I can't do anything for her if she's in jail."

"Well, hopefully she'll be out tomorrow. She's in for something that we all go through."

"So what's that?"

"Man trouble."

"Just what did she do? Try to kill him?"

"She wouldn't be gettin' out so easily for something like that."

"So what did my girl do? Crack his nuts or what?"

"Naw, she got the best of the other woman."

"My girl. What type of work is she looking for?"

"She just said anything to get started in changing her life around. Then she wants to go back to school."

"Well, since it's you, tell her to come by my office on Monday. But if she gets out in time tomorrow and can stop by..." Then she said, "Just tell her that I'll see her on Monday. To just stop by and we can talk. But I'm sure that I can find her something."

"Thanks, girl, and I know that I owe you one."

"Sure do, so how about hooking me up with one of those lawyers? Anyway, when are we going to get together and hang out?"

"Say, what are you doing tonight?"

"Nothing. Why, girl?"

"How about my place tonight? So that we can talk about everything and everybody. How about between six and six thirty?"

"Sounds good. See you then."

"Hey, Liz, thanks again."

"No problem. We girls have to stick together."

"You ain't never lied about that. I'll see you tonight."

"You sure will."

Okay, let me call Lanet and see if she wants to come over and join us.

Then we hung up the phone.

I dialed her phone. "Hey, Lanet, this is Rachael."

"What's up, Ray?"

"Are you busy tonight?"

"Not really, why? What's going on?"

"Well, some of the girls are coming over to have a little girl talk and to catch up on each other's goings-on."

"Well, count me in."

"Okay, my place tonight about six or six thirty."

"Okay, see you then."

When we hung up, it was time to close up shop. So I gathered up my things and left.

I stopped at the store and bought some things to snack on and a couple bottles of wine.

I was smiling to myself, thinking about the fun we have when we do get together.

I was really looking forward to tonight.

It was going to be good to see my sisters because I hadn't seen them in a while or the others, so it was going to be a nice night.

I also thought about Eugene, so when I got home, I decided to give him a call before everyone got there.

So I called; he answered, and I said, "Hey, baby."

"Hey, love of my life, what's going on?"

"Oh, nothing much. I just got in from the store."

"I take it the girls haven't gotten there yet?"

"You're right, and I wanted to talk to you before they do get here. Actually, I just wanted to hear your voice."

"Girl, you got me blushing like a kid."

"Good, I like doing that. I love that smile that you have."

"And I love everything about you plus that smile that you have. Even that frown that you get when you are teed off."

"Oh, so you saw that?"

"Yes, I did. I watch everything that you do when you are near me."

"How sweet."

"You sound pretty excited."

"I am. I can hardly wait to tell everybody about you."

"How we met, how Lisa tried to hook us up at first. Everything."

"Boy, I would love to be a fly on the wall. Just to hear how you tell them about our meeting, the very first time that you saw me because I had seen you long before you spotted me."

"Well, trust me. Everyone is going to be so jealous when I'm finished telling my side of the story."

"Then you know that Lisa is going to add her two cents."

"So what time are you coming over tonight?"

"Funny, you know that I am not coming over tonight."

"But if you change your mind?"

"If I do, then I'll call you. Otherwise, I'll see you tomorrow. Maybe we can have lunch. Oh, wait a minute. I take that back about lunch. That's going to be up in the air for now unless this girl doesn't show up for trial tomorrow so that she can press charges. But I hope that she doesn't show up."

"Why?"

"Because my client is one of those that got caught up and deserves another chance."

"But if we don't make lunch, then we'll talk, and I'll see you the day after."

"Whatever you say, my sweets." But I had plans on seeing him later the next night anyway. "Hey, where are you anyway?"

"I'm on my way back to the office. I've got a few things to wrap up, then I'll be headed home. I think that I'll go visit my parents since I haven't seen them in a couple of days."

"That's sweet. What about the children?"

"It's been a few days since I've seen them, but they don't miss a beat calling me. You would think that they were my parents. My son isn't as bad, but he gets his questions in too. I called them today and told them about Saturday, and they are very excited about meeting you."

"Really?"

"Yes, ma'am."

"Yes who?"

"I'm sorry. Yes, baby. Even my parents get out of here."

"I'm serious."

"Well, mine feel the same way."

"And I can't wait to meet them also."

"Well, my sweets, I'll talk to you tomorrow."

"All right, have a pleasant evening."

"All right, and you do the same."

"Now remember, after your company leaves and you still want to talk or come over, then feel free."

"Hey, thanks. I'll keep that in mind. But if I do come over and it's late, I don't want you to think that it's a booty call."

Eugene busted out laughing and said, "Girl, you are something else. But don't worry, I will." Then he started laughing again.

I had to laugh myself. I said, "I'll talk to you later."

"All right, my sweets. Behave yourself."

"I will."

"Hey, Ray."

"Yes?"

"Never mind."

"What is it?"

"It's just an old saying that I was going to say."

"What's that?"

"I know that my ears are going to be burning, but I'll know why they're burning this time."

"You know what, I believe in that old saying too. So keep a cool towel around to put out the fire on those ears of yours."

We had another laugh. Then we said our goodbyes.

After talking to Eugene, I went into the kitchen and started making snacks and poured myself a glass of wine.

After that, I sat down and thought about my life again with all its ups and downs. And now, I was on high; and hopefully, I'll stay this way forever.

I felt myself drifting off to sleep for what I thought was a few minutes, but it turned out to be a little over an hour. It was six fifteen when someone knocked on the door. It was Lisa.

"Hey, girl, what are you doing? Is Eugene here?"

"Naw, why?"

"Because I've been knocking on your door for an hour."

"Yeah right. How did you get in?"

"Someone was coming in, and I came in right behind them."

"Well, come on in. I was sitting on the couch, and I must have drifted off to sleep."

Just as soon as Lisa came in and sat down on the couch, the buzzer rang. I walked to the door, pressed the button, and said, "Who is it?"

The voice said, "Bitch, open the door." And I knew who it was.

Lisa hollered, "That's Wanda, isn't it?"

"Yeah, you know it?"

I buzzed her in, and a few minutes later, she and Denise came in.

"What's up?" We hugged because it's been a couple of weeks since I have seen either one of my sisters. But we talk on the phone regularly. And I've been busy.

They came in, Lisa stood up, and they hugged her too because they love her as much as I do because she stuck by me when I lost Shawn. She was right there in my corner. But they also knew that she was a pain in the ass at times too.

"Damn, Lisa, you gettin' fat as hell," Denise said. "You must really be content."

We all started laughing because we all knew that once you get married, you sometimes let yourself go and gain a little weight.

I said, "She's content all right. She's having a baby."

"What?" Denise and Wanda said at the same time, then looked at Lisa. "You go, girl."

Then Wanda said, "So when's the little crumb snatcher due?"

But before she could answer, the buzzer rang. It was Liz and Lanet. When they came in, everybody hugged. Wanda, Lanet, and Liz all had brought a bottle of wine. Lisa brought a quart of milk, saying, "I knew you didn't have any."

I got out glasses for everybody; then we all sat on the sofa—the love seat—and I put a pillow on the floor and sat down. We started some small talk about how everyone looked and how long it had been since we had seen each other.

After a second glass of wine, everyone got a little looser.

"Okay, everyone, who wants to go first and tell what's going on in their lives?"

Lisa said, "Why don't you go first?"

I was excited and didn't want anyone to come up with something better than what I was about to say. So I said, "Okay, I'll go first. Wanda and Denise, this is really for the two of you. I got a man. I spent the night at his house. We have slept together and everything. There is so much to tell, but I'll just give you some of what's happening for now."

Everybody was like "You go, girl."

But my sisters said, "Bitch, stop lying. You just don't want us to hook you up with Santa again." Everyone broke out laughing.

"I knew that the two of you wouldn't believe me, but I've got a witness. Lisa, would you tell them?"

"Why should we believe Lisa?"

"Because she tried to hook us up, but we still kept missing each other."

"So if she didn't get the two of you together, then who did, or how did you two meet?"

Everyone was saying, "You go, girl, kiss and tell."

"Well, let's see. I had just won a case and wanted to celebrate, so I decided to stop at Red Lobster to get a drink and get something to eat. So I sat at the bar and ordered a drink. Then this guy walked up and asked would I mind if he joined me, if I were alone at the moment. So I said who is it that wants to know if I'm alone or not? Then he told me his name. But at that point, it didn't ring a bell. So we kept on talking, and he mentioned where he worked. I said I work at that same building. He said that he knew that. So I said just how would you know that. He went on to say that he had seen me there before and at the casino, but didn't say anything because he wasn't sure it was me because I looked different in street clothes. That's why he didn't say anything to me when he saw me at the casino."

So one of the girls said, "So you actually got to meet him before Lisa had a chance to introduce you to each other?"

"Yeah. But the funny thing was I thought that the man was crazy because he would always just stand around looking. Sometimes he would play, but he did a lot of staring. He really did scare me. I mean, just about every time I went to the casino, he was there also, in the same places that I normally played at."

Wanda said, "So why did you think that he was crazy when you were doing the same thing that he was doing? If he was looking at you, then you had to be looking at him also, so what?"

"Shut up, girl. Because as it turned out, he did think that I was crazy too." We laughed. "He thought that I was following him around. Until he saw me at the job and realized that we both just liked playing the same type of games. So we laughed about it, then we just talked and talked. We finished lunch. He paid, then I said the next time that we run into each other, it'll be my treat. He said okay, then we left. About a month later, I saw him at a restaurant with—wait y'all—this crazy bitch. I was with Robert."

"Old crazy ass," Wanda said. "So how did you pull that off being with two people at one time?"

I said, "Forget you, Wanda." And we all laughed.

"But for real, he told me that she worked for him and that she had a thing for him. But he told her that he was not interested in a nice way because he was newly divorced and he never dated anyone that worked for him. So she up and quit and started working for someone that works upstairs in the same building but continued to harass him since she didn't work for him any longer. But again, he told her that he was not interested. But this chick just wouldn't go away. One day, I walked out of the courtroom and saw him talking to her, but at that time, I didn't know the story behind her. Anyway, as I was walking toward them, I thought should I say anything? I mean, after all, that was the same woman that I had seen him with at the restaurant."

"Damn, girl, it sounds like he has a real fatal attraction on his hands. Not only him, but you too. Has she been following you too?"

"Yeah, but this bitch has run across the wrong person this time. But anyway, when I got to where they were standing, Eugene put his arms around my waist and kissed me, then said, 'Veronica, this is my future wife.' I thought, damn, I didn't want to look too shocked, so I said, 'Hi. How are you, Veronica?' Then I shook her hand. There was a little more small talk, then Eugene and I walked away because we were headed out to lunch. While we were walking, he said, 'I'll explain later when we get in the car.' That's when I found out that she wanted him, and it was a one-sided thing. Anyway, every time that we are together, we have a really good time. But I'm going to be for real with you, guys. At first, I thought that something was wrong with this guy. I mean, he's the perfect gentleman. A single man, good-looking, and no woman.

But then I found out why. But anyway, I wanted to share this with family and friends. So now you all can stop trying to hook me up with your friends."

"Okay, so just how big and how long can a brother hang?" Wanda said; then everybody laughed.

I said, "Girl, I didn't give it up that fast."

Wanda said, "Bitch, you said you slept with him?"

"See there, that's how lies get out. I said that I spent the night at his house. I never said that we had sex together. There's a big difference. I'm going to make him wait until Saturday night."

"What's so special about Saturday night?" Lanet asked.

"Oh, Jaylen and his girlfriend are getting married, and we're all going to get together at his house. And I'm going to meet his family, and he's going to meet mine. So, everybody, get ready for a wedding in a couple of months. Okay, now who's next to tell what's been happening in her circle?"

Someone said, "Well, we all know what's been going on in Lisa's circle." We all laughed.

"Funny," Lisa said, looking somewhat down.

I hit her on the shoulder and said, "Girl, forget about them."

"All right, Liz, what's up?"

"My dress, shit."

Boy, did we laugh.

Then everybody started to talk at one time.

We all talked and laughed until it was eleven forty-five. We had drank four bottles of wine, snacked, then talked some more.

Then Lanet said, "It's been sweet, but I have got to go. We must do this again. Hey, next time we'll meet at my place."

"Sounds good," everyone said. Then everybody got up and started to leave.

Wanda, Denise, and Lisa were the last to leave. Then they asked about Jaylen's wedding.

I told them that as soon as I got a date, then I would let them know. "But again, you all will probably know before I have a chance to tell you. Because I know that once Shawnda finds out, which I know is going to be before Saturday, she'll tell Ceria, then the world will know."

"Say that again. My baby can't hold water," Denise said.

Wanda and Denise said, "Holla at you later." Then they left.

Lisa was still there and said, "Okay, now tell me the truth."

"The truth about what?"

"You and Eugene."

"What?"

"About you and him sleeping together."

"Girl, I did tell everybody the truth. We have not slept together yet, but we will this weekend if everything goes my way. It's gonna be on."

She looked kind of down.

I said, "What's wrong with you? I know you ain't hatin' when it was you in the first place that tried to bring us together."

"Naw, it's not that. I'm really happy for you because you could really use some real happiness for a change."

"So why the long face?"

"I just wish that I were as happy as you are."

"Girl, please. You got a husband who loves you. And a baby on the way. What more could you ask for?"

"Maybe that my husband wouldn't cheat."

"Look, you and I both know that men do a lot of things that they are not supposed to do, but they do them anyway. So there is no need for you to keep yourself upset about something that happened in the past. And besides, you don't know if he's cheating or not. Didn't he say that he would never do that again?"

"Yeah, but, girl."

"But my foot, Lisa. Get your *but* out of the way and stop looking for trouble. What he used to do does not mean that he is still doing it. If he says that he is not cheating, then somewhere down in you try and believe him. Find some kind of way to try and trust him again. I mean, after all, he just might be telling you the truth. But if you are going to just keep nagging him, he might pick up his old habits just to get away from all the arguing and trying to convince you that he's not cheating. My free advice to you is to stop nagging and start loving him like you used to. And you did say that he was smothering you. So start enjoying it. Be happy that you've got a junior on the way. All right, girl? Be happy with what you got because if you let him go, then there's no tellin' what you might get in exchange. So work with what you got. And, girl, I am stressing that fact. You need to let go of the past and live for the future. Now does that sound familiar? That's what you told me some time ago, and I listened. Now see what letting go of the past has got me. A new man with a lot of happiness from this day forward."

She said, "I truly thank you for your free advice for my problems. I'm so glad that I talked to you. I'm so glad that you brought it all out of me, or I would still be feeling down. But I got the hint. Eric is going to see a new me. I feel a lot better about my marriage. I'm really going to try and make things work."

She hugged me, then said, "Thank you, Rachael."

"You are so very welcome." We hugged some more; then she said, "I gotta go and try and make up with my husband. I'm not going to pour it on too thick because then he will think that something was wrong. I'm just gonna slowly blow his mind. I'm going to sweep him off his feet with kindness. He's not going to know what happened from this day forward."

We hugged again.

She said again, "I gotta go."

So she left. Then I started to clean up our mess.

I started to think about my new sweetheart and wondered if I should go over to his house or just wait until tomorrow and see him when I see him. I think I'll opt for waiting until I see him tomorrow. Because, after all, good things come to those who wait. And I've waited for a long time. Dammmmn, when was the last time that I did have sex? The weekend that I saw Eugene at the restaurant with Veronica, and I was with Robert. And just thinking about that weekend would blow a Negro's head off because he was a bad boy in bed, but sex is not everything. Those are the kind of thoughts that I have to let go of because I'm with a new man now. But I wonder if he's any good in bed. But according to Veronica, I'm in for a treat. But we'll see. Now that everything is back in order, I'll take a shower and let a movie take me out. While I was taking my shower, I thought about what Lanet had said about Eugene when I had told them how Eugene had asked me to be his lady.

She was totally shocked because she said that nowadays, it's a couple of movies, a couple of dinners, a few rounds in bed, and you automatically belong to him—without a word being said about you being his. Everyone was saying "now isn't that the truth" or "he's already packed his bags and moved in with you or he's asking you to move in with him, depending on who's making the most money?"

Then Wanda broke out and said, "Sometimes it's just about a good fuck. Then it's all over."

Then everybody started laughing.

That thought brought a smile on my face.

As I was getting out of the shower, I dried myself off, wrapped a towel around my head, and headed for my bedroom. I sat down on the bed and started putting on some lotion. I picked up the remote and cut the television on and started flipping through the channels and then saw one of my favorite movies on, so I decided to let that movie put me to sleep. I looked over at the clock, and it was twelve thirty. Damn, I've got to be in court at least by eight thirty.

I thought about Toya and was glad that I was going to give her some good news. Liz was going to give her a job. I know that she is going to be happy about that. I'm sure.

As I lay down, sleep came pretty fast. It seemed like I just closed my eyes good when it was morning already. I felt pretty good, so I got up and put on some water to make myself a cup of coffee and try to get my paper before my neighbor did.

I got the paper first and laid it on the kitchen counter. Then I went in the bathroom to freshen up, went back into the kitchen, and had a piece of toast to go with my coffee.

After eating breakfast, I gathered my things and headed for the office.

I could hear Sabrina and her husband talking; they were always talking loud, but they seemed to get along pretty good. They were not bad people, just paper thieves. I just smiled as I went out my door and looked at theirs and thought, *I beat you to my paper once again.* I was in good spirits when I left for work.

When I got to my office, my secretary was standing there with flowers in her hand, saying, "These just came, and they're for you."

"Oh yeah? Who are they from?"

"I don't know." Looking down with a smile, she said, "I don't know."

"Yeah right."

"For real, they didn't leave a card."

We laughed; then I said, "Girl, there isn't one thing that comes into this office that you don't know who or where it came from."

"But this time, I'm for real. They didn't leave a card. So I took the flowers and sat them on my desk. They were some beautiful yellow and white roses."

Janel stuck her head in my door and said, "Ms. Brunson, the delivery person did say that the person that sent the flowers did say to say that they were from an admirer. And that they would see you later. But no card."

"Girl, you can lose the Ms. Brunson when we are alone. But it's very professional when we're in front of company. Okay?"

"Okay, Ray."

Then we both smiled, and she shut the door.

I looked at my flowers. I was smiling and thinking, *Oh, Eugene, you think that you are so slick, trying to work your way into getting some this weekend, and it worked. It's on, just wait. When the family thing is all over, it's going to be just me and you. But you didn't have to send me flowers. You know I'm easy.* I thought to myself and then said, "Girl, you know you are something else." I almost laughed out loud.

Let me get out of here because I know Toya is going to be looking for me before court gets started. I know she's going to be wondering what happened to me and why I haven't been there to talk to her this morning.

"But I'm on my way, Toya."

When I left out, I reminded Janel to not let anyone in my office. She said okay.

Then I left. I had my flowers in my hand just in case I saw Eugene, and I could thank him for the flowers.

I looked down the hall to see if I could see him, but I didn't, so I went on to the courthouse.

When I got to the court, there he was standing, talking to no other but Veronica. I walked toward them, and Eugene looked my way and started smiling and said, "Hey, baby, I missed you last night."

He put his arms around my waist and kissed me.

I said, "I missed you too."

Then I looked over at Veronica and said, "Good morning."

She hesitated, then said "morning," and walked away.

"What was that all about?"

"She was here when I got off the elevator. I thought about questioning her about her whereabouts but decided to ask a few different questions, but I knew she was gonna lie."

"What did she say?"

"She just said that she hadn't been up to too much. Oh, she said that she has met someone and that they're dating. So I said good for you. And that was when you walked up."

"Well, good for her. Now I've got to run. Okay?"

"But how about lunch?"

I said, "I'll call your cell phone and leave a message and let you know."

"Okay, that sounds good."

"But if we can't do lunch together, then I'll see you at the house tonight when you get off work."

"What time should I meet you?"

"Let's say four thirty for now. But call me or I'll call you whenever we get off work."

"Okay, baby, but I got to go." He kissed me, and I ran off to my courtroom. I went into the courtroom and signed in. Then I had the guard to take me to the back so that I could talk to my client.

When I got in the back, I saw Toya. She looked so sad.

I said, "Hey, Toya."

She looked up and started smiling. "Hi, Rachael. I thought you had forgotten about me."

"Girl, please, you know I didn't forget about you. I got caught up for a minute. But don't you worry, everything is going to be all right. I've got good news for you."

"You do? What?"

"So far the girl has not shown up. Not only that, but Liz has found a job for you. Well, she's going to find you a job on Monday. She wants you to come to her office so she can get you all set up. I'll tell you what to do and where to go when you get out."

She was so happy she got up and just hugged me so tight and held on to me, saying, "Thank you. Thank you. I don't know what else to say."

"Just say you'll be there on Monday? And get ready to start a new life."

"Rachael, you don't know how happy I am. I don't even care if I don't have a place to go to right now, but you can bet I will in a couple of weeks. But until I get a paycheck, I'll just stay in a hotel."

"You go, girl. That's what I'm talking about. Better yourself. Look to a brighter future because you don't have to stay down if you don't want to. Wait a minute. What do you mean you don't have a place to stay? I thought you had a place to stay with your friends."

"I do, but I really don't want to be there, but I called over there to see if they had any of my money, and they didn't. So they probably spent it on some weed or just gettin' high. If I didn't need a change of clothes, I wouldn't even go back over there. But I'm a survivor. Trust me, Ms. Brunson. And I'm not talking about getting into any more trouble. I don't know yet. But I already made up my mind that I was not going to stay there anymore even if you didn't find me a job. I'm through with that kind of life. Maybe I'll call my mother and see where she's coming from. Hopefully, she'll say come home."

She was so sure of herself at that moment all I could do was hug her and say, "Everything is going to be all right with you."

I said, "So just keep the faith. Well, girl, I have got to get back into the courtroom so that I can work on getting you out. So I'll see you in a little bit."

By the time I got back into the courtroom, I didn't see any strange faces that wasn't there when I went back to talk to Toya. So I thought maybe she's not going to show up after all.

So I took a seat; then a few minutes later, the bailiff said, "All rise. Court is now in session. The Honorable Judge Louis Phillips is presiding."

I thought, *Why do we have to stand? This is only a man, not God.*

For a long time, this has always puzzled me. But I stood up anyway but wondered what would happen if I didn't stand up. But I'll do whatever pleases the court so long as I win; I'll kiss the judge's grave if he wanted me to as long as I got my way. But I really don't give a damn.

Before I could finish my thoughts, someone was calling out my name. And that broke my thoughts. I looked up, and it was the prosecutor who was calling my name, saying, "Can I talk to you for a minute?"

"Sure." So I got up and walked over to where he was.

He asked me if my client was going to plead guilty.

"No," I said, "my client was defending herself, so what's guilty about that?"

He said, "Okay. I just thought that I would ask before our case goes before the judge."

I looked at him and thought, *So your client has not showed up yet nor have you heard from her. And if she doesn't show up, you want the judge to know that my client has agreed to a guilty plea and get a dismissal in your favor so that you can bring her back to court for the same bullshit, but I got your number. You should know better than that. I'm too smart to fall into that little trap.* Sometimes people try to take advantage of your kindness, but I'm not that nice anymore. Been there, done that. But no more. Ms. Goody Two-shoes is going for the throat of anybody that is trying to go up against her or her family. Including my new man.

There were three cases called before mine, and each time, I went to the back to tell Toya that it won't be long now.

At last our case was called. When the bailiff brought Toya from the back, she looked around to see if she saw her accuser, but she didn't. She mouthed, "I don't see her."

But we still had to go through the motions.

Finally, the judge asked the prosecutor where his client was.

He said, "Your Honor, I don't know. I've tried to call her but never reached her this morning."

He said that he did talk to her last night, and she said that she was coming to court this morning.

"Well, Mr. Prosecutor, you did let your client know what time to be here this morning, didn't you?"

"Yes, I did, Your Honor."

"Well, on that note, does the defense attorney have anything to say?"

"Yes, Your Honor, I do. I ask that all charges brought against my client be dismissed."

"Do you agree, Mr. Prosecutor?"

"I do agree, Your Honor, but would like to add with prejudice."

"Well, Mr. Prosecutor, we will drop all charges against the defense attorney's client and will not add prejudice because your client has had plenty of time to get here. We have had a number of cases before yours, and she still hasn't made it. So case dismissed."

"Ms. Baker, just a word of advice: stay out of trouble. This kind is really not worth it."

"I will, Your Honor, and thank you."

After that, I walked over and told Toya to have a seat on the outside of the jury box while I got the paperwork together.

She was so happy she said, "You mean that I can really just get ready to walk up out of here without him after me for something?"

She was pointing at the bailiff.

"Yes, you can. But, Ms. Baker, there's a little more paperwork that I have to get, and I want you to wait because I have that information for you."

I went back in the courtroom and got her release papers, and twenty minutes later, we were standing on the outside.

Toya said, "Ms. Brunson, I can't thank you enough."

She just ran up and hugged me so tight, and it seemed as though she didn't want to let go. She said, "I'm telling you that nobody—I mean, nobody—has ever cared one bit about me whether I breathed or not. No, wait. I'll take that back because my friends did care. They cared enough about me that they did not come to see me, they cared if I ate, they cared enough to ask me when I got out would I hustle up enough money to pay my share of the rent and buy a few groceries."

She had tears rolling down her eyes; then she said, "I love you, Ms. Brunson, and I'm going to prove it to you. Just watch and see. I have had plenty of time to sit and think about what direction I was headed in. And sitting in a jail cell was not what I had in mind. You got people telling you what you can and cannot do. You have to ask if you can have a glass of water. No, Ms. Brunson, that's not for me."

She kept saying, "People tell you what time to get up, what time to go to bed. No, no, that's not for me."

"So, Toya, where are you going to go?"

"Well, I'm not sure if I want to call my mother or call my cousin's house. We always looked out for one another. But don't worry, I'll be fine."

"Okay, you've got the information that I gave you, right?"

"You bet I got it. I'll see her first thing Monday morning. You bet. I'll sleep in the emergency room if I have to. But you can bet I'll be there in her office come Monday morning. I really mean that I'm changing my life from this day forward."

She gave me one last hug; then we walked off in different directions.

I turned and watched her walk away. Then she started to run a little.

It was two thirty. I walked back inside the courthouse to prepare for another case. When I got the paperwork together, I went back to my office. When I walked back into my office, I saw the flowers that Eugene had sent. I had meant to take them with me this morning but had sat them back down while talking to Janel. And I ran off without them. But that was all right because I thought about who sent them— Eugene. So I decided to leave him a message on his cell phone and thank him for the flowers.

Boy, he's trying hard to get some of me. But I'm holding out until this weekend—Saturday night. Then it's on.

I left a message on his cell phone voice mail. So I know he'll call when he gets the message.

So I went to work on another case, getting all the witnesses' names and addresses together for the prosecutor to question.

But I would talk to them first. Even though this was a court-appointed case, I believe that everyone that I defend should get the best defense from their lawyer. No matter who was footing the bill.

Looking over the paperwork, this case was going to be a challenge, but I was up for it.

A young man is accused of raping a lady but says that he didn't do it. He says that he was with friends. All the friends agree that they were all together when this happened.

We'll see. I'll start on this first thing Monday morning.

I'll start by talking to some of the witnesses. I'll be able to handle this with no problem. I looked at my watch; it was three thirty. Time to go. I began putting things together for the following Monday morning.

When the phone rang, I pressed the intercom and said, "Yes, Janel?"

"Mr. Michaels is on line 1."

"Thanks."

"Hi, sweetie. I got your message, and you are welcome. Anything to put a smile on your face. Look, sweetheart, I'm going to be tied up here for another two hours. I'm still in court. I just stepped out for a minute to catch you before you got to my place. But, baby, you can come by here. I'm still in court, but I'll try to time you and give you enough time to get here. Then I can come down and give you the keys to the house so that you can go ahead there, and I'll meet you later. Baby, I'm sorry I didn't even ask you what you were about to do. I just took for granted my own thoughts for you. So let me back up and ask you if you have time to come by here to pick up the keys and meet me later."

"Well, sweetheart, I was just about to head over to your house. And I'm glad that you caught me. So yes, I can come by there and pick up the keys."

"Okay good, then I'll see you in about ten minutes, okay?"

"Yes, sir, see you then. Hey, Eugene."

"Hmm."

"Are you all right?"

"Yeah, why did you ask that?"

"Because you sound kinda down, sort of dry."

"Baby, I'm fine. We'll talk. It's probably just the case that I'm working on."

"Okay then, I'm on my way."

And he just hung up the phone.

Something is bothering him, I can tell. Although we've only been seeing each other for what—a few weeks—I can still sense something is not right. But I'll find out.

So I grabbed the flowers up in my arms. This time, I was not going to sit them down and leave them. I also grabbed my briefcase and left.

I told Janel that I was gone for the day and, if she walked away from her desk or out of sight from my office, to make sure that my door was locked.

She said, "Are you sure that everything is okay?"

"Yeah, everything is fine. I have got to run."

I hurried out of the building to meet Eugene. When I pulled up in front of the building, Eugene was walking out, looking so down. When he got to the truck, he walked around to my window and tried to smile. But I could still tell that something just didn't feel right.

So I asked him again, "Baby, are you sure you're okay? Are you sorry now that you sent me the flowers or what?"

He just smiled and didn't say a word about the flowers.

Then he said, "Let me show you which key is which. I'm kinda in a hurry, we're cross-examining next."

He showed me which key was for which door and said "you got it," trying to sound cheerful.

"I got it," I said.

Then he leaned in and kissed me and then took a quick look over at the flowers. Then he said, "I'll see you in a few hours."

I just looked at him walking away. I watched him walk back into the building; once he got back inside, I drove off.

I headed to my apartment to get a change of clothes for the weekend and an outfit for church on Sunday.

When I got to my apartment, I wondered if I should take the flowers up with me or take them to Eugene's house to show him how much I appreciated him sending me the flowers at work.

I gathered up my things, put them in a suitcase, and left.

I got to Eugene's house in about ten minutes later.

When I got inside his house, I just kinda stood there in one spot and looked around in amazement, saying, "God is good."

I thought about how different my life was from the time I lost my Shawn up until now.

I have had some good times and some wild times in between. And now I'm headed for yet another change. Hopefully, this will last the rest of my life.

My life has changed so much that it's almost unbelievable.

But I keep telling myself that good things come to those who wait and that life goes on; everything must change.

There's always a saying, but this time, it looks like all the above are true.

I think, regardless of how hard I've tried to keep from falling in love with Eugene, I'm falling fast. But I can't tell him just yet.

I know that I want to be with him all the time. But I try not to show it too much because sometimes, when you show a person just how much you care, they have a tendency to take you for granted or take advantage of you.

And I know that it happens on both sides.

That's why, for myself, I just want to take my time to make sure that he loves me.

I'll show him, but I won't say a word until I'm really ready.

I walked into the kitchen and looked in the fridge to see what was available to cook for him when he got home.

I had an hour and a half before Eugene would be home. I thought I would run and take a shower, then make a salad, put some steaks on the grill, and bake some potatoes.

Yeah, that's what I'll do. Then he can shower and just relax when he gets here. But I have got to find out what is bothering him. Oh, my flowers. I ran back outside and got the flowers out of the truck, came back in, and put the flowers in a vase; they smelled so good, so fresh.

I sat them on the kitchen counter and then went and took my shower.

The water felt great. I really didn't want to get out, but I knew that I had to get dinner started. So I hurried up with my shower, got out, and rubbed on some seductive lotion. I put on a bra, some panties, and a bathrobe.

I wrapped a towel around my head until I could get the grill going.

The steaks were already thawed, so I washed and seasoned them. I sat them to the side until I finished with the potatoes and salad.

I put the potatoes in some foil, then put them on the grill. This was one time that I was glad that he had a gas grill.

Because by the time I would have finished with a regular grill, Eugene would be home. Anyway, I went back in and started on the salad; I washed the lettuces and chopped tomatoes and bell pepper and everything else that I was going to use in the salad.

I got all that together, then went back outside to check on the fire. It was okay. When I walked back inside, Eugene was walking toward the back door.

He said, "Hey, baby."

"Hi, sweetie." He walked up, slipped his arm inside my robe, and wrapped his arm around my waist and said, "I love you, Rachael."

He looked so serious and had a funny look at the same time. But when he said that, all I could say was "Where did that come from?"

"It came from deep down inside my heart."

"Well, I love you too. Yes, I do. At first, I thought that you were going to be just… I don't know."

He said, "A one-night stand, huh?"

"Well, not really a one-night stand, but maybe a month or so give or take?"

"What? Then you thought that I would be gone."

"Well, yeah, because I know that some men will do and say a lot just to have sex with someone and then will find a way to say that I'm not really wanting a commitment. So I just thought that we'd be together for a while, then you would come up with some kind of excuse not to see each other again. But today, when I went to my place to get my things for the weekend to spend with you, I really thought about how much I wanted to be with you."

"Are you sure that it's just me that you want to be with and not your husband?"

When he said that, I backed away from him and looked him in the eyes and said, "He's my husband in name only, and in a few months, he won't even be that. He'll be my ex-husband, and anyway, why would you say something like that? You know, you really just hurt my feelings after I just told you that I love you. When I had told you that I wasn't going to say that unless I was sure, and I'm sure. But now you want to know if I love you and someone else? Well, I'll tell you…" Tears had begun to run down my cheeks as I said, "No, I don't just love you. I love you and me together. And that there's no one else. I just can't see why you would say something like that."

"I said it because I love you so much so soon, and I don't want my heart broken. And I didn't send you any flowers, and I thought that someone was trying to come back into your life. Rachael, I don't mean to make you upset, but I needed to know." He wiped the tears away with his shirt and said, "I'm sorry, baby. I'm sorry. I won't ever say anything like that again. Please forgive me."

I looked at him and said, "You are forgiven. But if you didn't send the flowers, then who did? Because there was no card. Then I thought is that why you were acting so funny and sounding so dry."

I had stepped up in his face and put his arms back around my waist.

"Wait a minute. Do you think that Veronica would do something like that? You know, I wouldn't put it past her not to do something like this."

"She almost got me upset, thinking that someone was trying to take my baby away from me already. I know that I have not been with you physically, but mentally I've been right there with you."

"I love you, Mr. Michaels, and nnnnooooooo one else. So it was the flowers that had you so messed up. That's what was bothering you. Baby, I'm sorry, but I thought they came from you. I wish you would have said something because you could have saved both of us some gray hairs. So, baby, the next time something happens—good or bad—please let's talk about it. You know, even before you asked me to be your lady, I had never seen you look so sad, and I really never want to see that again."

Before he could say anything, I grabbed his hand and pulled him toward the backyard to check on the steaks.

Then I said, "If we're going to make it, then we can't hold anything back from one another, no matter how big or how small. I can't stress that enough, baby, I love you. I didn't want to let you know because I wasn't sure that you really cared for me. But I can see that you do, so I felt comfortable telling you that I love you too."

We hugged and kissed. Then I said, "That's enough of that."

Eugene turned over the steaks. I said, "I got this. You go get your shower and hurry up. They'll be ready in a minute."

He started walking away, then turned back, and said, "I just didn't want to spoil your excitement about the flowers. You had so much joy in your voice that I didn't want to spoil it for you. I really thought that your husband was trying to get you back. I never thought about that sick girl Veronica."

I walked over to him and said, "This conversation is over, no more. Now go shower."

"Do you know how much better I feel? But if you ever feel like you want to see someone else, please let me know before you do."

"I will, and I want the same commitment from you. Because I know that you are not the little angel that you propose to be."

Eugene just smiled, then said, "Okay, I've had a few one-nighters a couple of times, but that was so far in my past. But I promise, from this day forward, no more."

He picked me up. Then we laughed.

I said, "Put me down." And he did, but not before he put his hands around my butt.

I could feel the bulge in his pants as he slid me down from holding me up in the air.

He said, "I'm about to go take a shower for real this time while you finish cooking. I love you, Rachael."

"And I love you too. Now hurry up. While I go out there and check on the steak and potatoes."

After flipping the steaks over, I went back into the house to work on the salad again. When the phone rang, I started to answer it but then decided not to.

I thought I'll just listen and see who it is that's calling him.

The machine kicked on, and I heard Eugene's voice saying that he could not come to the phone, so please leave a message, and he would return the call as soon as he had a chance to.

Then the voice said, "Hey there, pick up the phone." It was a female voice. Then it said, "Hey, love of my life, where are you?"

My heart went flip-flop.

Then the voice said, "Hey, Dad, where are you? Are you with my mom-to-be? I can't wait to meet her tomorrow. I love you, Dad, and I know if you care anything about her, then I know that she's going to be all right. Oh well, I'll see you tomorrow." Then she hung up the phone.

Boy, we women jump to conclusions pretty fast.

Because my first thoughts were he's been lying to me, and he does have someone else that he has been seeing. But then, even after listening to the message, I thought, why would he want me to move in with him if he was seeing someone else? So I had to get myself in check. And remember what I told Lisa and take my own advice that men do change. So I just kept on making our salad.

I think that I will make us a drink. "Hmm, that sounds like a winner. Let's see, strawberry daiquiri, sloe gin fizz, Long Island iced tea, or just a glass of wine? What shall I make?"

I decided on the sloe gin fizz. I pulled out the blender, walked over to the well-stocked bar, got everything that I needed, went back to the kitchen, and put everything that I was going to use on the counter.

Then I went back outside to check on the food. Since it was a gas grill, I had it on low heat so it could cook slowly. That way, it would make the steaks very tender. Everything was fine. So I went back in the kitchen and started the drinks.

Eugene came into the kitchen wearing shorts and a T-shirt, smelling like a million dollars.

"Hey, baby," he said. "It smells good in here."

"Thanks, I'm making—no, I'm not going to tell you just yet. I want you to guess the taste."

"Okay, I can do that."

"Oh, one of your daughters called."

"Which one?"

"She didn't leave her name."

"Why didn't you ask her name?"

"Because I didn't pick up the phone when it rang. I let your machine pick it up. But if it will help, she called you the love of her life. Maybe that will help. So do you know which one it was?"

"Yep, that was Britini."

"That little girl really loves her dad. What are the other girls' names?"

"Cerica, Candics, Chantell, and Eugene Candics III is the one who lives with her mother. She'll let her call me occasionally, otherwise I call her once or twice a week because I don't want her to forget her dad."

"I'm pretty sure that she won't forget her dad."

He picked up his drink.

And I said, "Do you know what it is that you are drinking?"

"Girl, yes, I do. It's a Long Island iced tea."

I said, "Yeah right."

Then he started to laugh and said, "Girl, I know it's gin, so what happened that you want gin? Is it because you know what is said about gin?"

"No, I don't know what is said about gin, so why don't you tell me just what is said about gin."

"Well, now since you have never heard what is said about drinking gin, let me tell you. It is said that gin, when it enters the bloodstream, makes the person who made it sexually aggressive."

"Oh, is that right?"

"That's what I heard on the news."

"Well, that must have been your very own private station. Because I have never seen or heard of it on the news stations that I watched, so what do you say to that?"

"I say wait until later, and I'll show you the channel that I'm talking about."

"Can't wait."

We laughed as I walked back outside. "I know that this food is ready now."

"Where do you want to eat?"

"Out here is fine."

"Okay, I'll bring out some plates and silverware. Are you sure you won't get cold? Because I know that you are wearing little to nothing under that robe."

"Well, guess again."

"Okay, if you are wearing more than just your panties and bra, then you can bypass watching my TV station. But if you are wearing that or less, then you are gonna have to watch my news station. What do you say to that?"

"I said, "Okay, but if you lose, then what do I win?"

"Whatever you want."
"And just what might that be?"
"I'm not sure yet."
"Okay, open that robe and let's see."

"Okay, close your eyes first."

"Oh no, so that you can get a chance to run and put something else on? No way. Now open."

"All right, here goes." I opened my robe and said, "I win. You see, I'm wearing a bra, panties, and a T-shirt. So you see, I win."

"Okay, you got me that time. Your wish is my command."

"I'll think of something later. Let's eat."

We ate outside; we laughed and talked, listening to the music that was playing softly. We really enjoyed ourselves until it got dark outside.

Then he said, "Let's go back inside, and I'll relight the fire."

We picked up all the dishes, took them inside, and put them in the dishwasher.

Eugene said, "Is there any more of your gin drink left? You mixed them so well, and dinner was very good too."

"Why thank you."

Then I went to go see if there was anything left in the blender.

I love putting things in the blender.

Eugene went and started the fire. I hollered, "I'm going to have to make another batch because this one is all gone."

I made another mixture, poured us a glassful, then took them into the den.

I sat on the floor next to the big fireplace. Eugene sat across from me; we both started talking at the same time.

He said, "Okay, you go first."

"I just wanted to say that every time we're together, I have a wonderful time with you. Now that was what I was going to say. Now it's your turn."

"Hey, don't call me a copycat, but I was going to say basically the same thing. Then I was going to add how much I love you. But you might think that I'm just trying to sway you into moving in with me." Then he smiled and said, "I love you, Rachael."

Then he slid over to me, took my face in his hands, and began kissing me all over my face.

"Hmm," I began to moan as he moved down to my neck. His hands began to take the belt a loose on my robe. I could feel his bare hands touch my skin. He reached behind me and took my bra a loose with one hand. Then he started kissing my chest.

I kissed his head and ran my hands up under his T-shirt, rubbing his back that felt so smooth.

He started playing with my nipples, one, then the other, saying we're not trying to let them get jealous of each other—one getting too much attention, then the other—as he slowly laid me flat on the floor. And he started rubbing my stomach and slowly moved his hand down until he reached my panties. When he reached the top, he just began rubbing between my legs.

Then he rubbed from the top of my panties to the bottom, up and down—never touching the inside, just playing on the outside.

As he was kissing my breast, I was about to faint with want. But he just kept on rubbing. I had gotten so wet.

I reached for his head and pulled it up to my face and kissed him very passionately on his lips, cheeks, eyes, and all over his upper body where I could reach in the position that I was in.

He whispered, "I want you, Rachael."

I threw my legs around his waist and slowly let him know that I wanted him too.

We started kissing again. Then he began to slid his hands inside my panties and let his hand move up and down my kitty; he let a finger slide inside of me. Eugene moaned.

But he just continued to play.

Somehow I managed to get him under me; then I was on top of him. Dammmmn, he was hard as a rock. He still had his T-shirt and underwear on. So I reached between his legs and took hold of his penis. I let my hand run along the length, but it seemed like I couldn't get to the end. It was long and thick.

Shit, I thought, *I'm going to have trouble with this, but it's going to be fun. And I've got friends who are nurses, just in case I hurt myself, so watch out. But I think that after a month or so, I'll be all right.* I rolled on him as if we were making out. I didn't want to give in just yet, so I began to kiss his face, and I licked his lips.

He said, "Oooh, baby, I want you. I want to taste you. I want to feel the inside of you. Ooooh, baby." He kept on moaning and whispering.

And I continued to play until he couldn't take much more.

But I whispered not yet; then I lowered my head and started sucking on his nipples slowly, letting my tongue run across his chest. His hands rubbed my back up and down. As I kissed his stomach, his hands played with my hair as he moaned, "Yes, baby."

I kissed my way down to the top of his boxers then back up to his stomach, his nipples, and again to his lips, licking all around his mouth. He was like a brick.

I thought I could handle this, but if I can't, then I'll learn because there was no way that I was ever going to let go of this man.

He turned me over, putting me back on the floor, as he began to let the tip of his tongue circle my stomach. As he lowered his kisses, the phone rang.

But he didn't stop until he heard the voice on the other end of the phone, saying, "Daddy, Daddy, are you there? I love you."

"Dammmn," he said as he got up to answer the phone. "Dammn," he said again.

When he stood up, he was as straight as a ruler but much, much thicker.

Oh my goodness, I thought as he was standing there.

He picked up the phone and said, "Hi, baby, Daddy was a little tied up, but I could hear your voice. How are you?" I heard him ask her. I got up and walked toward the bathroom. He reached out and grabbed my robe and pulled me back between his legs.

I saw that he had gone down some, but not much. He felt good, but I was glad that the phone rang and stopped us because I wanted to meet his mother and not have to lie to her in case she asked me if I fooled around with her baby yet.

This way, I could honestly say, "No, ma'am, not yet."

I just want to have clear conscience about him and I.

Eugene kissed me on the neck while I was standing between his legs and put me right back to where we had just left off.

He was still talking on the phone with his daughter as I pulled away from him and whispered to him that I was going to the bathroom.

He nodded okay and kept talking to his daughter on the phone.

I went on into the bathroom and turned on the shower.

While I was letting the water warm up, I went into the room that I was going to sleep in and got my lotion, which I will put on after I got out of the shower. I went back into the bathroom and started taking off my T-shirt and bra. Just as I was about to take off my panties and step into the shower, Eugene knocked on the door.

I quickly pulled my panties back up and opened the door.

He said, "I'm sorry about that, baby."

"Hey, you don't have to be sorry about that. You were talking on the phone to your baby. Sweetheart, we've got plenty of time to spend together," I said.

"Baby, I'm glad that you understand." Then he kissed me, but I stopped him.

He said, "What's wrong?"

"Nothing's wrong, nothing at all."

I leaned over, turned off the water in the shower, then took Eugene by the hand and led him into the room where I was going to sleep. I sat him down on the bed and said, "Look, there is nothing wrong. But there might have been if it was anybody else on the phone, and you stopped. But you never know what's going on when a child calls. But I was glad that the phone did ring. Because I wanted to meet your mother with a clear conscience, just in case she might ask me if we slept together yet. Maybe she won't ask, but just in case she does, I can honestly say, 'No, we have not had sex together yet.'"

"Why in the world would she ask that kind of question?"

"We parents—well, we mothers—sometimes ask our sons and daughters questions like that so that we can tell them to be careful if you don't want any babies and because we can. But do you remember earlier when you said your wish is my command. Well, I wish that we hold off on sex."

"Hold off," he said even before I could finish saying what I was saying.

"Wait, let me finish."

"Okay, hold off until when?"

"Next week."

"I know you're kidding."

"Why do I have to be kidding? So you're saying you're calling off the wish?"

"No, you can have it your way if that's what you want. I can wait. I can wait a month if that's what you want."

"Okay good."

He just shook his head and said okay as he got off the bed.

I pushed him back on the bed and said, "I was only kidding when I said a week because I want you just as bad. But this part is for real. I want to wait until after I meet your mother at least. Baby, it's just one more night."

"Okay." Then he kissed my nipple. I had forgotten that I was about to get in the shower and didn't have on any clothes except my panties.

"But can you do me a favor?"

"What's that?"

"Will you sleep with me?"

I looked at him, and he laughed and said, "I mean, will you sleep in the same bed with me?"

"Oh, I was about to say 'Didn't we agree to wait one more night?' But since you put it like that, let me think about it."

"Remember, we're just going to sleep in the same bed. I'm not going to touch you here." He touched between my legs. "Nor will I do this." He kissed my stomach.

I hit him and said, "Quit playing."

"Hey, I won't do any of that unless you lose control, then I'll just be defending myself."

"Funny but I'll take you up on that offer just to prove to you that I do have control."

"Okay good, then I'll see you when you get out of the shower."

"Hey, would you like to join me?"

"Oh no, you didn't go there? But don't worry because I'll join you tomorrow after the day is over. Or after you meet my parents, we can slip off and go have a quick shower. Huh, now what do you say to that?"

"Oh okay, tomorrow it is." I went and turned the shower back on.

Then I thought, *What have I done? I agreed to sleep in the same bed with him. What if that man kisses me one time. I know I'm going to lose all control. Okay, wait. I'm strong and horny all at the same time.*

But I can play his game better than he think.

When I got out of the shower, I put on some sexy-smelling lotion and my bathrobe. I thought, *I'll lie in the bed naked and see just how strong he can be.*

But I went and put a teddy on. This will make him sweat with his smart ass (sleep with me). Okay, here I come.

He was already in bed. He said, "Hey, you want to watch a movie?"

"Sure, pick one out."

"Okay, but before we get too comfortable, let's say our prayers."

So we held hands on the bed and said our prayers and thanked God for bringing us together. When we finished saying our prayers, I got up and went into the other bedroom that I was going to sleep in and cut the light off. Then I went back into the room with Eugene and got in bed.

Eugene had a movie on already, so I asked him what movie was he watching.

"*Heat*," he said.

"*Heat*." Then we both laughed. "But for real, this is a pretty good movie. You'll like it."

"Is it an adult movie?"

"Girl, if you don't stop… No, it's not an adult movie, but if you like, we can order one off cable."

"No thanks." I pulled the covers up and saw that Eugene didn't have a stitch on. He was butt naked. I tried not to look shocked.

But I guess it didn't work because he said, "This is how I sleep, in the buff."

"So do I, but I thought it would be nice to put on a little something."

"What? You can't handle lying next to me with nothing on? You might as well be naked. Look at what you're wearing. You're just trying to tease me, but I can handle myself."

"Me too." So he started the movie.

We both just lay there in silence for a few minutes before we both broke out laughing.

He grabbed me by the waist and pulled me close to him and said, "Don't worry, I'm not going to try anything. I just want to feel you next to me."

So I lay in his arms as he explained the movie to me.

He started to tell me about the movie, then stopped, and said, "Look, I don't want to tell you the whole movie because then you won't want to watch it with me. But I will say that you are going to like this movie." Then he laughed a little.

I could see that he had begun to rise a little, so I pulled away and turned on my side; he got right behind me. I could feel him, so I moved again. He said, "What's wrong?"

I said, "You know exactly what's wrong."

"Well, you shouldn't be lying here smelling so good. You did that on purpose so you could tease me, but I'm all right. You looking all sexy, you don't play fair."

"What?" I pulled the covers up and said, "Now look at you and say again, 'You don't play fair.'"

"Okay, can we do this since it's sticking out? Can I rest it between your legs? I won't try anything. Just let it rest right there, then it would be all right."

"Oh, you think that you are so slick, don't you?"

"No, it's just I don't know what else to do with it. But when it realizes that it's not going any further, then it'll go down. If you don't move."

"You are so funny. You think that you can lay it between my legs, and you won't go any further."

"I promise."

"Okay, if you can be that strong, then so can I."

So I raised my leg and let him put it between my legs. Dammmn.

"What?" he said.

"Nothing."

I could hear him smirk. He felt so warm and huge. *Dammn*, I thought, *I'm not going to last. Okay, let me get deep into the movie. I'll show him*. But he was rocking; I said, "Stop that."

"Stop what? It's doing that on its own."

I wanted to touch the head since it was sticking out from between my legs. I just wanted to wet my finger and touch the tip with his smart ass, but I didn't.

I can handle this. I thought it's going to be rough. But fun.

I tried to get him to tell me more about the movie to take the tension off what we were doing and not doing.

The more I talked to him about nothing, the more I could feel him going down. So I kept talking, and next thing I knew, he was snoring and still a little stiff. I started to touch it but thought better, so I just lay there and listened to my man sleep; then I drifted off to sleep myself.

It seemed like it had been hours, but it was only minutes before the movie was over, and the TV was making noises. So I reached for the remote, turned off the TV, and went back to sleep. Eugene was still snoring.

I felt so comfortable being with him, but before I knew it, Eugene was up and cooking breakfast.

Dang, that was fast. I just closed my eyes; now it was already time to get up.

Oh well, it's another day. So I got up and headed for the bathroom that was in Eugene's room.

I opened up a cabinet to see what he kept in it. It was stocked with everything, so I went across the hall to where my things were to get my toothbrush. While I was in the spare bedroom, I heard Eugene holler.

"Hey, it's about time you got out of bed."

I hollered back, "I'll be there in a minute." So I brushed my teeth, washed my face and body, then went into the kitchen.

Eugene had a glass of orange juice sitting on the counter for me.

"Good morning, sleepyhead."

"Good morning."

"How did you sleep?"

"Oh, very well, thanks. And how about yourself?"

"Couldn't sleep a wink."

"Oh really? Then I'll tell you someone who looks like you crawled in bed with us and was snoring his head off. He got in the bed without me feeling any movement in the bed. To tell you the truth, I didn't even feel you slid from between my legs. So can you please tell me who it was that was in bed with us? Whose arms was I lying in, in your bed?"

"Okay, okay, it was my twin."

"Well, tell him tonight be at the same place, same time."

He laughed and said okay as he came around the counter and

picked me up and sat me on top of the counter, stood between my legs, and said, "Don't worry, he'll be there with bells on."

He kissed me on the forehead and said, "I've got breakfast just about done."

He kissed me again, then lifted me up off the counter, and slid me very close to his body. I could feel the rise he had. But neither he nor I said anything.

He picked me up again and rubbed me up against his body as he put me back down.

This time, I said, "Quit playing."

"What? I'm just getting in a little weight lifting. What's wrong with that?"

"Nothing. Nothing at all."

"All right, let's eat." He had made our plates.

I took off my bathrobe; I was wearing my teddy, a very sleek one.

"Oh, you don't play fair."

"Hmm, and you do?"

"Okay, let's just eat."

"What you say, after we eat, we make out a list and go to the grocery store and pick up a few things for the gathering later this afternoon?"

"Can't we relax a little? After all, it's 8:00 a.m. in the morning."

"You're right. I'm just rushing the day to be over with so that you and I can really relax."

When we finished eating and putting away the dishes, I went and got on the sofa.

Eugene came in, got on his knees in front of me, and said, "Will you marry me?"

"Where did that come from?"

"It came from my heart. So will you marry me right now?"

"You're funny."

"I'm serious, and I know it's early in our relationship. But if we're going to be together, we might as well be together the right way."

"Eugene, why the hell not? As soon as I'm divorced, it's you and me. And this time, it'll be to death us do part."

"Are you for real?"

"Yes, I am. I love you, Mr. Michaels."

"And I love you, Mrs. Michaels. That sounds good." Then he laid his head on my lap.

I got hot instantly.

"Rachael."

"Yes?"

He raised his head. "Can I just touch you?"

"No, you cannot."

"Well, can I do this?" He pulled the strap that was holding my left tit down and kissed it oh so softly.

I couldn't say a word. I just laid my head back against the pillow.

Eugene said, "Just a little foreplay, nothing more."

He played from one tit to the other. Then he put his hand on my thigh and slowly moved it between my legs, parting them just a little, as he planted little kisses on my thigh. Then he touched my kitty as if he really didn't mean to.

I just moaned. He let his hand just sit there while I became wet as I could be.

Eugene came back up and was kissing my breast, then lowered his kisses until he got to my belly button; then he said, "Can I?"

"Eugene, please."

And then the old mighty phone rang.

He just dropped his head and waited to see who it was when the machine picked it up.

In the meantime, while his head was still on my lap, he kissed my kitty. I still had my panties on.

Then I said, "That's just another sign telling us to wait until dark."

We could hear the voice on the machine. This time, it was his mother. "Hey, baby, what are you doing?" He jumped up and grabbed the phone.

"Hey, Ma, how are you this morning?"

While he talked on the phone, it was my turn to play with him.

I kissed his chest, one nipple then the other.

I headed south on him. I looked up, and Eugene had a look on his face like payback.

I smiled and kept on heading south until I was right where I wanted to be. I looked at Eugene and whispered, "Can I?"

But I knew that I could because he was poking way out of his shorts. But I just wet my finger and touched the huge head sticking out.

I stood, smiled, and walked away.

He talked to his mother a little while longer, then got off the phone, and came back into the bedroom where I had gotten back in the bed and said, "You know, you are not right."

"What? Just a little foreplay, nothing more."

He grabbed my foot and started to tickle it; we were both laughing. When he stopped tickling me, he said, "My mother wants to know what she should bring." As he climbed in the bed, he added, "I told her to just bring Dad. She said, 'Are you sure, baby?' I said, 'Yes, Mother. I'm sure.' Then she said, 'I can't wait to meet Rachael, son.' I told her, 'You just don't know how bad I want you to meet her too.' Then she said, 'All right, I'll see you in a little while.' Girl, as soon as the two of you meet, I'm going to take you upstairs and make sweet love to you while we got a houseful of people. I want you just as bad. We have got just a few hours to go, then there's no stopping us after that. So just chill, let's watch the movie that we both fell asleep on."

"Hey, I tried to stay awake, but since Junior wasn't getting any action, he wanted us both to go to sleep, and we did. But I did try to keep my eyes open for a minute. Anyway, now that we are both awake, maybe we can watch it and try to stay awake. We'll start it from the beginning."

So we sat up with the bed pillows and watched the movie without any touching. We were about an hour into the movie when the doorbell rang.

"Who could that be this early in the morning?"

"Well, we know that it's not for me."

He got up, sat on the side of the bed for a minute, then got up, and went to see who it was at the door.

I said, "Do you want me to stop the movie while you see who it is at the door?"

"Yeah, do that." Then he disappeared out of the doorway.

But before he got all the way to the door, he looked out of the side window to see who it was. It was his parents. He said with a soft but loud whisper, "It's my parents."

I jumped up and ran into the other room and put on a jogging suit as fast as I could.

He called out my name and said, "Rachael, my parents are here."

I came out of the room looking and feeling stupid for no reason. But they didn't say anything for a minute.

But I know that they will probably say something to Eugene later.

I walked into the living room where they all were sitting. Eugene and his dad stood up.

Eugene said, "Rachael, these are my parents, Eugene Sr. and Rita Michaels. Mom, Dad, this is my Rachael."

"Hey, Rachael, how are you?" Extending her hand, Mrs. Michaels said, "We couldn't wait any longer to meet you. I told Eugene let's go now. What difference does a few hours make? We'll stop by, say hi, then we can leave. I mean, we are already in the area. So let's go and catch them fooling around. And it looks like we did just that." Then she laughed and said, "Girl, don't pay me any attention, were you fooling around?" His mother asked, looking at me.

"No, ma'am. We were not."

She got up, grabbed me by the hand, and walked me outside. When we were outside, she said, "I know you were doing something because he couldn't talk straight, uh-huh, when he was on the phone talking to me. That's when I knew that you were over here. But it's all right because he really likes you. A mother can tell. So are you sleeping with him, or are you making him wait?"

"Well, Mrs. Michaels, I'm making him wait."

"Good for you. Now how long are you gonna make him wait?"

"Well, now the waiting is over. Now it'll be when you guys leave." We started laughing.

She said, "I like you, and that's for real. Not because you let me ask you personal questions without saying none of your business. But because I can see that you are a very decent person. And my son is crazy about you. I couldn't wait for him to find himself someone that he could really be happy with, and now he has found you. Thank you, Rachael." And she hugged me.

"I think that the two of you deserve each other after all that the two of you have been through. I hope that you all will be very happy. I really do." We hugged again.

Then she said, "I'll let you get back to what you were doing. Rachael, you didn't mind me asking you if you had slept with him or not, did you?"

"No, I didn't. As a matter of fact, you were the reason that I didn't sleep with him as hard as he tried. I had told him that if you asked me that question, I wanted to be able to tell you the truth. And not avoid the question. But now that the hard part is over, if you don't mind me saying so, it's on now." We laughed, and she said, "You go, girl."

We walked back into the living room where Eugene and his father were.

Eugene looked like a younger version of his mother and father combined. They were a handsome couple.

After we sat around and talked a little bit more, his mother said, "Well, we'll be going now." She grabbed young Eugene by the hand as we walked toward the door. His father said, "Well, it was nice seeing you, Ms. Rachael." He hugged me and said, "We'll see you later this afternoon, okay?"

I said okay as they went to their car.

"Well now," Eugene said as he waved bye, "the hard part is over. What do you think about my parents?"

"Oh, your mom and I got along great."

"I could tell. Seems like the two of you were having your own little party out there."

"Hey, actually we did. I think she likes me."

"I think they both do from talking with my dad. He said that my mother almost busted open when she figured out you were over here. She just had to come right away and meet you before the others got here. He said that she told my two brothers and my two sisters that I was getting married again. So I won't be surprised if they show up. This is going to be fun. Do you mind if I invite my sisters and brothers over personally so that they won't be complaining about why I didn't invite them when they hear about it from mother?"

"Why not? We'll all be together sooner or later anyway. The more the merrier. I'll call my sisters and brothers too."

"Why not?" He picked me up and said, "We've got to get our list together for the store. It's already eleven. Let's get going."

"Well, put me down." And he did his usual way, sliding me down as close to him as he possibly could. I could feel his erection.

"Come on, Eugene, not now."

"Hey, you said after you meet my mother, and you just did. So now what do you have to say? I won't take no for answer."

He put his hands on my face and kissed me hungrily. Dammmn.

He then put one of his hands down inside my panties. First, he just rubbed my kitty back and forth. Then he let one of his fingers slide inside. I moaned as I reached for his erection, rubbing it through his pants.

We lay down right there in the living room, taking off our clothes. He kissed me, then went down, and tongued my breast.

I held his penis in my hand and rubbed it up and down. But I couldn't get a good hold of it because he was so big, and I needed two hands.

Then Eugene said, "That's right, baby, play with your big daddy. It's all yours."

I was holding it as best I could while trying to rub it against my kitty.

We were both moaning. He reached between us and started guiding it into me. "Ooooh… Oooooh…" He then slowed down and started to put the tip in, then pulled it out again and again until we both couldn't take it anymore.

He slowly entered me, giving me as much as I could take at a time. I screamed softly, and he said, "I'm sorry, baby, do you want me to stop?"

"No," I said, so Eugene moved in little slow circles—in and out, up and down. He tried to get as much in me as he could without hurting me. But I couldn't take it; I had to push him back a little.

We were still moving and kissing each other. I was digging my fingers in his back.

I was trying not to scratch his back up, but I think that I did put some marks on his back because I didn't have anything else to grab on to.

I tried to open up a little more by putting my legs higher around his waist. But he got harder and harder. That shit was hurting like crazy. Then he started saying, "Oooooh, shit, baby, oh, baby, you feel so good, baby." He whispered in my ear, "Give me a minute, and we can do this again."

"I would love to, but we have got company coming."

"Oh damn, you're right, but I don't feel like moving. At least for another two hours."

"Sorry, baby, but we got things to do. But after that, it'll be my turn on top."

"Oooooh, girl, you bet."

"Now as much as I would love to lay here and play with you, I can't. We've got to get going."

We got up and jumped in the shower together. "Well, I guess we're official now," I said.

He said, "I thought we were all along."

"We were, but it's really a done deal now."

"Well, all right then, you and me then."

We bathed each other.

We got out and dried each other off. We kissed; then he started to rise.

I grabbed him and said, "Baby, not now. Or we'll have people at the door while we lay naked in the dining room or wherever the mood hits us. So stop."

"How about one little quickie for the road? You see, I'm up for it."

"All right, one quickie." So I put my leg up on the tub as he entered me. He was kissing my back and squeezing my breast. Then he played with my kitty. Dammmn, it felt good. We were acting like this was our first time. After he would play with my kitty, he would grab my behind so that he could try to get himself in me a little deeper to get a better fit. He was so good it was almost like eating ice cream on a Sunday.

He was good.

I was holding on to the wall while we were having big fun. Then we both came. Then I said, "Please don't ever stop that spur-of-the-moment session."

"Don't worry, I won't. Just as long as you let me, I'm going to keep at you. When and wherever I can."

We held on to each other for a few minutes; then I said, "Let's get out of here right now."

"You're right." So we got back into the shower and washed again. This time, there was no horseplaying around. We washed, dried ourselves, dressed, and then left.

We didn't have time to make a list; he just said if we forget anything, then he'll run back to the store and pick it up.

When we got to the store, we started picking up everything; the cart was full before we knew it. We had ribs, steaks, shrimp, shish kebabs; we had all kinds of things in the cart. He said, "Baby, is there anything else that you want?"

I said, "Just you." Then I leaned over and kissed him. "Outside of that, there's nothing else that I want."

I was reaching in my purse to get my credit card out when Eugene said, "Hey, baby, will you go over there and get a bag of those chips?"

"Sure, what kind?" When I turned to get the chips, I asked again, looking over my shoulder to ask what kind again; and I saw that he had pulled out his card to pay for everything.

"Funny," I said; then I looked over to the next counter, and lo and behold, there stood Veronica, standing at the register next to us. She didn't say anything and neither did I.

We had everything, and I thought I saw someone with some paper plates, so I said, "Oh, honey, we forgot the plates, cups and napkins, forks and spoons. I'll go and get them while you put the groceries in the car."

"I'll just wait for you right here."

Before I could get away, Veronica said, "Are you guys having a party?"

"Yes, we are. As a matter of fact, we have invited guests over to make wedding plans."

She didn't say another word. She just looked like she could shoot bullets at me if she could. Talk about if looks could kill, I would surely be a goner.

While I was standing there, talking to Veronica, Eugene slipped past me and went and got the rest of the things we needed. I looked up, and he was walking up with an armful of stuff.

I helped him put the paper goods on the counter while the cashier rang them up.

Veronica looked at Eugene as she walked past him and didn't open her mouth to say a word to Eugene. She just threw her head up in the air and kept stepping.

I turned to look at Eugene who was looking very puzzled because Veronica just rolled her eyes.

I said, "Honey, she just asked me if we were having a party, and I said as a matter of fact, we are. It's a wedding-planning party. She just stood there with her mouth wide-open, not saying another word."

"That's what you said?"

"Sure did."

"Well, I'm surprised that you said that to her."

"Well, she asked. But I didn't tell her who the party was for."

"Maybe she figured it was for us. And that's why she stared at me so hard."

"Maybe so, but I can tell you that I know why she is having a hard time shaking you."

"Why is that?"

I whispered, "It's all of you, and the sex too."

He just blushed and said, "You know, I think the same about you and can hardly wait until we get home."

"Oh no, we've got company coming, and we at least have to have something cooked."

"Well, we'll throw hot dogs on the grill for starters. And to prove to you just how good you are, if it wasn't against the law, we could go at it right here. Because I want you just that bad. I can't get enough of you." Then he reached behind me and ran his hand across my butt.

"You better stop, or I'll do you right back."

We laughed, and the girl ringing up our groceries laughed right along with us.

"Girl, there ain't nothing wrong with a little affection and playfulness out in public with your man. Because my man and I are the same way. So you all enjoy yourselves," she said as she continue to ring up the groceries.

When we got back to the house, we were putting up the groceries when all of a sudden, Eugene walked up behind me, pressing himself up against me. I could feel that he was half erect and just rubbing himself up on me and playing with my breast.

"Dammmn, baby, I know that I said don't stop the spur-of-the-moment quickies. But, baby, I am so sore right now. You are going to have to let me get used to you so that whenever you or I are ready to go, there won't be a problem."

"Well, how will you get used to it if you won't let me?"

"Funny."

"I know. Let me play with it for you."

"But, baby, we have got to hurry up."

So I turned around, took out his weapon, got on my knees, and played with the head. He started saying, "Oooh, baby, I like the way you play with it."

But while playing with him, I got all heated up again. So a few minutes later, I told him that I needed him inside of me right then. "But, baby, be gentle."

"I will."

So I got up, and Eugene rubbed between my legs with my pants on; then he took off my pants and my panties. He started rubbing that kitty cat, and I started purring. I was so moist; then he guided himself into me oh so slow.

"Oh, my baby."

"Baby, I love this."

He licked the back of my neck, then played with my kitty as he moved in and out real slow. He was kissing my ears, playing with the kitty, and saying I love you. Then he started grabbing me tighter and tighter, and I knew that he was about to cum.

"Ooooooh, baby... Ooooooh, baby." And then he came. We actually came together.

We just leaned over the chair for a few minutes to get a grip of ourselves.

"Okay, baby, we are going to have to wait until tonight if you get in the mood again. After all, we've got a lifetime to look forward to."

"So I guess that I can wait a few more hours." Then he ran his hand between my legs, and we laughed. Then we went and had our shower.

While we were showering, he said, "I just can't believe that we are finally together. I thought about you a lot. Did you know that?"

"No, I didn't, but I thought that you were married."

He hugged me and said, "This is one time that I am glad that I am not married."

"Me too."

We got out of the shower and was drying each other off. I couldn't believe that this man was getting another erection. I said, "You better tell him ain't nothing happening for a few days. From the way that I'm feeling now, it might be even longer."

"A few days. Yeah right."

Eugene began to rub himself with Vaseline all over his body.

I rubbed some on myself also.

He said, "Do you want me to do that?"

"No, thank you. I can do it myself, but thanks for the offer."

We got dressed and finished putting away the groceries. Then we started getting things ready for the gathering.

"Eugene, I feel like I'm walking funny. Can you tell?"

"Well, let's see. Walk over there."

"I really don't feel like moving. I'm just that sore."

"Well, you really don't have to move. Just stay there and make the salad, and I'll watch you walk later. Let me get out there and get the grill going. Then I'll come back and start washing the meat off and get it seasoned. Baby?" he said.

"Yes?"

"You just keep standing there, and no one will know that you can't move."

"Funny," I said and threw some lettuce at him.

He said, "If you would have left me alone, you'd be all right. But no, you couldn't keep your hands off me. Now you want to blame me."

"Oh you." I looked for something else to throw at him, but he ran out of the kitchen.

I was walking around, taking baby steps, and glad that we had a few hours left before company was coming.

I hollered, "You laugh now. But just wait when I get fitted just right. You'll be the sore one."

"Oh, hurt me, baby, oh so good. I can't wait."

We laughed. And I started moving a little bit faster. We got the outside all set up. The bar was well stocked. We brought out the sound system. Not all of it but just enough so that the sounds would be sounding good.

I set up the tables. And when everything was in place, some of the meat was on the grill, and the salads were in the fridge, we sat down on the lounge chair and just chilled for a minute, sitting side by side. I looked at him and said, "Now, that didn't take that long. Two hours had passed while we were preparing for the party."

He looked at me, then kissed me, and said, "Thanks."

"For what?"

"For making me one happy man. Once again, you have put a smile back on my face."

"Hey, I can say the same thing, but I'll add. You have made me one happy and sore woman."

He squeezed my hand, and we sat without saying a word. We just enjoyed listening to the birds singing and all the quiet. It was so peaceful.

We were both drained, and I heard him snore a little, but then he caught himself. If we didn't have company coming, we probably would have slept right there for two days.

But we finally got up and was moving in slow motion. He flipped the ribs over; then we heard the doorbell ring.

He put the fork down and said, "Well, lady, let's start greeting our guests."

We opened the door up, and it was his parents. They said, "Are we the first ones here?"

"You sure are. Come on in. We were sitting out back."

His dad said, "It sure does smell good in here. Do you have any beer?"

"You know, I got just what you like, Pops. Would you like a beer too, Ma?"

"Yeah, why not?"

I said, "Eugene, I'll get the beer."

I walked into the kitchen to get the beers while they headed out for the patio.

While I was getting the beer out of the fridge, I heard his mother say, "So I see you had a good time." I turned around, and she said it again. "Did you enjoy yourself?"

I was looking at her, puzzled. Then she said, "I could tell that you two went at it."

"Oh, and just how can you tell that?"

"From the way that you were walking. You're barely moving."

"Well, I can't lie. We had a great time, Mrs. Michaels."

"Oh, call me Ma or Rita, whichever you feel comfortable with. Eugene Sr. always talks to me about what's going on with our boys. They all have a sit-down and talk to their father, and he tells me everything that they talk about. How all my boys are well-endowed, and a couple of them have lost a few women over of it. Girl, their father is the same way, that's why we had five children. I couldn't get enough of him and still can't. But in time, it'll get better. Take my word for it. You hear me?"

We laughed.

Then I said, "As sore as I am, even after we had a shower, I was ready again. But I just couldn't."

"Rachael, you don't mind me talking so personal to you, do you?"

"No, I don't mind at all. I talk the same way with my mother."

"The minute that I saw you, I knew that you were the right one for him, and that we were going to get along great."

"I can see that you are like me. Love yourself a big one."

"But let me get serious with you for a minute. I learned a long time ago that if you leave your back door open, someone will come in and close it for you. Meaning, if you two ever get angry with one another and he still wants to have sex, girl, give in and give it to him. Someone tried that shit on me. But I closed the door myself, so whenever Eugene wanted it, I gave it to him. I don't care how mad I might have been. I was there when he needed me and vice versa. Do you understand what I'm saying to you?"

"Yes, I understand. But what are you saying? that he had an affair?"

"Yes, years ago. But we worked it out, and I closed my own door, and we never had that problem again. Because I learned my lesson. I started paying more attention to him instead of always puttin' the kids first. He came first. Then we both looked after the kids. Girl, we still get our groove on."

"No wonder the two of you look so young."

"I might be a little older, but I am nowhere near the rocking chair. We still get at it at least three or four times a week."

We laughed, then hugged.

I said, "Thanks for the advice. I'm not letting anybody in my back door if I got anything to say about it."

"That's my girl."

Then the doorbell rang. We looked at each other and laughed as we went to open the door.

Before we got to the door, Rita said, "Look, you're going to be all right. Just keep moving. You'll be fine. The soreness will ease up in a while. This is the last thing that I'm going to say about it before we get to the door. Just keep working on it. It'll get better. Just let it hurt so good."

Then we opened the door. It was my mother and father.

"Hey, Mama." We were hugging; then I turned and introduced Rita to my mom and dad. They hugged and kissed.

Then I saw Jaylen pull up with Belinda. While they were getting out of the car, another car pulled up behind Jaylen with someone looking just like Eugene. I knew that he had to be one of Eugene's brothers because they looked so much alike.

Everyone was coming at the same time. When Eugene's brother came in, I reached out to shake his hand; but he grabbed me and hugged me, saying, "Hey there, sister-in-law."

Then his mother said, "Ray, this is Greg."

"Hi, Greg." I was trying to say that this is my son Jaylen, but Greg just shook his hand and said, "Hey there, young man, and you are?"

"Jaylen," my son said.

"Oh, so you're the reason that we are all getting together, and you are…"

"Belinda," Jaylen said; then Greg hugged her.

Then he turned to my mother, and I said, "This is my mother, Julia. And my father, Larry."

Looking at Greg was like looking at Eugene. Only he looked just a bit younger. They were the same height and looked like they weigh the same.

We all started walking toward the patio, and Eugene was coming toward us. When he saw his brother, they hugged and said, "What's up, man?" They acted as though they had not seen each other in a long while.

But they make it a point to see each other at least twice a week, and they stay on the phone daily, even their sisters.

I've talked to them a couple of times since I've been coming over; they are all very close.

After they hugged, Eugene said, "Hey, everybody."

Then I started introducing my family to Eugene because everyone else had already met.

We were all in the backyard when the doorbell rang. Eugene said, "I'll get it."

When he opened the door, it was Shawn, Shawnda, my two grandbabies, and April. Eugene introduced himself, hugged them, then walked them to the back where there were more introductions.

Everyone was laughing and talking; then Greg asked, "Who would like to taste one of my mixed drinks?" Everyone said I do, so he made all kinds of drinks.

Eugene flipped the meat, took some off, and added more.

I checked on the pasta for the spaghetti.

We all were having a good time. It was as though everyone had known each other for a long time. My mother and Gene's mother were talking. Even Eugene's father and my dad, Larry, were laughing and talking.

I was standing in the kitchen, looking out at everyone, when Eugene came in, put his arm around my waist, and asked, "Are you all right?"

"Sure, I'm fine. Why did you ask that?"

"Because remember I told you that I was going to sweep you away and make love to you while we had a house full of company." Then he started kissing my ear and said, "Well…"

Thinking about what his mother and I had talked about, I said, "Let's go."

He said, "Girl, that's why I love you, you are something else."

Then the doorbell rang; he said, "I got it."

It was Eugene's sisters, Candace and Ciera; and behind them were my two sisters, Wanda and Denise. And all their husbands—Keith, Tyrone, Edward, and Rodney.

Then behind them, another car pulls up with another one of Eugene's look-alike brothers. He was with a lady. Eugene said that she was his wife, Gwen.

We all headed for the patio where Eugene introduced everyone. His brother's name was Noel.

The three brothers got together with their father and hugged each other. They talked a little before Eugene walked Noel over to personally introduce me as his wife-to-be.

Noel hugged me and said, "Welcome to the family."

Then Greg said, "All right, everybody, my drinks are ready."

Eugene said, "If anybody is going to taste his drinks, then you won't be driving home."

Everyone laughed, then walked over to taste what he had made.

After that, I took Eugene over to meet my two sisters and their husbands. He shook the husbands' hands and said, "Well, sisters-in-law, you don't have to look anymore. She has me now."

They said, "Okay good." Then Wanda said, "The hunt is over." We all laughed.

Then we walked over to his sisters and their husbands. We all talked; then my family walked over to where we were standing, and everyone joined in on the conversation that was going on.

Everyone was there except my brothers and their wives. My brother Warren and his wife, Yvonne, should be back from their vacation. I had left a message on his machine, just in case they got back in time; but I know if he's back, he'll be here. My other brother Delvon and his wife, Ericka, should be here by now.

I must have spoken them up because as I was thinking about them, the doorbell rang, and it was them.

Once again, everyone was introduced; everyone was mingling. Everyone was at ease with each other. There were people all over the place. Eugene's kids were talking with mine; everything was going great. Eugene introduced me to his children, the four that were there: Nicole, Champane, Sharrell, and Eugene III. His other daughter Roselyn was with her mother, Christiana, in Atlanta.

Eugene had some good-looking children, and I know that mine looked good.

We were all just enjoying ourselves and had forgotten all about the reason that we were all together.

All the meat had been cooked. We brought out the food from the inside; everyone was eating. And some old-school music came on, and Wanda and her husband got up and started slow dancing.

I looked over at my daughter and saw that Eugene's brother Greg had taken a liking to my grandchildren and their mother.

I didn't say a word because she was a grown woman, and I thought that she needed someone in her life outside of her children's semen donor. I just looked at them occasionally. I'd just wait and see what she had to say about him. After all, they were about the same age. He was a couple of years older than she was, but it was all good. They actually looked good together, playing with the kids and all.

I walked inside to fill the ice bucket up. And Eugene came in while I was getting the ice. He thought I didn't see him as he tried to sneak up behind me.

He put his arms around my waist. I turned around to face him, and he said, "Are you enjoying yourself?"

I put my arms around his neck and said, "I sure am," and kissed him.

Eugene said, "Girl, don't you start something that you can't finish. And I mean finish right now. Not when everyone is gone."

"Hey, I'm game. No one will miss us anyway."

"Girl, you need to quit playing, you know. Someone will look for us."

"Oh, so what you doing? Turning me down?"

He just laughed and grabbed me by the hand and was leading me to the back when his daughter Champane came in the kitchen and asked for the ice. We just looked at each other and laughed.

He said, "Payback, baby, just wait."

I handed her the ice bucket. She said thanks, turned, and walked out of the kitchen.

He said, "Did you see Greg and Shawnda?"

"Oh yes, I did notice them too. I thought that I was the only one who noticed that. But if you and I noticed them, then everyone else did too, but who cares? I don't."

"And neither do I. Whatever is fair is fair."

Eugene and I were standing in the kitchen talking when the doorbell rang. "Who could that be?" he said.

"Maybe it's some of your nieces and nephews, or maybe it's some of my nieces and nephews."

We went to open the door, and it was Belinda's parents with Belinda's sister, brother, and their guest. I had forgotten to ask Belinda if her siblings were married or not. We had forgotten all about them; everyone was having such a good time. We actually had forgotten once again the reason we were all together.

We introduced ourselves and walked them out to the patio where everyone was; we introduced them to everyone, and they fell right in with the crowd.

I decided that before everyone gets to pleasing high, we had better get down to the business as to why we were all there. So I said, "Everyone, may I have your attention? First, let me reintroduce my son and his wife-to-be so that we could get the wedding plans together."

I pulled Belinda's parents to the side and asked them if it would be all right if I asked everyone for their opinion on the plans. Not that we were going to use it but to make everyone feel like they helped.

They said, "Sure, let's do it." Then Belinda's mother said, "I see that there are a lot of glasses turned up. Do you mind if we have some of what everyone is drinking?"

"Sure, just go right over there, and Eugene's brother will be glad to make you a drink or feel free to make your own."

Then I said, "Everyone, your attention please. I would like to introduce my son and his wife-to-be to those who didn't get to meet them."

Then my sister Wanda hollered out, "You have already done that a few minutes ago. So now is the date set already, or do you want me to set one for you, Jay? Because you know that I will. I've got no problem doing that."

Jaylen said, "I know that, Auntie, but we have set a date. We've decided on Christmas day if it's all right with our parents since they are the ones paying for it."

Belinda's father said, "That's fine with us, son."

"It's okay with me too."

Then Eugene said, "Okay, everyone, let's toast to the Christmas celebration."

As we were toasting, the doorbell rang. Eugene said, "I'll get it." It was my brother Warren and his wife, Yvonne.

Eugene took them to the back to introduce them to everyone. Warren and Eugene had already talked at the door after introducing them to everyone.

Warren said, "What's up? All you said on the machine was come over to this address if we got back in time. What's going on?"

"Well, your nephew is getting married, and I have a new man in my life, and this is a wedding-planning party. Eugene and I thought that this would be a good time for our families to meet. So how long have you been home? Or are you just getting in or what?"

"We had just got in, and I wanted to stay home and relax. But Yvonne wanted to come over here, so here we are."

I kissed them both on the cheek and put my arm through theirs as we walked toward our sisters.

Wanda said, "Did you bring back our souvenirs?"

"Girl, would I forget and have to hear your mouth? Yes, I did, but you are gonna have to come and get them."

"What is it?"

"Wait and see."

Everyone was still eating and shouting out what they thought would be nice for the wedding every now and then.

I told Eugene, "Let's just get Jaylen, BB, and her parents and put this thing together ourselves since no one is really paying any attention. Let's just let them continue doing what it is their doing while we make the plans."

So I gathered the main people together and went inside to make the plans.

We sat down and made all the plans for a beautiful Christmas wedding; then I said, "We've made all these plans, but no one has said where the wedding's going to take place. Have you all talked to a preacher yet?"

Belinda's mother said, "If you haven't, then I'll be glad to talk with my preacher. But I know that he will want you to go through marriage counseling first."

"That's fine, Ma, we don't mind going to counseling. Just let us know what he says, and we'll be there."

"Okay, now can we get back to the party?" Belinda said.

So we all headed for the patio. Eugene touched me and said, "Can you wait a minute?"

"What's wrong?"

"Nothing's wrong. I just want to spend another minute with you alone. And give you this." He kissed me so passionately and held me so tight that I could feel the bulge in his pants.

"Eugene, stop."

"Stop what?"

"You know what." And I touched his pants and said, "You just wait a little while longer."

He just smiled and said, "Okay, okay."

Then we went back and joined the others. By now, it was getting a little dark, so Eugene turned on the floodlights, which made the water in the pool glisten. We had walked to the other side of the pool and was looking in the water when Eugene's mother walked over and said, "So when are you guys going to make your announcement about your wedding?"

"Mama," Eugene said.

Then he let go of my hand and went back into the house.

I thought that he had gotten mad at his mother for asking about us announcing our wedding plans; but a few minutes later, Eugene came out of the house and stood on a chair and said, "Everyone, can I have your attention again please?"

Then he said, "Baby, can you come over here for a minute please?"

He got off the chair and got down on one knee.

I looked at him in disbelief. "Eugene, what are you doing?" I whispered.

He said, "I'm asking you in front of everyone here, will you marry me?"

I was just standing there in total shock, and he said it again, "Rachael, will you marry me?"

I was still standing and just looking at him when someone hollered out "answer him."

I leaned down, put my hands on his face, and said, "Yes, I'll marry you."

He said, "I know that I have already asked you, but I wanted to make it really, really official. All our children knew and your brothers and my brothers knew. Everyone knew that I was going to ask you to marry me tonight."

He got up off his knees and said, "Noel had this." He picked up my left hand and slid a big diamond ring on my finger.

All I could do was hug him with tears running down my face.

Everyone started clapping.

Then Eugene said, "Everyone, I had talked it over with Jaylen and Belinda before I decided to ask her in front of everyone. Because after all, this was for them. But they didn't mind, and I wanted the world to know how I felt about my baby, Rachael."

"That's my boy," his mother said.

Everyone could see how my ring was shining. Wanda hollered, "Dammmn, look at that ring shining like new money."

Eugene said, "I got this ring from my mother, who got it from her mother, who told me, 'One day, when you really find the one woman that you feel like spending the rest of your life with and you know that she is the right one, then I want you to give her this ring.' And I have found you, Rachael Ericka Brunson, soon-to-be Mrs. Michaels."

I started crying all over again and just hugged him.

He said, "I love you, girl."

"I love you too, Mr. Michaels."

Everyone started congratulating us and saying good luck.

Then my brothers walked over and asked Eugene if they could talk to him for a minute. Then they walked inside.

Although they already knew that Eugene was going to ask me to marry him, I knew what they were going to say.

Probably the same speech that they gave my other husbands, but I'll just wait and see.

I'll find out when everyone is gone.

Eugene's mother touched me on the shoulder and said, "I really think that he has found the… How can I say this, I want to say the perfect woman. But I know that there is no such person except Jesus, so I'll just say that he has found himself a very good woman."

"Thank you, Mrs. Michaels."

"Oh, just call me Rita or Ma like I said earlier. Whatever you prefer." We were hugging when Eugene's four children walked up and said, "We heard what Grandma was saying, and we totally agree."

"Thank you." And I hugged each one of them with tears rolling down my cheeks because I really didn't know how his children were going to react once they met me in person.

But I felt like they were sincere and really cared for me.

They were saying that they were crazy about their new little niece and nephew.

"And it looked like Uncle Greg was also crazy about them too."

Eugene's son said, "Enough of this mushy stuff. Now back to the food."

That's when my crew came over and basically said the same things to Eugene that his children had said to me.

He hugged Shawnda and shook the boys' hands.

We looked around, and there was a lot of dancing going on. Even my mother and dad were out there dancing; Greg and Shawnda, my sisters, and my brothers were out dancing with their wives. Eugene grabbed my hand and said, "Shall we?" And we joined the slow dancing.

I was looking around and thinking this is really something special. We finally had something good to celebrate.

But then, out of nowhere, Toya popped in my mind; and I wondered how she was doing. She stayed on my mind off and on for the rest of the night.

Eugene would walk over and say, "Are you all right?"

And I'd say sure because we had agreed that we would not bring our work home. We would leave them at the door of the building when we walked out. It would be behind us.

But for some reason, I couldn't shake the feelings I had about Toya's last word to me about sleeping in the emergency room. I tried to toss the feeling out of my mind and enjoy the rest of the evening. I squeezed Eugene tighter and whispered, "I love you, baby."

And he said, "And I love you, baby, always."

Looking around at everyone, you would think that we had known each other for years.

But at this point, Eugene and I had only known each other for four weeks. But if you wanted to count the time we spent chasing each other at the casino, then it would be seven weeks or more. But it still feels as though we had known each other for a longer period of time.

We got along great. We laughed a lot together, and we talked about everything.

"Hey, Rachael, Rachael." I heard someone calling out my name. I was lost in my own wonderful world of happiness, thinking about Eugene.

When I turned to look, it was Eugene calling me to come and dance with him.

At first he kinda caught me off guard. I just stood there looking at him.

Then he said, "Hey, girl, don't get shy on me now. We're all family."

I said, "Oh please." I walked out and started shaking my butt, raising my arms, rocking to the beat.

Eugene said, "Oh, you think you got rhythm, huh?" So he started doing what I was doing and moving in closer. I started turning around, and he was right up on me. So I just rubbed up against him, and he whispered, "All right, girl."

But I just kept right on dancing.

Then a slow record came on; everyone was dancing—children and all.

Then Eugene said, "Honey, you know what?"

"What?" I said.

"You have made this one happy day for me and my children,

mother, father, sisters, and brothers. I'll say this for all of us. Thank you."

"No, baby, I thank you for entering into my life and putting a smile back on my face. I thank you." Then I laid my head on his chest as we slow danced. Although it seemed like we were just standing in one spot, rocking back and forth. Then the music changed to a little faster beat.

But Eugene and I just pulled out to sit and watch everyone else enjoy themselves.

Finally, the music stopped. And Eugene said, "Just hold on, everybody. I'll fix that."

Then my brother said, "You don't have to fix that. On my account, I really enjoyed myself. But I have got to put you good people down."

It looked as though everyone was waiting for someone to say good night first because as soon as he said it, everyone started saying "me too."

So we stood up and said, "Well, we enjoyed everyone and hope that you all had a good time and want you to come back again. As a matter of fact, let's all just get together whenever we can once or twice a month at each other's house, we'll rotate."

Everyone agreed and said that we'll talk soon to see whose house we'll meet at next.

Then my sister Wanda said, "We can meet at my place. I'll just let Rachael or Eugene know, and then it's on."

They said, "Okay, let's make this a family thing from now on."

My mother hugged Eugene and said, "You two make a great couple. Take care of each other."

Eugene said, "I promise to do my best to take care of my baby, Ms. Johnson."

"Oh, you can call me Julia or Ma if you like."

I hugged my mother and dad as we walked to the door.

My sisters and their husbands came up behind us, hugging Mama and Dad, saying how much fun they had had.

My brothers came up and hugged Mama; then Warren told Mama that he would bring her and Dad's gifts over tomorrow. Yvonne hugged Mama, Dad, then Eugene and said that she had a wonderful time and was glad to meet him.

He told her that it was nice meeting her also.

Eugene said, "I know that you all were tired after just getting back from a long trip, but thanks for coming over."

"I really would not have missed meeting you and being with the family and meeting your family. I really have enjoyed myself. We'll be seeing each other some more and some more and some more, brother-in-law."

Then Eugene and my brother hugged.

Everyone had begun to get into their cars and began leaving.

Eugene's family was still inside along with my children, so after saying our goodbyes, we went back inside and talked a little while longer. Then Greg and Shawnda started putting on her children's sweaters. They were acting as though they were a married couple.

Eugene and I didn't say a word. We just looked at each other, waiting to see if they were going to say anything.

Shawn and April came over, saying how much they had enjoyed themselves; then Eugene asked if they were already married.

Shawn kind of smiled and said, "One day soon."

Then April smiled and said, "If he continues to behave, I might just marry him."

Then we all laughed.

As they were leaving, I was walking them to the door. Shawn turned to me and said out loud, "Mama, he seems to be an okay kind of guy. I hope that the two of you will be very happy."

Then he walked back up to us and said, "Mama, you know that the two of you will not always agree on everything, so before you blow up, try to work things out. I say that because you are my mother, and I know you very well."

Then he kissed my cheek and shook Eugene's hand.

I said, "If things get out of control, then I promise that we'll talk it through."

He said, "That's my girl." He kissed my cheek again, then went and got in the car.

I said, "The two of you need to pay attention to the advice that you have just given me. And you'll be together for a long time."

"We will, Ms. Brunson," April said. She hugged me; then they left.

We went back inside, but everyone was headed around to the front from the backyard, so I walked back through the house to meet them in the front. Jaylen and Belinda said, "Thanks again, Mama and Eugene. I'll give you a call sometime during the week."

Shawnda and Greg both said, "We'll talk to you later." And they walked away.

Eugene and his other brother was still standing there talking. They looked so handsome, and so did Greg, the youngest brother.

Noel's wife was holding on to his arm.

I walked up to Eugene, and he put his arm around me and asked his brother right in front of me what did he think of me.

He said, "I think that Gene here has himself a winner, and she's made a good choice by choosing you. So together the two of you are going to be all right, and I wish the both of you all the best."

"And so do I," Noel's wife said.

I said, "Why thanks, both of you."

Eugene's brother Greg said, "The two of you make a handsome couple."

"Thank you."

Then Greg said, "Hey, man, we're going to go so that the two of you can relax a little."

But then Eugene's mother, father, sisters, and their husbands all came out from the back.

While we were saying our goodbyes to his brothers, they all hugged me and said congratulations to us again; then they said that they had a wonderful time and would see us again at the next gathering, which would be at Wanda's house.

One of his sisters said, "All right, sister-in-law."

I just smiled and said, "We'll get together soon."

"Good," they said, and out they went.

Eugene and his sisters were standing outside, making plans for the next time that they were going to hang out together; then they said, "Hey, Pops, we'll see you later, and Rachael, it was nice meeting you in person. And once again, congratulations. We'll see you soon." Then they got into their cars and left.

Before his mother and father had taken off, his mother called me over to the car and said, "Baby, don't let him make you that sore again. Make him take his time and play with that thang."

"Rita," his father said and pulled her arm.

I just laughed.

She said, "For real," and laughed again. "I'll call you tomorrow, Ray."

I waved as they were pulling out of the driveway.

I walked toward Eugene. When I reached him, he put his arm around my neck and asked, "What did she want?"

"I'll tell you if you tell me what my brothers wanted, and before you go there with 'It was a man thang,' I don't want to hear it."

"So if you tell me what my brothers said to you, then I'll tell you what your mother said."

He said, "But, baby, it was just a man thang."

I said funny; then I started tickling him on his side. "Okay, then what your mother and I said was girl talk."

"No, it wasn't."

"How can you say that it wasn't girl talk?"

"Because my pops was in the car, so it wasn't a girl thang. He was in the car, and he knows what you were talking about. So out with it."

"You know what, I really don't think that you want to hear what we were talking about."

"Yes, I do. Because if I know my mother, she was talking about something pertaining to sex, wasn't she?"

I smiled and said, "You're right."

"So what did she say?"

"Come on now, can't I keep that to myself?"

"No, not this time."

Then he started tickling me.

"Okay, okay, she said for me to make you take your time so that I won't be so sore. You know, she teased me earlier. She noticed the way that I was moving."

"Oh, baby, I'm sorry. I'll be gentler," he said as he put his hands between my legs.

"Hey, stop that. I want to take a shower first. I feel sticky."

"Well, can I join you?"

"Mm, let me think, okay?" So we got everything that we needed for our shower. I was gonna wash my hair or have him do it for me.

After I got my shampoo, I turned on the water in the shower and turned around, and he was standing there in the buff.

I looked down, and he was ready to go. I just smiled, took off my clothes, and stepped in the shower with him right behind me.

When we got in, I said, "I hope that the water isn't too hot for you."

He said, "If it is, then I'll just throw you up front," and started laughing.

"You, rat."

"Damn." Looking at him from behind, his body was looking good. He was in shape from his head down to his toes.

He had a slight erection that was bigger than some of the guys that I used to date back in high school.

The water was a little too hot for him, so he said, "What are you trying to do? Cook us? You were supposed to test the water first."

"I did. I like it like this, so get used to it if you're going to be taking a shower with me or a bubble bath. I like it hot."

He said, "I like you hot, but we'll compromise—my way sometimes and your way other times."

"Sure," I said, thinking he'll see things my way because I'll always beat him to the shower.

I grabbed the bar of soap and started to bathe him. He was fully erect now, but I acted like I didn't notice it and kept right on bathing him.

I put his erect penis in one hand and washed it with the other. I looked him straight in the eyes and said, "I love you."

"And I love you back." He then held my face in his hands and started kissing me very passionately. He let go and got a washcloth and began to wash my arms, neck, shoulders—paying close attention to not miss a spot.

He bathed me just like a mother bathing her child until he got down to my kitty. He washed ever so gently; then he rinsed the suds out and washed the kitty with clear water.

Then when I thought that he was finished and was about to put my leg down, he said, "Hold it. I'm not finished yet." He started rubbing my kitty with his bare hand, saying, "Does this make it feel better, baby?"

With his other hand, he grabbed the back of my head and pushed it toward him and stuck his tongue down my throat.

I was rubbing him with both hands, but I felt as though I was falling to the floor as the water just ran down us.

Eugene turned off the water and began to make little circles on my tits with his tongue, first one, then the other. He continued playing with my tits with his tongue while his fingers played with my kitty. Then he slid one finger inside me, moving it in and out slowly and saying, "Does this make you feel better, baby? Does it take some of the pain away?"

Then his kisses left my tits and headed down to my stomach, then my navel; and as much as I dislike my navel being touched, it felt great. It was too good to say anything to stop him.

Before I could say anything, he was already kissing the top of my kitty; then he went down a little farther and put my leg over his shoulder and acted as though he was at Thirty-One Flavors.

I leaned my head back against the shower walls.

All I could do was play with his hair and whisper his name.

He planted little kisses all over my kitty, then let his tongue move in and out of me.

All I could do to keep from melting down to the floor was hold on to the walls of the shower. While he continued to enjoy himself, tasting all my juices mixed with water that was dripping off my body, I came again and again. He continued to play with my kitty with his tongue.

"Shit," I moaned. Then he started to kiss his way back up to my chest.

I grabbed his head and kissed him real hard.

Eugene put one of my legs around his waist as he entered me slowly.

"Oh, baby, oh, baby," he kept on saying as he moved ever so slowly at first then a little faster.

He picked me up and stepped out of the shower. He carried me to the bed, then started a little foreplay. He entered me again, this time moving a little faster.

I could feel him getting harder. I knew that he was about to cum, so I reached down and squeezed his penis to make it feel tighter for him; he loved that. "Oooooh, baby," he screamed as he slowly stopped moving and just lay on top of me.

"Baby," he said, "I know I'm heavy, but just give me a minute."

We just lay in silence for a while, enjoying each other. His erection was finally beginning to fade. But it still felt overwhelming. We continued to just lay still; he moved off me a little to take some of the weight off.

Then he said, "Girl, what are you trying to do to me?"

"Love you, that's all." Then I leaned over and kissed his forehead.

I reached for a pillow and told Eugene to raise up his head.

By now he had rolled off me and was lying flat on his back. He raised his head, and I put the pillow under it.

"Now raise your body so that I can pull the covers back."

At first he didn't want to move, but he lifted himself up and said, "Girl, you are wearing me out." We got under the covers and just held each other.

Then I said, "Okay, I don't mean to wear you out, so we'll take a break from sex. Oh, let's say for about a week?"

"Oh, you do have jokes, don't you?"

"What I said was just a figure of speech. It didn't mean anything."

He kissed my nose, and we both drifted off to sleep in each other's arms.

The next morning, we got up, showered, had breakfast, and got ready for church. We were both kind of quiet.

Then I said, "A penny for your thoughts."

Eugene just looked at me and said, "I just don't want to lose you."

"What do you mean by lose me? I'm not going anywhere."

"I was just thinking about those roses that someone sent you. And that you are still married."

I picked up his hand, led him to the bed, sat him down on the bed, then said, "I know that I am still married, but I have filed for divorce. But even before that, my marriage was over. Okay, I know that we were still having sex from time to time. But I had even put a stop to that. Now I know that you can understand that because you went through the same thing with your second wife. But now that's over, so, baby, please don't think about the past. It's behind us now. And we have each other from this day forward."

"But do you still love him?"

"I love him but not like you might think."

"It's just that I don't want anything to happen to you kind of thing, nothing more."

"We just had sex. There was no real feelings—at least not on my side. I can't speak for him, but I am pretty sure that the feeling were the same. And the flower thing, we don't even know who sent them. So let's not go there anymore, okay, baby?"

He pulled me down on top of him and said, "Okay, it's over, you're mine now. Let's get that shower."

I said, "Sweetheart, you and I both have been through a lot. We've had a lot of good times, and at times, it seemed as though the bad outweighed the good. So I think—well, I know—that you really meant what you said, and you really have enough room in your heart for me. I'm not looking back, only forward to spending the rest of my life loving you because I believe that fate has found a way to bring us together. I mean, look at how we first met at the casino where we both thought that the other was a stalker."

We both laughed. Then he said, "I really did think that you were stalking me."

I hit him, then kissed him, and said, "I really was so that should let you know how really bad I wanted you."

He just squeezed me and said, "I'm glad that you kept it up until I gave in." Then he laughed.

"But for real, I am so serious. There is no one that I'd rather spend the rest of my life, all my days and nights, with than you. It looks as though we're rushing, but actually we're not. So, baby, I say to you once again if you have room enough in your heart for me, then I'm all yours until death do us part."

He put his arms around my waist, kissed me, then said, "Let's go."

I said, "Oh, that's how you feel?"

"What?"

"All you got to say is let's go after I poured my heart out to you."

He turned and said, "Isn't that the way it works after you know that you got someone you act like whatever they say is okay."

"Oh you!"

But he picked me up and said, "I can't wait until your divorce is final so that you can be all mine the right way."

"Me too. Now let's go," I said. We just laughed.

He said, "Thanks, baby, for helping me with my insecurities," as we headed out the door.

When we got to the church, it seemed like every head turned and looked at us.

But that could have been just my imagination or guilt feeling because I was married. But no one in the church knew that except the two of us. So we sat down and enjoyed the service.

When it was over and we were leaving, a number of women rolled their eyes at me and spoke to Eugene.

I didn't say a word; he was holding my hand as we left out of the church.

I just smiled at the thought because more than likely those ladies were wishing that it was their hand that he was holding instead of mine.

Eugene asked if I wanted to go out to dinner or pick up something to eat.

I said that I was still full from breakfast, and all I wanted to do was get some sleep.

"Good, that's what I want too."

So we headed to his house.

When we got there, I took off my shoes and started undressing as soon as the door was shut.

Eugene said, "You were serious."

"Weren't you?"

I headed straight for the bedroom.

Eugene said, "What should I take out for dinner?"

"Doesn't matter. I'll see you in a couple of hours. I feel so drained."

He just laughed a little and went on into the kitchen.

I fell across the bed, and that was it for me. I didn't remember much after that.

Eugene woke me up by playing with my feet and kissing my

stomach.

"Hey, sweetie. Well, sleepyhead, dinner is done. Your children and mine both called. I've been on the phone for hours. It seems like ever since you fell a sleep, I watched you sleep for a while. I started to climb in with you, but you looked so peaceful, so I decided to wait until later to rape you."

Then he laughed, bent down, and kissed my kitty with my panties still on.

Then he said, "Let me stop or our food will get cold."

"I feel like I could go back to sleep."

"Well, right now, it's time to get up, and it's so nice outside. Would you like to eat outside, or would you like for me to bring your food in here?"

"I'll get up. Maybe some fresh air will wake me up. What did you fix?"

"Come and see, sleepyhead."

He left. I went into the bathroom to freshen up. My mind, for some reason, stayed on Toya. I don't know why, but it did.

I hope that she has not gotten into any more trouble because if she did, I was going to be finished with her, but I know that she hasn't.

I finished in the bathroom and put on a shirt that belonged to Eugene. It came down to my knees. I walked outside where Eugene had made seafood shish kebabs and seafood fettuccine and a salad. He poured me a glass of orange juice and had everything set up before he asked if I wanted to eat outside.

Boy, I thought, no wonder his wife was so possessive of him. He was a great catch that was hard to find. But now that he found me, there was going to be no letting go. No matter what issues came up. We were going to discuss them, anything that might have come up. We were going to work it out.

Anything that might want to get in the middle of our relationship, we were going to fix it.

I walked right past Eugene who was in the kitchen.

He came up behind me and put his arms around my waist and kissed my neck.

Then he said, "I'll give you a penny for your thoughts."

"What did you say?"

"I said I'd give you a penny for your thoughts. Where were you? I had called your name when you walked past, but you didn't hear me."

I turned around to face him and said, "I was right here, thinking about you."

"Sure you were, and I like that. That's my baby."

We kissed; then he sat me down at the table while he went inside and started bringing out the food. When he was finished bringing out the food, he sat down, picked up my hand, and said, "Let's say grace." And we did.

I tasted the fettuccini. "Hmm, this is very good. Who taught you how to cook?"

"I would say my mother, but I just kinda learned on my own after my wife passed away. And I had the children. At first we ate out a lot. But my mother said, 'That's not good, those children eating fast foods everyday. Do you want me to come down to Atlanta and cook for you?' I said, 'No, Ma.' And after that, I started cooking different things and experimenting with stuff until I met wife number 2. At first she wanted to come over and cook for us because she didn't have any children. And she took to mine, which eventually led to us getting married. We were together for six years. In the first year, she got pregnant, and things started changing. Then she started getting very jealous, but I just thought it was hormones or something, but things only got worst. I wanted out so bad. She would call me at work, she would page me, she would burn up my cell phone, she would accuse me of sleeping with clients. It didn't matter if I was at home or not, I was sleeping with someone. Lord, don't let me not answer a page or answer the cell phone right away because when I did, I knew all the hell that I was going to catch. I mean, it got so bad that she would come and sit in the courtroom when I was defending someone that was on trial until finally my mother said, 'What are you going to do? Let her make you lose your job?' Then I tried even harder to talk to her about her jealously thing she had going on, but she wasn't trying to hear me. She just kept on nagging. I started asking my mother to look for me a house in case I just had to leave. I started checking into law firms here until I just couldn't take it anymore. Finally, I packed up the kids that weren't kids anymore and left."

"You mean that you didn't let her know that you were leaving?"

"Oh sure, I let her know that I had had enough and was leaving. She said that she was sorry and would change."

"What did you say?"

"Oh, I fell for it for about another month. She changed for about a week, then went back to her old self. She started accusing me of having an affair here since this is where I wanted to move to. Outside of my family and a few people here and there, I really didn't know anybody. Gradually, I started meeting people. You know, even when we would come here to Chicago to visit my mother and father, we would all get together with my brothers and sisters and hang out, have a good time, so I thought. But as soon as we got in bed, here it would come. She'd say you just brought me along so that I could see you flirt with that bitch that I saw staring at you."

"So I do remember you talking about how people use to approach you. So just how many women did you take up on their offer?"

"Truthfully?"

"Yes, out with it."

"Okay, okay, five."

"Five different women?"

"Well yeah."

"And you slept with all of them?"

"Yes, I did. But I cut that out because it wasn't doing me any good. They each knew that I was married first of all. And they knew that I was seeing other people. But they wouldn't leave me alone, so that's why I started hanging out at the casino. I had been hanging out there long before I met you. But during that time, Veronica decided that she would be my companion. But at that point in my life, I had had enough of women, plus dealing with my wife. Man, I thought I was about to lose my mind. But I slowed my pace to get myself together."

"Oh, so you were still sleeping with her too?"

"Well yeah, I won't lie to you, but that's all in my past now, and that was the only way that she would let me see my baby girl. I already told you about that. But anyway, I had to put a stop to that as soon as we were divorced. But I was still nice to her, or she would have taken everything that I had during the divorce. I mean, I didn't have much, but what I did have was for my other children. If I had been alone, it would not have mattered. I hated that I had to lie to her and have her thinking that we were going to get back together. I had to lie or she wouldn't let me see my baby girl if I didn't. I would tell her let's just use this as a cooling-down period. And she agreed."

"So is she still under the impression that the two of you are going to get back together?"

"You know what, I don't know what she may be thinking because I have not talked to her in a long while. I've talked to my daughter but not to her, and you know the last time that I talked to my baby girl."

"So why haven't you talked to her or called her since then?"

"I don't know, but I'll call her tonight."

I took a sip of my orange juice and just looked at Eugene.

He said, "What's the matter?"

"Nothing really, it's just that I got so much out of you just by asking you who taught you how to cook."

He started laughing and said, "You sure did. I don't know where all of that came from. But maybe I needed to get that off my chest."

"And that you did. So tell me again about all of these different ladies."

"There's nothing else to tell outside of what I've already said. That was my checkered past."

I said, "Hummmmmmmmm hum."

Then he got up and took all the leftover food back into the house and put the dishes in the dishwasher.

After that, Eugene asked me what I feel like doing.

I said, "Nothing really. I've got to get my things together for work in the morning. After that, then I don't know. What do you feel like doing?"

"Just about the same. A nice hot shower and some sleep will do it for me."

"That sounds good to me." So I got my clothes together, and we headed for the shower.

I knew that Eugene was tired because he didn't try any of his slick moves.

I know if he felt like I did when we got home from church, then all he really wanted to do was sleep.

So I didn't try to make him have sex even though I wanted some.

When we got out of the shower and got into bed, he asked me what I wanted to watch on cable.

I said that I was going to watch the news.

"All right," he said as he snuggled up behind me. A few minutes later, he was snoring. So I turned the TV's volume down and lay in the warmth of his arms and watched the ten-o'clock news until I drifted off to sleep, listening to the tune of Eugene's snoring.

Again I was awakened by the smell of bacon cooking.

So I got up, went into the bathroom, brushed my teeth, washed up, and went into the kitchen.

"Good morning, sweetheart."

"Good morning yourself."

"A few more minutes and you would have had breakfast in bed."

"Oh, it's not too late. I can still get back in there, you know. I still feel tired, maybe I'm coming down with something."

"I know what you're coming down with, and it's not the flu."

"Oh really? Then tell me what you think I might be coming down with."

"It's another little Eugene."

"Oh please, I'm too old to be having a baby, so you can keep those evil thoughts to yourself."

He just smiled.

I said, "That's not anything that I would even consider. It's just a head cold probably."

"Well, do you feel well enough to go to work today?"

"I thought about staying home, but I've got to go. But if I start to feel worse, then I'll go home."

"So why go?

"I feel fine, I really do. I just have that Monday-morning-blues feeling. That's all. Haven't you ever felt like that, like just staying in bed?"

"I sure have. So why don't we just stay here and call in sick? Play hooky for once?"

"I don't know."

"Do you feel like eating your breakfast? I won't feel bad if you don't feel like eating."

"No, I'll eat. Maybe it'll help me feel better." He had made omelets with bacon and hash browns and had poured me a glass of orange juice.

I started eating and noticed that he was not eating, so I said, "Aren't you going to eat?"

He said, "I've already exercised and eaten."

"What? It's only 6:00 a.m., so what time did you get up?"

"About five, now I'm about to take me a quick shower, or do you want me to wait for you?"

"No, go right ahead. I'll have my shower after I finish eating, so don't wait for me."

"All right." He kissed my forehead and went into the bathroom.

He had made such a large breakfast I couldn't eat it all; so I put it to the side, got up, and joined him in the shower.

He was surprised when I opened the shower door and stepped in to join him.

We played for a little while before washing each other up.

He said, "Hey, girl, I love you this morning." Then he started singing "I Love You More Today Than Yesterday."

I put my arms around him and said, "I love you more today than yesterday also."

Then we started to make love. I felt like pleasing him, so after getting him hard as a brick and playing with him—kissing his neck, his shoulders, his nipples—I just started kissing my way south on his body. It was his turn to grab hold of the shower walls and moan. I had to hold him with both hands as I kissed the head, running my tongue from side to side, up and down, before taking him inside my warm mouth.

"Ooooooooh shit," he moaned as I continued to pull on him with my lips. "Oooooh yes, yes." His head was laid back as I continued to work on him. I could feel him hardening up even more.

But he reached down and pulled me up. We stepped out of the shower with the water still running; he started kissing my stomach.

Then he went all the way down to my kitty. He went straight for it like he couldn't wait to taste me.

He had managed to put one of my legs up on top of the toilet while he enjoyed himself. He then began to kiss his way back up while letting his fingers finish where he left off. He was inside of me with his fingers and his tongue kissing me at the same time. He took my leg off the toilet as we headed for the floor where he entered me slowly, moving as if he was sneaking up on something.

"Eugene," I moaned as he moved ever so gently in and out, slow at first then a little faster. I could feel him about to cum.

"Oooh, baby, oh, baby," he sighed, then said, "I love making love to you, and I love the way you make me feel in or out of bed."

We just lay on the floor, talking and holding each other.

I was trying to keep him inside of me for as long as I could because he felt so good.

"Girl, just think, when we get married, we can do this all day or whenever we feel like it."

I said, "We do that now. And we are not married yet."

"But I mean, we can do it without having any guilty feelings."

"You're right, and I can't wait to become Mrs. Michaels."

"Damn, I can't wait until you are divorced, and it's final."

We just lay in silence for a few minutes; then I said, "Honey, we have got to go to work."

"Oh, that's right."

We lay there for a few more seconds, then got up, and got back in the water that was still running.

In the shower, he said, "Girl, girl, girl, what are you doing to me?"

"I'm just taking care of my man, that's all, while my man takes care of his woman."

We got out of the shower. I was still feeling like shit, but I didn't want Eugene to worry about me, so I kept up the pretense that I was feeling much better and went on into work.

I was thinking when I get off work today, I was going to go home instead of going back to Eugene's house. It seemed like I had forgotten where I lived since being with Eugene. I felt so comfortable being with him.

When I got inside my office, my secretary was already there as usual.

"Hey, Rachael, how was your weekend?"

"I had such an amazing weekend. You wouldn't believe it. And how was yours?"

"I had a pretty good one, I must say so myself."

I walked inside my office; and there, on my desk, sat another dozen of yellow roses. They were beautiful. I stepped out and asked Janel if she knew who delivered the flowers.

She said that the flowers were on her desk when she got there this morning.

She said that after glancing at the card that came with the flowers, she thought that Mr. Michaels had sent them.

"What card?"

"Oh, it's on the side of the flowers."

I walked back into the office, looked around the flowers, and spotted the card.

It read, "Hey, baby. I enjoyed this past weekend and all the time that we spent together, all the things that we did, and all places we went."

After reading that part, I knew that the flowers didn't come from Eugene because we didn't go anywhere. We had company Saturday, and Sunday, we went to church. And after that, we got our groove on the rest of the time. The thought of getting our groove on brought chills down my spine. We had great lovemaking sessions.

"Oooooo, this morning, boy oh boy. Dammmn, now this."

I wonder who the hell is sending me these flowers.

Someone who doesn't want to see Eugene and I together, and somehow I'm going to find out just who is sending these damn flowers. I've got to let Eugene know about them before he finds out from someone else. Although no one ever sees anything that goes on around here, but the gossip never seems to cease.

I really don't feel like being bothered today with anyone, but I've got a couple of clients that I've got to talk to and a case that's supposed to go to trial this morning. So I've got to pull myself together.

So I gathered some paperwork together and my briefcase and headed for the courthouse.

Eugene was already there. That's where his first stop was for the morning.

When I got to the courthouse, I went straight to the third floor where I was defending a man who was supposed to have beaten up a young woman.

I knew that this is going to take a very long time.

It was going to take all day just to get a jury together, so I prepared myself to be in court all day.

My mind drifted back to the flowers. Dammmn, I've got to let that thought go and concentrate on what I'm doing before I let the wrong juror stay on this trial. And I know that that would not be good for me or my client.

So as court got started and we began to pick and question jurors, time was moving; and out of the eight that we questioned, we only agreed on two so far.

I knew that this was going to be a long day, but time was moving kinda fast. Before I knew it, it was lunchtime already, and the judge called for recess and said court will resume in one hour.

I put my things together and walked out into the hallway, and who was standing there? Old troubled Veronica. I ignored her as much as possible, but I did speak to her.

I started dialing my cell phone to call Eugene.

"Hello," he said.

"Hi, honey."

"Hey, there's my girl. You have been on my mind all morning. How are you feeling?"

"Well, I could be better, but I'm all right. Are you free for lunch?"

"Not for another half hour, where are you?"

"I'm on the third floor, trying to avoid saying anything to your girl."

"My girl? What do you mean? You've started talking to yourself now or what?"

"Oh, you do have jokes, sweetheart. But I'm talking about Veronica."

"She's not bothering you, is she?"

"No, she's not, but we need to talk, okay? Where are you?"

"I'm on the tenth floor."

"Okay, I'm on my way up. I'll just wait in the hall for you until you are finished."

"Okay, I won't be long. I'll see you in a few."

I decided to just sit there for a minute before heading up to see him.

I had laid my head back against the wall when Veronica came over and asked if everything was all right.

I lifted my head and said, "Excuse me?"

She said it again. "Is everything all right?"

I kinda just stared at her for a minute, then said, "Sure, everything is fine."

"You were looking kind of down."

"Hey, thanks for the concern, but everything is fine."

She had a little smirk on her face.

So I thought that I'd wipe it off by saying, "I think that I might be coming down with the flu. But Eugene thinks that I might be having another little Eugene."

She shot fire at me with her eyes.

Then I said, "Oh, I'm on my way up to see him right now."

She threw her head up in the air and walked away.

That made me think that she was the one that sent the flowers so that Eugene would think that someone else was sending them and that our relationship would end.

But I got news for you, my sister, that is not going to be happening.

I got up and went over and waited for the elevator to come. They take forever to come, but finally it came. I got on and pressed the Tenth Floor button.

When I got off the elevator, there was some movement that caught me out of the corner of my eye. I turned but didn't see anybody, so I kept walking toward the courtroom where Eugene was.

As I was walking, I just decided to look back, and there was Veronica heading for the elevator.

I thought, *Now that's one sick bitch. What she thought? I was lying to her or something. Hello.*

But to tell the truth, I can't blame her for wanting what she wants, but it's too late now. He's all mine. And I don't share, not my man anyway.

I sat down on the bench across the courtroom and waited for

Eugene to come out.

About ten minutes later, he walked his fine ass out, looking good.

"Hey, baby," he said.

I stood up to greet him. "Hey yourself."

"So how's your day going?"

"So far, my day is moving pretty fast. How about yours?"

"After talking to you, the day seems to be as smooth as silk. I love you."

Then he kissed me on the cheek.

"Hey, Veronica hasn't said or done anything out of the way to you, has she?"

"Naw." I didn't bother to say anything about her following me up here because, after all, she has a right to be wherever she wants to be.

Eugene suggested that we just take a walk out to the hot dog stand and just sit at one of the picnic tables and talk.

"That sounds good to me, but you mean we won't be eating any hot dogs? just talking?" I smiled.

He said, "Now who got jokes?"

As we walked to the elevator, when the doors opened up, Veronica was standing inside. We stepped in, and Eugene spoke to her, and she spoke back.

There was silence in the elevator until Eugene said, "What do you want me to cook for dinner?"

"I'm not sure. What do you have a taste for?"

"You," he said.

"Well, I don't have a problem with that, but you said that I wasn't feeling enough for you."

"Well, we'll see."

I sensed movement after that comment. So I said, "Yeah, we'll wait and see what happens when we get home now, won't we?"

He kissed my head and said, "You're something else. That's why I love you so much."

We laughed a little, then stepped out of the elevator.

We went outside and bought sausage with sauerkraut. He had a pop, but I had orange juice.

We sat on the bench and had a little small talk about the cases that we were working on.

Then he asked me, "What was it that we needed to talk about?"

"Oh, someone sent me another dozen of yellow rose with a card that said… Well, here, read it for yourself."

His smile went away.

"Hey," I said as I sat my food down and held his face in my hands. "Honey, it's all right because no one can buy me with two dozen roses unless it's you because I'm not that cheap." Then I kissed him on the lips, and he smiled.

Eugene said, "I know, baby, it's just that it bothers me that whoever is doing this is trying to get you and I both upset."

"Well, we're not going to let it upset us because we're past that now. And we know where we stand, and that's with each other until death do us part. Nothing is going to come between us unless we let it, and I don't intend on that happening. Do you?"

"Girl, please."

"All right then." I kissed him again, then said, "Now eat."

We finished our food, then talked for a few more minutes about the weather and people walking by; we had a few laughs. Then I looked at my watch. It was time for me to go back to work. Eugene walked me back inside to the elevator.

I said, "Honey, you don't have to go all the way back up with me when the door opened."

But he said, "I'm going to go up with you anyway."

So we walked inside the elevator, and as soon as the doors closed, Eugene pulled me into his arms and kissed me with so much passion that I felt the bulge in his pants, and I couldn't help but to feel it.

"Oooooooooh, baby," he whispered.

"Stop, Eugene," I said; and as soon as we let go of one another, the doors opened up.

"Dammmn," he muttered.

Good thing he was wearing a suit. Otherwise someone could have seen the bulge in his pants, but only if you looked hard enough; but not really too hard, you could see his suit jacket a little puffed out.

We got to my courtroom, and I said, "Okay, sweetie, I'll see you later."

He looked around to see if anyone was looking; then he ran his hand across my behind.

I said, "Don't start something that you can't finish, and I mean finish right now."

"Oh, I can finish right now. Where is the closet?"

We laughed. I hit him on the shoulder and went into the courtroom.

At the end of the day, I was feeling a little better; we got out of court early.

So I went by my place. It seemed so at peace, so I decided to relax and run myself a bath since I haven't had one in a while. So I turned on the water, put some bubbles in, then went into the kitchen, opened up the fridge, and poured myself a glass of wine.

Then I went back into the bathroom and looked at the bubbles that had risen almost over the top of the tub. I turned the water off and started undressing. Once I undressed, I stepped in the water; it felt so good. I sat down in the water. I had turned on the CD player and put Whitney Houston, Rachelle Ferrell, and Will Downing in the player. I put my bath pillow behind my head and lay back and enjoyed the moment.

I hadn't done this in such a long time that I was angry with myself.

I stayed in the bathtub for about an hour, letting the water run out only to refill it again as it cooled off. I had to get out of the water and go get the bottle of wine out of the fridge. As I was running through the house without a stitch on, I heard my cell phone ringing. I knew it was Eugene. And when I picked it up, it was Eugene. I answered it, "Hey, baby," as I sat back down in the water.

"Where are you?" he said with a dry tone in his voice. "I don't see your truck out here."

"I'm at my apartment. Oh, you know that I have not been here in so long. I just came here when I got out of court."

"So what are you doing?"

"Oh, I'm having a hot bath. I'm soaking in the tub and drinking a glass of wine."

"That sounds good. Can I join you?"

"Why sure you can."

"I'm on my way." He hung up before I could tell him my apartment number.

I started to get out of the tub and unlock the door, but then I thought the doorman is going to have to buzz me first anyway, so I'll just wait until he gets here.

I decided to let out all the water and wait a few minutes before filling it up again so that it would still be hot when he got here, nothing like a fresh bath for me and my baby.

I got another glass out of the cabinet for Eugene, but I should make him do like he did me and let him look for what he needs, but I'll be nice this time.

I sat on the sofa, laid my head back, and daydreamed about our lovemaking.

I was all in when a knock came on the door. Oh, he's here. I got up, ran to the door, opened it, and had the biggest shock.

There stood Robert and Eugene.

"Robert, what are you doing here?"

Then I said, "I'm sorry, come in." I grabbed Eugene by the hand and led him in.

It was obvious that they had been talking.

So I said, "You two know each other?"

"No, we just met coming up in the elevator together," Eugene said.

So I said, "Well, let me introduce you to each other. Eugene, this is Robert, my husband—soon-to-be ex-husband. And Robert, this is Eugene, my future husband."

They shook hands; then Robert said, "Isn't this the guy that we saw at the restaurant, and you couldn't take your eyes off each other?"

"Yes, one and the same. But back to my question, what are you doing here?"

"I was in town and in your neighborhood, so I thought that I would stop by and say hello."

I thought to myself, *Yeah right, you thought that you were going to come up here and taste me, but no more of that.*

I saw Eugene looking at me kind of funny and thought this couldn't happen at a worthwhile time.

I said, "That was nice of you, but I'm fine as you can see."

Robert said, "I also wanted to talk to you about something."

"Well, go right ahead and say just what it is that you came to say."

"Naw, that wouldn't be right."

"No, go ahead. Eugene and I are not keeping anything from each other."

"Go ahead," Eugene said.

"Okay, but I'm not meaning any disrespect. But you did say go ahead and say what I came here to say. All right then. Rachael, before I left town, I came here to see if you would give me another chance to make up with you and let me take away some of the hurt and pain that I caused you."

I could feel the hurt in his voice as he talked.

When he said that, Eugene looked at me, and I looked at him and raised my eyebrows.

He said, "I want to ask you one last time. Will you be my wife again, Rachael, please?"

I almost cried, but I had strength standing next to me.

So I took his hand.

He said, "Rachael, before you say anything, I just want to say that I learned a lot about love with you. You taught me a lot not just about love but to really love someone outside of myself. I know that I have messed up really, really bad, but after realizing that there will never be anyone out there to compare to you, I knew—rather hoped—that you would let me make it up to you. Rachael, I know that it's going to take time for you to trust me again, but please give me that chance.

"Please, Rachael? I realized that to me you are everything, and I hope that in your heart of hearts you will forgive me and take me back even if it's on a trial basis. Ray, you just don't know all the changes I've been going through, all the growing up that I've done since I've been away from you, Rachael," he said before his face flooded with tears.

The CD player crooned, "Anyone who ever loved could look at me and know that I love you," as if on cue.

At that moment, Eugene said, "I think that I'll leave so that you two can finish talking."

"No, Eugene, don't leave. What I have to say to Robert is no secret. I've told you that there is nothing between us anymore."

I turned to Robert and said, "Robert, I know that you may still have feelings for me. But you are going to have to let me go in your heart. When you and I were together, I gave you 100 percent in our marriage, and so did you, in the beginning. But then things changed, and when they did, I started getting uneasy feelings. Because of what I had been through with Shawn, you know that I don't mean to throw this back in your face, but you knew that I couldn't handle you and your drug problem. I just couldn't. But you didn't seem to care, and you just continued, and to add to that, you had many affairs. I don't mean to make you feel bad. But I have someone new in my life now. And we both have had our share of bad luck with the men and the women that we have had in our lives. As a matter of fact, I almost missed out on him because of all the things that I have been through with the men in my life. Robert, I love you, but I'm not in love with you anymore. I thank you for thinking about me and wanting a second chance with me. That in itself lets me know that I wasn't a bad person to be with. But I have moved on with my life."

I put my arm through Eugene's and laid my head on his shoulder—well, close to his shoulder because of his height. "Robert, Eugene and I are going to be married as soon as our divorce is final. So all I can say to you is that I wish you the best in your next relationship. And just a little advice if I might. Keep it real with her and you'll be all right. Robert, what it really boils down to is there will always be a place in my heart where you once were. But even if I didn't have Eugene in my life, it was already over for us. Even before you left."

"But, Rachael, if you felt that way, then why did you keep sleeping with me?"

"Because I was still attracted to you sexually. But then, I put a stop to that, didn't I?"

He didn't say anything.

So I said it again. "Didn't I stop having sex with you before you left, Robert? And I mean prior to the last week that we were together?"

"Yes, Rachael, you did. Look, I'm feeling like such a big dummy."

"Well, Rachael, I am truly happy for you. And I wish the best for you and Eugene."

He turned to Eugene and stretched out his hand and said,

"Someone had to lose. But I'm glad that you won. You've got one hella lady there, and I hope that you don't make the same mistakes that I did."

"Don't worry," Eugene said, "I don't intend to do anything to hurt her. I'm out to steal only one thing from her."

"What's that?"

"Her heart. I plan to get it and keep it right beside mine for as long as she'll let me."

"Man, I'm sorry for my behavior. But I love her, and I wanted her to know that. And I needed to know for sure that she didn't want me anymore."

Eugene said, "Robert, I can understand that."

Then Robert said, "I guess sending those flowers didn't help persuade you any."

"No, they didn't. So that was you?"

"Yeah."

"So why didn't you put your name on the card?"

"I just thought that you would know right off who sent them because I did that all the time when we were together. But you don't have to worry. I won't be sending anymore."

He hugged me and said, "Best of luck to both of you." Then he left.

Eugene and I didn't say anything for a minute.

Then Eugene said, "I knew it was him when I first learned about the flowers. And this last time, I had this gut feeling as you women would say. But I knew indeed that they had come from an ex, whether it was a husband or a boyfriend. See, I know from experience that sending flowers work better when trying to make up. That's why I was a little uneasy when you thought that they came from me." Holding each other, he said, "Dammmn, now that was a little scary."

"Why'd you say that?"

"Because he was pouring out his heart, and maybe if I wasn't here, you might have given in to him."

"Oh, you think so?"

"Baby, I'm saying that man wanted his wife back, and he pulled out all the stops to try and get you back. I mean, everything he had. Baby, even though you told him who I was, that didn't stop him. Nothing mattered to him. He was on a mission. And I can understand why. You're everything that a man wants in a wife or woman, girlfriend or whatever. You are all that rolled into one. I knew that the first time that I saw you."

"Oh really, and just how would you know that?"

"Trust me, men can tell. It's called a man's instinct." Then he winked and said, "A man can tell a lot about a woman after seeing her a few times. It doesn't even matter where he saw her. That's why I was trying so hard. Because I knew that if you were not taken, then I still had a chance. And you see, I was right. One man's junk is another man's treasure. And I found the pot of gold. I'm glad that no one else had a chance to see in you what I saw. You tried to be tough, but I was tougher. Girl, you were meant to be my wife. Look at all the ways that we ran into each other. All the hit and misses, and finally here we are. Together forever. Girl, just think we kissed at the casino, we met at the restaurant, we work in the same building, go to the same church. I mean, it was just meant to be."

I just smiled.

He kissed my head, then let me go, and said, "So this is where you were hiding from me. All the time I was thinking about you. Before I really knew who you were, Rachael, you would be on my mind all the time, especially after we met—well, not met but ran into each other at the Red Lobster. You were all I could think about. Then you broke my heart when I saw you and Robert together at the restaurant."

"Oh yeah, when you were out with Veronica."

"Hold it. I was not out with her. She found out where I was going from my secretary. I already told you that."

"I know, I was just checking."

"Girl." Then he grabbed me and hugged me real tight, then his hands started roaming.

He thought about the reason that he had come over, then said, "Do you know that you are not wearing any clothes up under that robe?"

"Sure, I know that. I was waiting for you so that you could get naked and join me in a nice hot bath."

"That's right." Then he started undressing.

"I got to let all the water out again because I know that that water is like ice. I had let it out once while waiting for you but tried to time you and put some more in so that the water would still be hot. But we got thrown off course.”

“Hey, we’ll heat it up then.”

“Yeah right.”

He had taken off everything except his underpants. Dammmn. He’s built, not overbuilt like I said before but just right. Everywhere and in all the right places. I just watched him walk around in the bedroom.

Then he asked if I had anything to drink.

“There is something. Look on the bar or in the fridge. It depends on what you want to drink. I know what you can drink.”

“What’s that?”

“Never mind.”

“Hey, don’t back down now. Say what you were gonna say.”

“I’ll save it for later.”

“Girl, go get the water ready.” Then he smiled.

I went and checked on the water and put some bubble bath in the bathtub and watched as the bubbles began to rise.

I was just standing and looking into the water when I started thinking about all the things that Robert had said. My heart went out to him, and I was glad that Eugene was here. Because I just might have given into him simply because I know that he really did, or still do love me, and he and I did have a real good time together. But I’m just glad that Eugene was with me.

Dammmmn, I’m glad that I’ve got someone in my corner that has been through all the mess that life has taken us through, and we’re still standing.

Just as I was really getting into my thoughts, Eugene walked up behind me and kissed me on the neck and said, “A nickel for your thoughts.”

He put his arms around my waist and continued to whisper in my ear while holding two glasses of something in his hands.

“What’s in the glasses?”

“Oh, don’t try and change the subject.”

“What did you say?”

“You know what I said. What were you thinking about when I came in and broke up your thoughts?"

"Well, if you must know, I was thinking about you," I said as I turned around to kiss him and put my arms around his waist.

"What about me?"

"I was thinking just how lucky I am to have you in my life."

"Baby, I feel the same way about you, but are you having any second thoughts about us?"

Tears rolled down my cheeks as I looked him in the eyes and said, "You don't realize the love that I have for you. It's real, and I only want you for the rest of my life and then some. So please don't ever think that I want anything to do with anyone but you. You are going to be my life, and I'm going to do all I can to keep you happy."

Eugene kissed my head and said, "I'm going to do the same for you. Just keep your eyes on me, and you'll see just how much I want you in my life. But you know I can show you better than I can tell you."

We stood overlooking the mountains and blue skies while confessing our love for each other.

Then I raised my head off his chest and said, "You know what you are to me?"

"No, what am I to you?"

"You are my casino lover."

* * *

Well, it's been two years now, and Eugene and I are married now. Twice a month, we rent a room across the water to keep our love fresh as if we just met, and we both love it. We still have our family gatherings. Veronica couldn't stand watching us any longer so she left the building, and we never heard from her again.